MANDA McGRATH

WISE VIRGIN

Complete and Unabridged

ULVERSCROFT
Leicester

First published in Great Britain

First Large Print Edition
published 1999

British Library CIP Data

McGrath, Manda
 Wise virgin.—Large print ed.—
 Ulverscroft large print series: romance
 1. Love stories
 2. Large type books
 I. Title
 823.9′14 [F]

ISBN 0–7089–4061–7

Published by
F. A. Thorpe (Publishing) Ltd.
Anstey, Leicestershire
Set by Words & Graphics Ltd.
Anstey, Leicestershire
Printed and bound in Great Britain by
T. J. International Ltd., Padstow, Cornwall

This book is printed on acid-free paper

SPECIAL MESSAGE TO READERS

WISE VIRGIN

Sisters Jean and Ailsa Leslie live on a small farm in the Scottish Grampians. Andrew Esplin, the local blacksmith, keeps a brotherly eye on the girls, loving Ailsa, the younger sister, from afar. Ailsa is in love with Stewart Morrison, who is working in Greenock. Jean is engaged to Alan Drummond, who has gone to Australia, intending to send for her when his prospects are good. But Jean shocks everyone when she elopes with Dunton from the big house . . .

Books by Manda McGrath
Published by The House of Ulverscroft:

EAST OF SINGAPORE
FOOTLIGHTS
THE LAST DITCH

1

Glen Eck lay in a wide verdant valley amid the windswept Grampians. To its few inhabitants it was known merely as The Glen, and it lived by its cattle and its agriculture, and was content to remain what it had been for close on three centuries — a humble village, set in particularly beautiful surroundings, with no ambition other than to retain its peace and quietude.

The village itself was a small affair, comprising half a dozen shops, a smithy — which still contrived to flourish, despite the reign of the motor car, a chapel and an inn. The farms upon whose produce it depended were scattered over an area of some five miles — chiefly small holdings of from twenty to five hundred acres. Behind the chapel was a park, well stocked with game and deer, and by courtesy of its owner open to the villagers on Sundays and national holidays.

The big house — Aberdinnie — situated in the park, at the highest point of elevation, was a rambling mansion of sixteenth century construction, in which the ancestors of the present 'laird' had lived and gazed across the hills a good century before the first brick was laid in the Glen.

Andrew Esplin, the blacksmith, from the window of whose forge the big white house could be seen at its best, was convinced it was haunted, and his conviction carried such weight that half the villagers came to believe it.

'I've heard Father tell of the Lady Jane, who jumped from the top window in eighteen sixty-three,' he said. 'In those days it was impossible to find a body who gang nigh the place after dark. The ghost — '

The dark-haired girl to whom he was speaking broke into a peal of healthy laughter. Andrew knitted his brows as if he resented this scepticism, but the next moment he was smiling at her.

'Very weel, Ailsa. Have it yer ain way. But there are more things in heaven and earth — '

'That's cribbing, Andrew. It's Shakespeare.'

'No the worse for that,' he muttered.

He gave a last rub with the file on the new shoe which he had just fitted to the pony's hind foot and stood up to mop his brow with his leather apron.

'He'll do now.' He passed his hand over the pony's silken neck and made a few sounds with his lips, which the animal seemed to understand. 'What might his age be now?' he asked.

'Nearly five years. I had him on my fifteenth birthday, and he was one year old then — so the dealer said.'

'So you'll be nearly nineteen yersel'?'

Ailsa nodded and brushed back her mop of dark short curls with a brown hand. She was aware that Andrew was regarding her very keenly, but felt no embarrassment, as she had known him since she was a child. Laughing merrily, she raised her hands above her head and pirouetted gracefully before him.

'Have you quite finished, Andrew?' she asked.

'Ay, but it's wonderful!'

'What is wonderful?'

'How a wee slip of a bairn with bib and tucker can grow into a bonnie lass in sich a short time. Why, it was I who gave you your furrst walking lesson, when your dear mother was abed with sickness.'

Ailsa's brown eyes lost some of their brightness at this reminder of the past. Long ago as it was, she could well remember the face of her mother, who had passed away after an illness which lasted nearly five years. It had left her and her sister, Jean, at the mercy of an uncle of not too affectionate a nature. Under his rigid disciplinary methods she had missed all the love that her ailing mother had lavished on her. It was this tremendous contrast which had helped to preserve most vividly those tender memories.

'You knew my mother, Andrew,' she said. 'Was she like me — or Jean?'

'You favour your mother, Ailsa. Jean takes after her father. Your mother was a beautiful woman.'

'That is where I don't take after her.'

'But I see her every time I look at you.'

'Quite likely — but I'm plain, and know it. Jean is different. Somehow she got all the family looks. Why, when we were at school together they used to call us 'beauty and the beast.' '

'I'd like to hear them,' growled Andrew.

'What does it matter? Life is more than looks, anyway.'

'Ay, but you're as bonnie — '

She wagged her finger to stop his compliments, and held up her foot as a sign that she wished him to assist her to mount the pony. With a grin he extended his great horny hand and hoisted her into the saddle.

'Going home, lass?'

'Yes. We've got to start getting the hay in.'

She nodded rather coldly to a slim, dark man in a small car who passed the forge at that moment; Andrew pursed his lips and followed the line of blue smoke until the car disappeared round a bend in the road.

'Has he shot all the pheasants yet?' he asked.

'Who? Mr.Dunton? I don't know.'

'I hear his tenancy of Aberdinnie is up shortly, and I shan't be sorry either.'

'You don't like him?'

'No, I don't.'

Whatever Andrew's reason might be for disliking the temporary tenant of the big house, he preferred to keep it to himself. With a wave of his hand he bade her godspeed and went on with his work.

★ ★ ★

Ailsa Leslie entered the farmhouse to find her sister engaged in opening a large flat box which had evidently just been brought up by the Glen postie.

'What have you got there, Jean?' she asked.

Jean seemed a trifle embarrassed as she drew off the lid of the box and brought to light its contents — a new and very fashionable costume. She took it between

5

her fingers and held it up, waiting for Ailsa's approval.

'Where did you get it?' demanded Ailsa.

'Glasgow. I saw it advertised, and couldn't resist it. Now dinna be angry, Ailsa. It was high time I had something new to my back. I've been going about in rags for the last six months.'

'How much did it cost?'

'Only eight guineas.'

Ailsa's eyes blazed. She had found it hard enough to make ends meet on the little Glen Eck farm without throwing money away. All the responsibility of the farm had fallen upon her shoulders ever since their uncle's death, and she was Jean's exact opposite, both in looks and temperament.

Jean was fair as a Saxon, with long-lashed blue eyes that looked all the bluer by contrast with her golden curls, which clustered about her ears in effective abandon. It was by contrast with this wraith-like beauty that Ailsa looked plain. She lacked Jean's perfection of feature and Jean's incomparable complexion, but she possessed something which her sister lacked — character.

'Eight guineas!' Ailsa echoed bitterly. 'Jean, have you no idea of values whatever? You know we canna afford to have new dresses just now. And what's the use of it in the Glen?

6

It will only make you look conspicuous.'

'Conspicuous!' retorted Jean. 'I shan't be half so conspicuous as I am in rags. I hate all those people at the big house looking at me as if I were a beggar.'

'We're not beggars,' said Ailsa; 'but we're poor. As for the guests at Aberdinnie, what does it matter what they think? Their world and ours are quite different. Jean, why can't you be satisfied with your lot?'

'Are *you* satisfied?'

'Yes. At least I will be when Stewart passes his final examination and we — '

She was going to say, 'when we are married,' but as Stewart Morrison had not yet proposed it seemed rather premature. Stewart was in Greenock, working at full pressure in a drawing office. His letters were full of the future, and she divined that when next they met she would wear an engagement ring.

'All very well for you,' grumbled Jean, 'with Stewart within a few hours, but what about me? Alan's over thirteen thousand miles away, and it may be years before he sends for me. Why shouldn't I look nice, even if I have to live in a deadly place like this.'

Alan Drummond was Jean's fiancé, and in the old days had lived in the Glen within a mile of the Leslies. On the death of his father three years back Alan had decided to seek fortune farther afield, and, having sold his small inheritance, sailed a few months later to Australia. Before leaving he had unburdened his heart to Jean, to whom this unexpected departure had come as a shock. She had promised to go out to him whenever his prospects justified sending for her.

Ailsa remembered Alan as a dour, rather serious-minded youth, with not a little of his father's intolerance ingrained in his character. He was the very opposite of Jean, with her imperious ways and devil-may-care disposition, but despite this the two got on extremely well together, and Ailsa, like Jean, looked forward to the day when love's young dream would be brought to fruition.

'Jean,' she murmured, 'you must have patience. As for the Glen being a deadly place — why, it's beautiful.'

Jean clenched her hands and stared out of the window. Ailsa, puzzled by the expression on her face, put her hands on her shoulders and gazed wistfully at her.

'Is anything the matter, dear?' she asked.

'What do you mean?'

'You've seemed so preoccupied of late — so different.'

'Havers! There is nothing the matter with

me except that I'm tired of slaving away here. It doesn't seem right. We deserve something better than this.'

Ailsa saw that argument in the circumstances was useless. Jean would never look facts in the face. Her remark about 'slaving' was scarcely true, for she did very little work in the house and troubled herself hardly at all about the farm. Her personal appearance occupied most of her time. She tried to live the life she dreamed about — the life of the people of Aberdinnie House, who shot over the hills and gave themselves up to pleasure all day and every day.

Ailsa continued to put in sixteen hours a day, never sparing herself in her determination to pull things through satisfactorily. During the next week Jean was absent a great deal in the evenings, excusing herself on the plea that the weather was oppressive and she felt the need of fresh air.

It disturbed Ailsa a little, but there were good grounds for the excuse. The heat-wave increased, and the stifling heat of the day hung over the Glen long after the fierce sun had set. One evening Jean set out for her customary walk. Ailsa, who was busy churning, looked up to see her sister clad in the new costume, with her hair particularly well dressed and her face slightly powdered.

'My, it's hot,' she remarked. 'You'll be boiled in that costume. Dinna go far, Jean. There's a storm brewing.'

Jean nodded. Her eyes seemed brighter than usual, and she stopped on her way to the door, but if she was going to say something she evidently thought better of it, and a moment later vanished. Ailsa continued at her work for another hour, when the low rumble of thunder sent her to the window.

Her eyes swept the stretch of road that wandered through the towering Grampians, to lose itself in the purple haze of the mountains. Great angry clouds were hovering over the hills, shutting out the sun. In the hollow, down the brae from the little farm, lay the Kirkton of Eck, just a scattered group of cottar houses huddling around the old-fashioned kirk, whose sturdy square tower rose high above them all. Back from the road, between Andrew Esplin's smiddy and the school, stood the Eck Arms, rebuilt and aggressively new. And just behind it all the river leaped and swirled over the white, gleaming boulders. Gorgeous the view in the summer sunshine, but awesome now in the leaden stillness that hinted of the coming storm.

Away over the hills rolled the vanguard of the approaching storm, red and threatening

10

at the edge and inky black behind. Even as she looked the sun declined and the aspect grew more awful. She hoped Jean would turn back when she saw the state of the elements.

It grew dark, and the rumbling thunder increased. Then without warning the clouds opened and the rain came down in lashing streams, tumbling in floods down the gullies in the hillside to the river. It proved to be merely the beginning. The thunder crashed louder and louder and awful forked lightning smote through the blackness. At eleven o'clock the storm was still playing havoc and the rain was still dense.

The nearest village to the Kirkton of Eck was some four miles away, and there was scant shelter anywhere else. At half-past eleven she began to grow nervous on Jean's account. Had she taken shelter in one of the outlying farms she would have been driven back in some conveyance by this time. Yet she came not. Haunted by horrible fears, she put on a mackintosh, and rounded up the ploughman and his son.

'Munro, Jean is out in the Glen. We'll have to search for her.'

'That's bad,' muttered Munro. 'But maybe she'll hae ta'en shelter.'

'I — I hope so. We must call at all the

11

farms. Bring a lantern.'

The search began five minutes later in a drizzling rain. Andrew Esplin, who had been working late on a special job, saw them as he was leaving the smiddy.

'Anything amiss?' he asked, anxiety in his tone.

'Jean is missing,' she said.

'Missing! When did she go out?'

'An hour before the storm broke. I — I'm afraid, Andrew.'

'Hold on,' said Andrew. 'I'm coming with ye.'

He ran into his cottage, and a few minutes later emerged with another lantern in his hand. Beating their way through the rain and wind, the party set out over the rough Glen road. After three hours of fruitless hunting they came back to the farm to find that Jean had not returned. Ailsa, now thoroughly alarmed, was biting her lip in despair.

'What can we do now?' she whispered.

Munro, who was dog-tired, yawned and rubbed his eyes, and the boy looked near to collapse.

'Send thae twa to bed,' whispered Andrew. 'There's a'e place we havena tried yet.'

Ailsa dismissed the pair, and then looked at Andrew questioningly.

'We havena tried Aberdinnie. There's just a possibility — '

'But if she had gone to Aberdinnie she could have got home in half an hour,' Ailsa argued.

Andrew shrugged his shoulders.

'You go inside, Miss Ailsa, and leave this to me. I'll come and report to you later.'

'But — '

Andrew insisted, and reluctantly she went indoors. To go to bed was impossible in the circumstances, so she sat and waited, reflecting on Andrew's rather queer behaviour. Over an hour passed before she heard a knock on the door and ran to open it. Andrew stood there, looking exceedingly fierce.

'Not there?' she gasped.

'Not there,' he grunted. 'But I've discovered something. Can I come in?'

She nodded and gazed at him with anxious eyes as he stepped into the sitting-room and stood facing her.

2

By his expression it was clear that something serious had happened, and Ailsa's heart thumped rapidly in her breast. What could it be but some dreadful injury — or even worse?

'Tell me, Andrew,' she begged in a hoarse whisper, 'what — what have you discovered?'

'The guests left Aberdinnie this morning.'

'Well?'

'Mister Dunton left at the back o' seven by the last train.'

'But I don't understand. What — '

She stopped as a terrible suspicion arose in her mind, but it seemed too fantastic and impossible to harbour.

'Can't you guess where Jean has gone?'

'No, Andrew. You don't mean that she has — has gone away with Mister Dunton?' she almost screamed.

'I do.'

Horror took the place of amazement. Andrew commenced speaking in a low, tense voice.

'I gaed to Aberdinnie and found only the house-keeper there. She told me Mr. Dunton had given up possession to-day and that he motored doon the Glen to the junction to catch the last train to Glasgow.'

'But wouldn't he go by road?'

'That had been his intention, but at the last meenit he had trouble wi' his car and decided to put it on the rail. It was as much as he could do to get it to move at all. Now, considering the weather, and the fact that his car was hung up, it looked to me as if he was in a mighty big hurry. I gaed to the junction and found it shut, but I knocked up the booking clerk, and I learnt that Mr. Dunton bought two first-class tickets to Glasgow.'

'Two!'

'Ay; and what's mair, the clerk minds seeing a young lady near the ticket office. He thought it was one of the guests from Aberdinnie, and I let him think so.'

Ailsa's brain reeled under this shock.

'Andrew, there must be a mistake. What you suggest is terrible — impossible. Jean didn't even know Mr. Dunton, but even if she did she wouldn't do that. You know she wouldn't.'

She looked fierce in her defence of her sister, but it had no effect upon Andrew.

'Fac's are chiels that winna ding, Ailsa, and one fact is that Jean did ken that scamp better than you imagine. I've seen them together twice when I've been traivellin' to Lindsay's place across the water. She tried to hide her face from me, but I've kent her ower mony years to be fooled.'

'Then why didn't you tell me?' she cried.

'I'm no clipe. I tried to think there was nothing to worry about — that it was just an innocent flirtation that any bonnie lassie might be guilty of.' He thumped his big fist on the table. 'If I had guessed it would come to this I'd — I'd have knocked his head off, I would.'

He looked quite capable of carrying this out to the letter. His great chest expanded as he took a mighty breath, and the fingers which gripped the edge of the table quivered in a strange way. Ailsa saw in him the staunch friend who would sacrifice anything for her, or even for the wayward Jean. She touched him on the arm, and aroused him from his fierce reflections.

'Andrew, what am I to do?'

'Do? Find him and her. Glasgow's no' so big that it can hide them for long. I saw his car at the junction waiting for the morning goods train. I took the number. I guess that will put us close on his heels.'

'But, Andrew, I don't want the police to interfere. The news will reach the Glen, and

Jean's life will be awful. No one must know about this.'

'There's nae reason why they should. I'll get Dunton's address withoot telling the real reason.' He caught her by the hands and smiled into her distressed face. 'Now, lassie, try to sleep. We can do nothing until the morn. Be at the junction at ten o'clock, and I'll meet you.'

'You — you'll come with me to Glasgow?'

'Ay. Wha else should come but me? Do ye think I'll sit still and see a poor lassie's life ruined because she made a mistake? There, tak' he'rt — it will a' come richt.'

Lying in bed with sleepless eyes, she wondered whether it would come right. She knew Jean's impetuous spirit, her devil-may-care view of things. She knew, too, the lure of a man of Dunton's social position. That his motives were not honourable she had not the slightest doubt. And here she was powerless, whilst Jean might be in dreadful danger.

The long hours passed, and at last morning broke over the hills — a glorious morn ushered in with bird music outside her window. She wished she could sing as they sang. With moist eyes she knelt by the bed and prayed fervently that she might not be too late. Then feeling a little more composed, she dressed and went down to attend to a hundred and one things that needed doing before breakfast.

She met Andrew later at the junction, having got a lift in one of the Glen farmer's traps. It seemed an age before the tedious journey to Glasgow came to an end. Soon after the first disappointment came — Andrew discovered that the registration number of Dunton's car was taken out in Aberdeen. Looking for Jean's face in the crowded streets of the city would be a waste of time.

'Let's look in the telephone book,' suggested Andrew.

But the telephone book contained no Dunton of the same initials, neither did the directory. It was then that Ailsa thought of an idea.

'The car — he will have to take delivery of the car at the station.'

It held some promise, and Andrew decided to act on it. They hurried to the station and arrived there almost simultaneously with the car. Then commenced the monotonous task of watching. For the remainder of the day they hung about the goods yard, but the car never came out.

They went to find rooms for the night. The next morning they were at the station early, resigned to their vigil. It was afternoon

18

when two mechanics turned up in a car and one of them alighted and went into the goods yard.

'At last,' muttered Andrew. 'Ailsa, will you run and get a taxi and bring it round here?'

She saw his intentions, and started off. In ten minutes she was back again inside the taxi. The driver pulled up near Andrew just as the mechanic came out of the yard driving the small sporting car. Andrew jumped into the taxi.

'Where to?' queried the driver.

'Follow that car.'

After a mile or so of tortuous streets their quarry pulled into a garage. Andrew immediately stopped the taxi and paid the driver. Soon after, the slim figure of Dunton arrived in a taxi. Ailsa caught her breath with a little hiss, and Andrew clenched his fist. Dunton came out again after a quarter of an hour and commenced to walk briskly up the street. They shadowed him successfully until he disappeared into the Central Station Hotel.

A glance at the hotel register told them the number of Dunton's room — 328. They were rushed up to the third floor in the lift. At length they reached 328 and halted. Ailsa began to exhibit signs of nervousness, but

Andrew knocked without hesitation.

'Come in,' said a voice.

They entered the next moment, and found Dunton in the act of packing. He wrinkled his brow as he saw Andrew's big figure and Ailsa's rather pale face. Then he stood bolt upright as Andrew calmly locked the door and pocketed the key.

'What do you want? How dare you come in here!'

'Maybe you mind o' me?' said Andrew.

'I don't. Unlock that — '

He halted as his eyes fell again on Ailsa, and a look of fear entered them.

'I see you remember me,' said Ailsa. 'I've come to know what you have done with my sister.'

Dunton simulated a smile of amusement.

'Really, I don't understand you. I remember seeing you at Glen Eck, but this — this is preposterous.'

Andrew, who considered that enough time had been wasted already, stepped across the room and stopped within a foot of Dunton. The smile left Dunton's face as he gazed into Andrew's eyes. He saw before him as pugnacious a man as ever he set eyes on in all his life. His gaze wandered from the great shoulders to the knotted hands, and he felt afraid.

'I — I don't understand — ' he commenced.

'Well, understand now,' roared Andrew. 'The night before last you travelled to Glasgow with Jean Leslie. You're going to tell us where she is, and you're going to come wi' us there.'

'You — you must be insane!'

To Ailsa's horror Andrew stretched out his long arm and caught Dunton by the scruff of his neck, shaking him as a terrier does a rat.

'Andrew!' she gasped.

But the burly smith was sure of his ground, and, being sure, he had no mercy. Dunton's teeth chattered like castanets. He fought, but he was like a child in that iron grip. When at last Andrew released him he fell back on a couch and almost choked.

'Now you can go and call the police, Ailsa,' said Andrew.

Dunton's alarmed face came to view. He held up his hands and muttered something.

'Better go, Ailsa,' said Andrew.

'Stop!' moaned Dunton. 'She's all right — your sister. I did bring her to Glasgow, but only to give her a good time.'

'Where is she?' growled Andrew.

'At Bridge Street — No. 20. You'll find she is — '

'No, no, ye dinna,' muttered Andrew.

'You were ower busy packing when we came in for me to feel like leaving you. You're coming along, too.'

'All right — I'll come.'

Andrew unlocked the door, and Dunton, after making himself more presentable, prepared to lead them. They arrived at Bridge Street to find it full of tenement houses. No. 20 was like all the rest, and approached by a flight of steps from the street. Dunton knocked somewhat timidly, and the house-keeper appeared and nodded pleasantly. The trio went up the stairs and halted outside the door.

'She is inside — I think,' stammered Dunton.

'Lead the way, then.'

He knocked, and from inside came a voice which brought a sharp cry from Ailsa. In an instant she was through the door embracing her sister.

'Ailsa! Ailsa!'

The tears were streaming down Jean's face. Some seconds passed before she realised that other persons were present — Dunton in the foreground and Andrew close behind him. She hung her head as her eyes fell on Dunton, and Ailsa saw the blood mounting to her face.

'Jean, tell me everything.'

Jean raised her head and looked at Dunton, who fidgeted with his cane and seemed incapable of words.

'You — you didn't come,' she almost sobbed. 'I've waited and waited. Tell them — tell them why I — Oh, God, can't you see what they must think of me!'

'It — it was a mistake,' mumbled Dunton.

'A mistake! Then you didn't mean to marry me?'

'I did, but when I thought things over it — it was impossible. I was going to write to you to-night — '

Jean passed her hand before her eyes and tottered towards Ailsa, who clasped her in her arms tenderly.

'Don't — don't cry, dear. Tell me — about it.'

'I — I loved him. I wanted to tell you, but he asked me not to, because of the guests at Aberdinnie. He wanted me to elope with him and be married before the sheriff. He had arranged everything, and we were to go to the lawyer in Renfield Street to-day, and then up to the Sheriff Court. Until just now I thought he meant it.'

'I did mean it,' replied Dunton hoarsely. 'But don't you see how impossible it is?'

Andrew made a noise in his throat and

pushed past Dunton roughly. He hesitated a second and then touched Jean on the shoulder. She looked up with swimming eyes.

'Miss Jeannie, would you marry him now?'

'I — I — ' she stammered.

'Do you love him?'

'Y — yes,' falteringly.

'That's good enough.' He swung round on Dunton, his eyes literally blazing. 'You're going to marry her now. Ailsa, run out and bring a lawyer.'

'I tell you — ' cried Dunton.

'You'll tell me nothing,' snapped Andrew. 'Where's your manhood? Where's your pride? Where's your decency? You're goin' to do the richt thing by the lassie.'

Ailsa was staring at Andrew in amazement. She found her breath at last, and came close to him.

'Is it wisest?' she murmured.

'I believe so, lassie,' he replied huskily. 'You heard her say she loves him still.' He turned to the pallid figure of Dunton and commenced to whisper to him with not a few gesticulations. Whatever he said had its effects. Dunton moved towards Jean very abjectly.

'If you'll have me I'm — I'm ready,' he said.

And so in that room an hour later the wedding was celebrated with some tears and a little laughter, and registered later at the Sheriff Court, but where it was going to lead no one foresaw.

3

Jean's married life was of brief duration. She had commenced by vowing to be a model wife to Dunton, and he on his part strove to forget the rather sordid affair which had brought them together. But marriages are truly made in heaven, and it took no more than a week or two for each to discover that they were totally unsuited.

Ailsa read between the lines of the letters she received from Glasgow, and sensed the tragedy. She had arranged to go and visit Jean one weekend when the unexpected happened — Dunton was killed in a train collision. The telegram from Jean sent her to Glasgow post haste. She found her sister pale and distraught, and strove to impart what comfort she could.

'I — I want to think well of him now this dreadful thing has happened,' sobbed Jean. 'But he treated me badly, Ailsa. I can't tell you what I have suffered these few weeks.'

Ailsa kissed her and cast her eyes about the humble room with no little astonishment.

'I thought he was rich,' she said.

'It was all a pose. He was well-connected,

but his folk got to hear of the wedding and refused to recognise me. He told me they had stopped his allowance until such time as he could — could get rid of me.'

Fierce anger leaped in Ailsa's eyes at the knowledge of this inhuman attitude on the part of the dead man's relatives, but she choked it down as she reflected that perhaps they were not aware of the circumstances which had brought the wedding about.

'What are you going to do now, Jean?'

'I don't know. I believe he has left me unprovided for. Even this furniture is hired.'

'You're coming home with me,' said Ailsa. Jean shuddered.

'I couldn't. How can I face the folk at the Glen? They must know — '

They know nothing. When you first went away I gave them to understand that you had gone to some distant relatives for a holiday. It is barely a month since, and I have never told them any different. Andrew is the only man who knows the truth, and he is staunch. You can trust Andrew to mind his own business.'

'Yes, but what about Munro and the boy?'

They quite believe you ran away to Aunt Mary's. You can come back in a day or two, and we can resume the old life. Jean, dear, time will make amends.'

'I know,' murmured Jean tearfully. 'But there's Alan.'

'Yes, there's Alan.' Ailsa bit her lip at this reminder. 'Didn't you write and tell Alan about it?'

Jean shook her head.

'I was going to when — when this happened. Ailsa, Ailsa, I don't want to tell him now. He is all I have left in the world. I made a terrible mistake — in — getting married. I thought I loved Dunton. I was carried away by his promises. There is no reason why Alan should ever know. It would only hurt him, and no good purpose would be served.'

'But it would not be right to keep him ignorant — '

'Why not? Nothing has changed. I love him more than ever. I want to go to him when he is ready. If I tell him about this it can never be the same again between us. You know Alan — he is an idealist. Maybe he still wants me, but he would never forget this. It would be the one cloud in our happiness. Ailsa, promise me you'll say nothing. Help me to forget that this ever happened.'

'Very well,' said Ailsa a little reluctantly. 'If you think it's for the good of all concerned, I promise.'

So Jean returned to the Glen a week later and tried to forget the past by putting a little more enthusiasm into the work of the farm. But the enthusiasm waned after a bit. Her temperament was not such as to permit her to settle down. She still pined for something more exciting than the Glen could offer.

'She looks a little different,' whispered Andrew to Ailsa.

'Of course. She'll never be quite the same again.'

Andrew ran his eagle eye over Ailsa's trim figure. Her eyes seemed brighter than usual, and she appeared to be in the grip of an uncontrollable excitement.

'You look as gay as the mornin',' he remarked.

'Do I? Stewart Morrison is coming down tomorrow. He has passed his final examination.'

'So, that's it,' mused Andrew. 'Well, it's no surprise to me. That young fellow was bound to get on. Maybe he'll mind I'm still here?'

'You'll keep silent — about Jean?'

'You can trust me, Miss Ailsa. I'm too busy a man to engage in gossip with my neighbours.'

Stewart Morrison turned up the following day. He was two years older than Ailsa, and a splendid figure of a lad. With Stewart in the vicinity there was scant time for work. He was like a whirlwind — full of exuberance after months of hard study.

'What a train service!' he ejaculated. 'And the station bus seemed to crawl up the Glen. I could have walked here quicker. And how are the chickens and kye and — everything? Ailsa, you've grown an inch.'

Ailsa laughed joyously as she suffered her hand to be pumped up and down for a full minute. Then Jean came in and was treated likewise.

'So you passed?' said Ailsa.

'Yes; I heard only yesterday.' His brow clouded a little, and then he added: 'I'm going to Barrow next week.'

'What for?'

'It was the manager's idea. I'm to work there for a year, and if I do well I'm to come back to the Clyde again and take up a good post.'

Ailsa's disappointment was written all over her face, but she strove to look on the brighter side — towards that future when Stewart would have won his spurs.

That evening they walked together over the hills in the beautiful autumn moonlight. Stewart began to talk of the future and the things he had planned. Whilst doing so his hand was busy fumbling in his waistcoat pocket. She caught a glimpse of something brilliant and held her breath.

'Ailsa, dear, I — I have brought — brought — '

He gulped, and then held a ring within a few inches of her nose.

'Stewart, it's beautiful.'

'Then you'll wear it?'

'If you want me to. You're sure you want me to?'

He slipped it on her finger, and then caught her gently by the shoulders, gazing wistfully into her large, enraptured eyes.

'I've wanted to give it you for months past, Ailsa, but I thought I ought to wait until I could tell you I had gone a little way towards success.'

'You darling!'

Her arms went round his neck, and she felt his passionate kiss on her lips. It was to mean a year of waiting, but what was a year when maybe half a century of sublime happiness lay beyond?

'How long have you loved me, Stewart?' she whispered.

'Since first we played together in the burn ten years ago. I've always dreamed of the day when I could take you in my arms — like this — like this — '

That evening was like a dream, never to be forgotten. When she ultimately bade him good-bye at the junction her young heart was beating like a drum. Loving at a distance was so different from this. She thought she could feel his strong arms about her now — feel that tingling delicious kiss —

Thereafter came letters from Barrow, filled with endearments and lover's secrets. A new thing was born into her life, filling it to the brim with unmarred happiness. So great was the spell over her that for a time she failed to notice a change in Jean. But there came a time when it was impossible to overlook it. Jean grew pale and listless, and at times her eyes filled with an unmistakable fear.

Then one evening Ailsa arrived home earlier than she was expected to find her sister busy at some kind of needlework — a thing unusual with her. To Ailsa's surprise she slipped the thing she was making behind her with a startled cry.

'What is the matter?' queried Ailsa.

'Nothing — I — '

But the small garment was only half-hidden. It arrested Ailsa's gaze, and she picked it up before Jean could prevent her. Then the truth was made manifest. She heard a great sob from Jean, and took her in her arms with compassionate murmurs.

'It's all right, dear. But why didn't you tell me before?'

'I don't know.'

With the sharing of her secret Jean seemed much happier. She soon came to talk of the coming child quite casually and to show its clothes to Ailsa with no little pride. Then in the midst of this excitement came a letter from far-away Australia. Ailsa happened to be out when it arrived, so Jean thought it best to say nothing of it. It brought her news of her old sweetheart. He was well, but found money not too plentiful. Nevertheless, he was filled with optimism, and begged her to trust him to win through.

That made the problem of the future more acute, for she had always shunned realities, and in replying made no mention of the escapade which had brought about the pending event. Her letter was no less affectionate and hopeful than his. It was good to pour out her heart to one who really loved.

The months slipped along with astonishing speed. Autumn merged into winter, and winter into spring and early summer. With the great domestic event close at hand Ailsa had no time to spare in the village. Jean called for all her attention, and got it. In order to keep the matter secret they had mutually agreed to dispense with the services of a doctor and to resort to an old wife who lived some three miles away. When the time came Ailsa was for cancelling this decision, but Jean was against any change of plan. If the truth had to be known, she wanted it to be at a time when she was well enough to explain everything.

The child was born — a fine healthy boy. Its manifold requirements and its care were sufficient to sweep away all other considerations. His majesty the baby was the first thing in the minds of both Jean and Ailsa.

'Jean, may I tell Stewart?' pleaded Ailsa, in the middle of writing a letter.

'No, no.'

'But he's right away in Barrow.'

'He has some relatives in Sydney. Alan might easily get to know.'

She had raised the question which for months had occupied Ailsa's mind as well as her own. Ailsa would have mentioned it before, had not Jean's health acted as a deterrent. The problem had to be faced, and she meant to face it now.

'You must write to Alan at once and tell him the truth, Jean.'

Jean gulped and turned her frightened eyes on her sister.

'You said you — '

'We didn't guess then about the baby. It makes all the difference. Alan has the right to know, and you must tell him.'

'I — I dare not.'

'You must.'

'What — what can I say? How can I confess that I made such a terrible mistake. I couldn't write the words — I couldn't.'

'Then I'll write them for you,' said Ailsa determinedly. 'You've got to face the issue, and it's better to face it now.'

Jean folded the baby close to her breast and wept over it softly. All Ailsa's sympathy went out to her, but she felt that this course she had taken was the only decent one in the circumstances.

It was less than a week later that a bolt came crashing out of the blue. Ailsa was returning from the fields in the dusk of even when she saw the figure of a man approaching the house from the road. There was something familiar in the walk and in the proud poise of the head, and she tried to remember where she had seen him before. Then suddenly recognition came. It was Alan Drummond.

She ran to intercept him before he could reach the door, but he arrived there first, and she heard him knock. The next moment she was beside him with wild eyes.

'Alan!'

'Ailsa! S-sh. I came to spring a surprise on Jean. I only landed yesterday.'

'You'll frighten her. Please, please go away, and let me warn her — '

But it was too late to do that, for the door opened and Jean's fair head came round it. She opened her mouth to say something, and then gave vent to an ejaculation of huge amazement. Believing he had frightened her, and regretting his conduct, Alan took her in his arms.

'I thought it would be great fun to turn up unexpected. There, it's all right. I'm no ghost.'

He raised her hands to his lips and kissed them fondly, then, seeing no apparent objection, pulled her closer and kissed her on the lips. Ailsa uttered a wild cry, but Alan heard nothing — saw nothing but the face he had dreamed about for three long years.

'Well, aren't you going to ask me in?' he laughed.

'Yes, yes. Come in and tell us everything.'

He was far too excited to notice anything amiss with the two girls — the furtive glances towards the stairs above which the baby was sleeping. Ailsa saw at once that the letter written after so much pleading was wasted. Months must elapse before it reached Drummond, and in the meantime here was Jean obviously head over heels in love.

'I never dreamed I should be home like this,' said Alan. 'I had the greatest piece of luck in the world. Jean, I'm going to buy you the best house in the district. I'm rich. The railway syndicate wanted my land and paid me a tremendous price for it.'

Jean's eyes were shining like stars at the good news. Here was the man she loved — young, handsome, rich. She met Ailsa's challenging eyes, and knew exactly what was going on in that dark head.

'No more farming, Jean,' laughed Alan. 'Ailsa can do that — she loves it.'

Ailsa made no reply, for she thought she had heard a cry from upstairs, and instinctively her head was inclined that way. Alan noticed it.

'What are you listening for, Ailsa?'

'N — nothing.'

He began to talk to Jean again, when from the room above came the penetrating hunger cry of the baby. The smile left Drummond's face as he heard it. He turned to Jean with trembling lips.

'It's a baby!'

'Y — yes,' she stammered.

'Great heavens, but — '

Ailsa was at the foot of the stairs, her hand on the balustrade and her eyes fixed on Jean. She was waiting for the confession, but it never came. In Jean's terrified eyes was a great and irresistible appeal. Ailsa saw her fate hanging in the balance, and her heart went out to her sister.

In one respect Jean had been correct. The truth would have shattered for ever the love between these two. She saw it in Drummond's eyes. It seemed to be written in letters of fire before her. The happiness of two lives was at stake, and she meant to preserve that happiness, be the cost what it might.

'Whose — whose child is that?' asked Drummond.

'He's mine,' said Ailsa calmly. 'I — I must go to him.'

4

It were easier to pass a camel through the eye of the proverbial needle than to keep a secret in the Glen. How the thing got about it was not easy to discover, but it rapidly grew from a mere whisper to open gossip. In due course it reached as far as Andrew Esplin's smiddy.

Andrew was busy at his anvil when one of the farmers dropped in with a horse which wanted shoeing. Whilst waiting the man hailed a friend across the road, and the latter walked over to pass the time of day. Some of the conversation which followed could not fail to reach Andrew's ears.

'There's a bairn in the hoose, sure enough. I've heard it mysel', and other folk as weel.'

'Maybe it's only a kitlin.'

'A kitlin! Havers! Think I canna tell a kitlin's cry frae a bairn's? It's the talk o' the Glen.'

'Weel, I've kent Ailsa and Jeannie Leslie these fifteen years, and I'm telling you it's a lie.'

The scandal-monger took umbrage at the

remark and raised his voice to a higher pitch.

'Then hoo do ye accoont for't? And hoo do ye accoont for the buyin' o' a feedin' bottle, powders, and sic like things frae 'Lizbeth Tamson's shoppie? Hoo is it that baith o' them hae shunned the Kirkton thae past months? Auld Munro or the laddie rins a' the errands noo, and they ken more'n they dare lay tongue tae. I'm tellin' ye there's a lot o' talk i' the Glen.'

'If there is it's nane o' oor business.'

'No, but it's a peety for a young lassie like Ailsa Leslie — '

'Wha says it's Ailsa?'

'It maun be. Jean is tae be mairrit to Mister Drummond this day week. I'm sorry for Ailsa. She was aye a kindly lassie.'

Andrew, who had caught the last part of this gossip, put down his hammer and strode across to the gossipers.

'What's that you're sayin'?' he growled.

'I was speakin' aboot Ailsa Leslie.'

'An' what aboot Ailsa Leslie?'

'Her an' her bairn.'

Andrew's huge hand suddenly gripped him by the collar and shook him as a terrier might a rat. The man's teeth rattled in his head, until Andrew finally released him and shot him out of the smiddy.

40

'I'll hae the law on you for this, Andrew Esplin!' he fumed.

'Law! Listen, you rat! If I hear another dirty word like that from your lips it's you who will be brought up before the law. Tak' your horse and get him shoed whaur you like. I'll hae naething tae dae wi' you.'

Andrew's rage was tremendous. Ailsa Leslie, the darling of his heart, the subject of gossip in the Glen! It put him off work for the day, and made him more uncivil than he had been in all his life. He closed the smiddy earlier than usual and went to the Eck Arms to slake an enormous thirst. But to his horror the subject being debated there was the very one which had caused him to lose a good customer.

Unable to listen to such things, and fearing that he might lose control of himself, he left in a hurry. That there was seldom smoke without fire he knew, and that there was some ground for this painful rumour he had little doubt. But Ailsa — it was impossible. Nothing in the world could persuade him that the delightful, generous, pure-hearted Ailsa was anything than he had always believed.

He experienced an irresistible desire to see her. Not to question her, but to warn her of the stories that were being whispered

41

abroad. He approached the farm, and then his stout heart failed him. How could he go to her and mention such a thing? True and trusted friend as he was, he might hurt her unwittingly.

He was turning away, when a faint cry fell on his ear. He halted and heard it again. Beyond question it was the hunger cry of a child, and it caused him to draw in his breath with a hiss of astonishment. Then light dawned on him as he remembered the trip to Glasgow and what followed. Here was the result of poor Jean's runaway marriage. Those fools had not known the truth. But the truth must be published now, that was certain. Then he gasped as he remembered Drummond and the approaching wedding. Was it possible Drummond did not know? Was it possible Ailsa had sacrificed herself in order to save her sister's happiness?

Bewildered and horrified at such a possibility, he grasped his courage in both hands and went straight to the door of the house. Ailsa herself opened it, and uttered a little cry of pleasure as she recognised her old friend.

'I've just called to see if onything was amiss,' he explained. 'I havena seen ye for ower twa months, Miss Ailsa.'

'Come in, Andrew,' she quavered. 'You know I'm always pleased to see you.'

He stepped inside the cosy sitting-room, and Ailsa, after closing the door, joined him. She smiled a little wistfully as she surveyed his grim face.

'There's something troubling you, Andrew?'

'Aye, there is. There are things bein' said in the Kirkton which no man can hearken to without losing his head and feeling like murder.'

The blood mounted to her cheeks, and he saw at once that she was not entirely ignorant of the rumour.

'You ken what it is, lassie?'

'Yes. We — we tried to keep it quiet, but it had to come out. Perhaps it's as well.'

'As well? Lassie, do you ken exactly what they are saying?'

She nodded.

'And you're letting 'em say it?'

'It's best that way, Andrew.'

'Best!' Her composure left him breathless. He saw from her eyes that she was in deadly earnest and that argument on that score was useless. Nevertheless he felt it his duty to point out where her sacrifice would lead her.

'When a woman's down in the world, or even when it appears she is down, folks kick her hard,' he said fiercely.

'I know.'

'It's going to be mortal hard work for you, Ailsa.'

She inclined her head, and then took his big hand in hers with a smile on her face.

'Andrew, you, of course, know the truth?'

'Aye, but it was only the nicht I guessed it. You've taken on another's burden?'

'There was no other way. Jean loves the child, but I think she loves Alan more. If Alan knew the truth there would be no wedding next week. For Jean's sake we have to keep her secret, Andrew. I can rely upon you?'

Andrew passed his hand across his brow and set his mouth firmly.

'Aye, you can rely upon me,' he muttered. 'But there's someone else who'll have to know the real truth.'

She looked at him swiftly, and saw the name of her sweetheart framed on his lips. For the first time her face lost its composure and her hands trembled.

'No one else must know,' she said, in an almost inaudible whisper. 'I've given my promise.'

Andrew's face was more grim than ever as he foresaw terrible complications.

'Then I withdraw my promise,' he said.

'Andrew!'

'I mean it. Do you think I'm goin' to sit

44

still and see all your future happiness ebbing away? It's inhuman, lass, and I winna stand for it. Can ye no' trust him to keep a still tongue?'

'Yes, yes, but — '

'There's no but aboot it. Whaur's your sister?'

'Upstairs.'

'Tell her I'm here. Tell her that unless she consents to your telling Stewart Morrison whose bairn that is I'll spread the truth a' through the Glen.'

He looked as intractable as his own anvil, and clearly meant to carry out his threat. She attempted to plead with him, but he remained firm. A few seconds later Jean came downstairs and nodded in an embarrassed way as she entered the room and saw Andrew.

'I — I thought it was your voice, Andrew,' she stammered.

'Aye, it's me,' growled Andrew.

Jean turned her frightened eyes from the burly smith to the somewhat-agitated Ailsa. She saw there was some hitch, and was waiting to know what it was.

'Tell her,' said Andrew.

Ailsa took her sister's hand and gazed tenderly into her face.

'Jean, Andrew knows the truth.'

'I — I suppose he does.'

'But he's stubborn. He — he wants me to tell Stewart.'

'No, no!'

Andrew came forward with his big hands clenched and his shaggy head thrust forward pugnaciously.

'Miss Jean, your sister has done a mighty big thing for you.'

'I know.'

'She's placed herself at the mercy of all the gossipers of the Glen. Everybody's door will be shut against her. Wherever she goes unkind words will follow her — '

'Don't — don't!'

Jean turned her pale face to her sister.

'Andrew's right,' she murmured. 'You must tell Stewart.'

Ailsa nodded with shining eyes, and Andrew looked immensely relieved.

'God bless you, Andrew. You were always my best friend.'

'Please God, I'll 'bide so.'

When he had gone Ailsa approached the somewhat agitated Jean.

'You're not worrying, dear?'

'I'm — I'm ashamed, Ailsa. I — I feel I can't look you in the face. If I didn't love Alan so much I'd go now and tell him everything. But I canna — I canna!'

'Cheer up!' smiled Ailsa. 'Only Andrew knows, and you know how trustworthy he is. As for Stewart — he will understand. He's the dearest lad alive.'

'Are you going to write and tell him?'

'Not yet. I — I must think out what to say. If I — '

She started as a rat-tat sounded on the outer door. Jean knew the knock, and her face betrayed her immense joy.

'It's Alan back from Glasgow. He said he would look in before he went home. I'll go.'

She ran to the door, and a few moments later returned with Drummond, whose face bore signs of considerable excitement.

'I've got it!' he ejaculated.

'Got what?'

'Aberdinnie! Jean, I kept it as a surprise for you. The house was in the market, and I made a bid for it.'

Ailsa's eyes opened with astonishment. Aberdinnie, the big house of the Glen, to be the future residence of Jean! It sounded impossible.

'Is that why you went to Glasgow?' asked Jean.

'Yes. Sir William is abroad, and has decided to remain there. The war hit him hard financially, and it is as much as he can do to live comfortably in a small villa on the Riviera. I dealt with his agent, and I've bought the place — lock, stock, and barrel. Jean, you're going to be a lady of importance — '

Ailsa, feeling that she might be in the way, stole up to the bedroom and sat by the side of the sleeping child. That Drummond had bought Aberdinnie surprised her only from the point of view of finance. Given sufficient money, that was the kind of thing she would have expected of him. Even in his young days he had shown a desire for social eminence, and Australia had only been the means to an end. Given a beautiful wife and a beautiful house, not to mention a fair education and ample means, what could he not achieve?

She felt a trace of bitterness as she looked down at the sleeping child and reflected upon the situation. But she banished this when she remembered that she, too, might ere long be a wife, and a wife with nothing to hide from her husband. That brought her to the question of the explanation which was due to Stewart. A letter would be inadequate to tell the whole story. She decided to wait until he came to the Glen, as he had promised to a fortnight hence, and then tell him the story with her own lips.

When she ultimately went downstairs

Drummond was on the point of leaving. He kissed Jean fondly and nodded smilingly at herself, but behind the smile she saw a frown. He could not forget that he was to marry the sister of a girl under a cloud, and it hurt his pride not a little.

'Oh, dear!' murmured Jean. 'I'm so happy!'

'Are you?'

'Delirious! To think of Alan buying Aberdinnie! It's like a dream come true.' Then, very seriously, 'Ailsa, when I'm — I'm married you'll let me see my — my baby whenever I want to?'

'Of course.'

'And he's got to be christened. I want to call him Peter.'

'Peter! It sounds nice.'

She said nothing of her natural dread of the christening ceremony, with the kindly eyes of the minister searching her very soul. Only now was she beginning to pay the full price of her great sacrifice.

5

The christening of the baby took place in the Glen Kirk on the following Sabbath, four days before Jean's wedding. To Ailsa it was a veritable Calvary, for all the Glen folk were there.

'A stoot he'rt tae a stey brae,' whispered Andrew. 'Dinna break down now, lass. You've been so brave.'

Under the scrutiny of a hundred pairs of eyes she faced the ordeal, whispered the boy's name, and heard the minister echo it in solemn tones. But her courage only made things worse for her. Such brazen effrontery helped to kill any sympathy there might have been. Even the kindly minister appeared to be upset.

When she eventually arrived home she broke down and wept tears of anguish. She was finding what a bitter censorian the world was when its social laws were presumably outraged.

'Ailsa, don't cry,' pleaded Jean. 'You make me feel so — so — '

'I can't help it. People are so harsh. Even if what they think were true they have no right to be cruel. It seems that only God can forgive.'

But the following day proved that she was wrong. In the afternoon there came a timid knock at the door, and she opened it to find the white-haired minister there.

'I — I haven't called on you for so long,' he demurred, 'I thought it high time I did so.'

'Please — please come in.'

They engaged in purely local topics for some time, the minister laughing occasionally as he narrated some amusing incident of the Glen, but in the end he approached the subject which she knew was the real object of his visit.

'And how is Peter?'

'Splendid. He gets bigger and bigger every day. He's asleep now in the garden.'

She was aware that the grey eyes were regarding her critically, and wished she were able to rid him of the pain which he evidently felt.

'Ailsa, what are you going to do about it?'

'About what?'

'This business. I don't ask you to tell me anything about it — that is between you and God. It's the boy I'm thinking about. In Glen Eck he will feel his position keenly when he gets old enough to understand. Unfortunately there will always be people anxious to remind him. One day he must make a start in the business of life. He ought to start on a fair footing. He'll never have that in Glen Eck. As soon as his little brain is capable of understanding he'll feel the smart.'

A little cry of pain escaped her, but he put his hand on her arm in kindly fashion.

'What is done is done, Ailsa. I haven't come here to make you feel your position more keenly than you do. I'm just thinking of the future — your future and his. Glen Eck is no place for him now.'

She saw in a flash what he was driving at. He was asking her — advising her — to leave Glen Eck and the house in which she was born. He was suggesting she should leave everything and seek new fields because of this. It occurred to her that she had intended giving up the farm when she was married to Stewart, but that was different — a voluntary surrender in the cause of love. What he now proposed was flight from the Glen gossips. The blood mounted to her cheeks as she shook her head determinedly.

'No, I won't do it — not if every soul in the Glen treats me as a leper. This is my battle, and I'm going to fight it, unless — '

'Unless what?'

'Unless Stewart asks me to go — when we are married. That will be different.'

She saw his mouth close tightly, and realised it would have been more discreet to have left her sweetheart's name out of it. But it was too late now. She could not explain her intentions nor clear away the huge doubt which was obviously obsessing him.

'Stewart — Stewart will understand,' she murmured.

'I hope so, my dear — I hope so. I confess your composure and your courage are overwhelming. I trust that this trouble has not hardened your heart, Ailsa — that you will continue to come to the kirk as you used to?'

She shook her head stubbornly.

'No, it would be full of those who fling stones without trying to understand.'

'Not full, Ailsa. There would be another Presence there who does understand. Don't isolate yourself from Him, for you may need Him more than ever in the future. There is no need to be ashamed to come to church, Ailsa.'

'I'm not ashamed of anything,' she said quickly; then stammering: 'Yes, yes, I am. Oh, I wish I could tell you — '

'Don't tell me anything you would rather

not. But, Ailsa, there is one thing I would like to ask — forgive me for asking it. The man — Peter's — isn't it possible for you to come together?'

He stopped abruptly as he saw the small hands open and close spasmodically.

'I beg your pardon — '

'It's all right. That was a natural remark; but he is dead.'

He lowered his head.

'Perhaps you are right, Ailsa, to stay,' he murmured. 'Whatever folks may say, you are and always will be the bravest little woman in the world. Good-night, my dear.'

He left her feeling more determined than ever to fight the voice of gossip. In all Glen Eck she counted but two friends — Andrew, who knew the truth, and the minister, who did not. When Jean arrived home from a walk with her prospective husband she found Ailsa brighter than she had been for some time.

'Back from love's excursions?' she queried with a smile.

'Yes, Alan took me over to Perth to introduce me to some friends of his. He is going to Glasgow tomorrow to buy a car, so that we can have a motoring honeymoon.'

'You're a lucky girl, Jean.'

'I suppose I am. But I'll never forget,

Ailsa, it was you who helped me through the wood.'

She was sincere enough, but Ailsa wondered whether this marriage would not open up a gulf between herself and her sister. The most she could expect, or indeed wished for, from Stewart was a comfortable home and an income sufficient to make both ends met and leave a trifle for the 'rainy day.' She was wise enough to know that money worked social miracles, and that Drummond with his ambitions, would not be content even to remain in his present position.

When the wedding day arrived it found Jean as beautiful a bride as ever faced the minister. But Ailsa did not attend the ceremony, which took place in Perth at Drummond's special request. She had a hundred reasons for not being present — some obvious and some not. She placed Peter as the first obstacle and the harvest as the second. But the real reason was that she felt she was not wanted. Jean had tried to persuade her, but even in her sister's eyes she read the truth — she was an outcast in the opinion of Drummond, one who, while commanding his sympathy, would be decidedly unwanted among the wedding guests.

'I wish you the best of luck, dear,' she

whispered to Jean, immediately prior to her departure. 'Write me a letter and tell me all about it.'

'I will; but you will read about it in the paper. Do I look all right?'

'You look beautiful. I wish I might look half as beautiful when — when my time comes.'

Jean's smiling face grew serious as the remark set certain thoughts in motion.

'Ailsa, is Stewart coming over on Sunday?'

'Yes.'

'And then you'll tell him everything?'

'Yes.'

'Oh, if — '

'Have no fear. Stewart will never break a promise made to me. Your happiness will be as much his concern as mine. Cheer up, dear; here comes the car. Oh, there's Peter. You haven't said good-bye to Peter.'

She ran into the garden and brought the plump baby into the room in her arms. Jean took it from her tenderly and gazed wistfully into the dimpled face. She crooned over it for a few moments and kissed its mouth, eyes, and hands. When she finally gave it to Ailsa her eyes were wet with tears.

'You'll write and tell me about him?' she almost sobbed.

'Of course I will.'

'Ailsa, you've been awfully good to me. If it hadn't been for you I shouldn't be wearing a bride's dress now.'

'Don't talk about it,' murmured Ailsa. 'If the circumstances were changed you would have done the same for me.'

Jean shook her head as she wiped away a tear with the corner of her pocket handkerchief.

'I shouldn't. It's no use ignoring plain facts. I've always been a coward and you've always been strong. Even now I'm afraid.'

'Afraid on your wedding morn! There is nothing to be afraid of, Jean.'

'There is. You have forgotten one thing.'

'What thing?'

'That letter you sent to Alan. One day it will come back from Australia. If it should ever reach Alan — '

But Ailsa had not overlooked the letter. Though she had made no mention of it before, it had always been before her mind.

'You must not meet troubles half way,' she urged. 'In all probability it will be returned here, for it is unlikely that Alan left any address to which letters could be forwarded.'

'But he did. One came only the other day. At this very moment that incriminating letter is on its way here. I have seen it in my dreams. I have seen it — '

Ailsa saw she was getting distressed again, and put her arm about her shoulders to comfort her.

'You've got to forget it to-day, Jean. Don't let it spoil the happiest day of your life. In any case it can't be forwarded to Alan during the honeymoon, as you will be motoring from place to place. When the trouble comes we will meet it.'

Jean forced a smile to her face and, lifting her veil, kissed Ailsa fondly. In the quiet brown eyes Jean read love and unending sacrifice. By the time she stepped into the waiting car, to greet the bridesmaids who had come all the way from Perth to fetch her, her eyes were shining with happiness, and her heart was light again. She waved her hand to the window as the car moved forward, and heard Ailsa's voice above the drone of the motor.

'Good-bye, Jean. Good luck to you.'

Then old Munro, who suddenly appeared from behind a hayrick, flung a huge slipper, which hit the back of the luxurious car with a thud.

Ailsa, with the baby in her arms, watched the car disappear down the road and then drooped her head and gazed into the blue wondering eyes of the child.

'She's gone, Peter,' she murmured. 'Gone and left us all alone — you and me. It doesn't matter so long as she's happy and we're happy too. And we're going to be happy, aren't we? I'm going to be your mummy now and for ever. How do you like that, you dimpled darling?'

Peter looked as if he liked it very much, for his chubby fists moved up and played with her lips and nose until she laughed with joy and smothered him with kisses.

6

The departure of Jean left the house strangely vacant, but Ailsa was too occupied with her manifold duties to let it worry her unduly. She found that the care of Peter took up a great amount of her time, and the business of the farm suffered accordingly, for Munro and his son were of the placid and irresponsible type, and only did things when they were absolutely necessary.

Ailsa, who disliked any haphazard methods of business, looked about her for a woman who could assist in the domestic work, thus permitting her to devote more time to the supervision of the two ploughmen. To her astonishment she found that even a daily woman suffered from a certain amount of bias, and was not at all anxious to work in a house which was being talked about.

'Human beings are strange creatures, aren't they, Andrew?' she remarked to the smith. 'I am not asking them for friendship. All I offer is honest work, and it goes a-begging.'

Andrew breathed deeply and expanded his magnificent chest. Of late he had been getting into bad odour with his friends through his vociferous defence of Ailsa, and the fact did not hurt him so much as it enraged him.

'Most of it is outside show, Miss Ailsa,' he grunted. 'Their hearts are good, but every man is afraid of what his neighbour might think of him. I wish I could tell them what I ken. I'd like to see their faces go red with shame. I'd like to see them on their knees asking pardon — '

'Andrew, you must remember your promise.'

'Ay, I'm remembering it, lass. Have you heard from your sister yet?'

'Yes, this morning. She is going up the side of the canal to Inverness with her husband. The first night they couldn't get into a hotel and had to sleep in the car. Her letter was brimming over with happiness.'

Andrew frowned, and Ailsa shook her finger at him reprovingly.

'You mustn't think badly of her, Andrew. You'll hurt me if you do.'

'I wouldn't hurt you for world, lass, but it doesn't seem right to me.'

'It's right so long as people are happy.'

'I'm no philosopher, Ailsa, but it appears to me there's a right and wrong to everything, whether folk are happy or not.'

'I won't argue with you, Andrew. I'm far too busy to argue with anyone — least of all with Andrew Esplin, who, when he chooses, can be the most obstinate man in Scotland.'

Andrew grinned and got rid of his bad temper, which had been engendered by a stormy argument but an hour before.

'You're like a ray of June sunshine, Miss Ailsa,' he laughed. 'Now, about that woman you're wanting — you leave it to me. I'll send one along before evening, or my name's not Andrew.'

'You're a treasure, Andrew.'

'I'm a hornet in the Glen these days. My, I've been stinging some of them mighty hard.'

He laughed, and began to work the bellows with his muscular arm. She bade him good day, and was turning away when he called her back.

'Is it to-morrow Stewart Morrison is coming?' he queried.

'Y — yes.'

'And then you're going to tell him?'

'Yes, I'm going to meet him at the station. Andrew, if you can get that woman I'll bless you. I want her to mind Peter to-morrow while I go over the hill with Stewart.'

'I'll get her,' said Andrew doggedly.

He was as good as his word, and that evening a rather dour woman called at the farm and informed Ailsa that Andrew Esplin had sent her. Whatever persuasive methods the smith had used to bring about this remarkable result Ailsa never knew, but the terms were agreed, and the woman promised to start work the following morning.

Sunday dawned warm and bright. The woman turned up on the minute; Ailsa looked forward to a day of immense happiness. She referred to Stewart's last letter, and noted the time of the train by which he was due to arrive.

'Your uncle's coming this morning, Peter,' she crooned to the baby. 'He'll be a little surprised to find he has a nephew as big and bonnie as you.'

But Fate had in store as cruel a blow as ever it had inflicted. So small a thing as the alteration of a train in the time-table was the means by which this was brought about. Stewart discovered it at the last moment, but it was too late to write and inform Ailsa, and he guessed that a telegram would not reach her in time.

He stepped out of the train at the junction into warm and dazzling sunshine, with his heart full of the impending meeting. Looking far across the valley, he could see the northern wing of the big house among the trees, and beyond it, higher up on the hill, the farm where Ailsa had her being. The signalman, recognising a familiar figure, poked his head from his box and waved his hand.

'Good morning, Andy,' shouted Stewart. How is everybody?'

'Same as ever. Auld Gillespie, the shepherd, is dead, though, and Sandy Kidd has influenza. Jeannie Leslie was mairrit on Thursday tae Alan Drummond, who cam' back rich frae Australia. Did you ken that?'

'Yes, Ailsa told me, of course.'

Andy's face wore a queer expression as Ailsa was mentioned. Stewart could not fail to notice it, and wondered what had caused it.

'Ailsa's all right, isn't she, Andy?' he asked.

But Andy discovered that he had work to attend to, and withdrew his head suddenly. Stewart wrinkled his forehead.

'Andy!'

But Andy was deaf to further inquiries. At first he imagined that Stewart knew about everything, but now he felt convinced that the contrary was the case, and like a wise man, preferred to keep his own counsel.

Stewart, with disturbed mind, hastened from the wayside station and set his face for the Glen. Andy's behaviour aroused the wildest possibilities. Ailsa might be dangerously ill or the victim of an accident. In such eventuality she might have preferred to keep him in ignorance of the fact lest he should worry unduly.

With these sombre thoughts revolving in his mind he hurried down the winding lane. A quarter of a mile from the farm calamity awaited him. He met a man with a dog strolling lazily along. The man was none other than the victim of Andrew's wrath, whom the latter had flung out of the smiddy a week or so before. Seeing Stewart obviously making for the farm, he stopped and stared at him.

'Hullo, Mains!' remarked Stewart. 'Seen a ghost?'

'It's Stewart Morrison, isn't it?'

'That's so. Did you imagine I was dead!'

'No, but — '

He turned his gaze towards the farm, and Stewart saw again evidence of a mystery. He strode up to the farmer and looked at him tensely.

'Mains, is there anything wrong at the farm? Why do you look at me like that?'

'I — I thought you knew until I saw you making — '

'Knew what? For God's sake speak! Is — is anything wrong with Ailsa Leslie?'

The farmer remained silent.

'Is she ill?' gasped Stewart.

'No, not now,' stammered Mains.

'So, she's been ill? Why can't you answer?'

The farmer crouched back into the hedge. Against his desire to spread the gossip was fear of the blazing eyes of the agitated questioner. Stewart, tormented by suspense, caught him by the shoulder.

'For heaven's sake tell me what is wrong?'

'You — you really want tae ken?'

'Yes.'

'It's — it's a bairn,' stammered Mains.

'A bairn! What bairn?'

'Her bairn — Ailsa Leslie's bairn. I thocht — '

Stewart reeled like a drunken man. His face went ghastly white, and his lips moved in anguish. Then uncontrollable rage boiled within him. He sprang at Mains and caught him by the throat.

'You liar! You infernal scoundrel to try and tell me that. I'll — I'll — '

'Let go!' gasped Mains. 'You asked me tae tell you, and I've only tell't you what a'body i' the Glen kens. Ask Andrew Esplin. Ask anybody — '

He wrenched himself free, and sprang away from the infuriated Stewart. What more he said Stewart did not know. His one desire was to get away before he committed some crime of violence. Mains was drunk, he thought, or mad. And yet Andy had exhibited — It was impossible, unthinkable.

He lurched rather than walked towards the farm. It was yet early, and no one was about the place. With halting steps he made for the door. It was open, and from inside came Ailsa's musical voice, prattling for the baby's benefit.

'Mummy won't be long, darling. Give her a big fat kiss, and then go to seepy-bye.'

He stumbled through the door to behold her leaning over the baby's cot with her head bent. A great sob escaped him as he realised it was true. There was a baby. Mains had not been mad or drunk. Here it was before his eyes.

Ailsa heard the cry of bitter anguish, and turned swiftly to see the distraught figure leaning against the doorpost. So unexpected was the intrusion that she uttered a faint cry and stood as if rooted to the spot.

'So, it's true — true!' A horrible laugh came from his throat. 'You, Ailsa, you — '

'Stewart!' she cried out.

'And — you've written to me — lies, lies, lies — '

He turned away, muttering things inaudible

to her — sounds that cut deep into her tortured heart.

'Stewart, wait!'

He halted as if against his will. A few words could put it right now, but the words were never spoken. On the verge of framing them her pride revolted. He believed this of her — the man she loved more than anything in the world believed her worthless on the mere evidence of his eyes! That knowledge sank deep into her soul, bringing such agony as she had never known before. For the space of ten seconds they stood facing each other with the gulf ever widening. Then he turned and left her — and she let him go.

7

These were days of despair for Ailsa. With Stewart gone out of her life there seemed little enough to live for. All the dreams of the future, all the castles she had built shattered for ever. The moment after Stewart had left she rushed to the door, his name on her lips. The desire to call him back — to explain away the hideous thoughts in his mind — was almost irresistible. On the verge of doing so came the most painful thought of all — that his love was shallow enough for him to believe her capable of faithlessness.

An hour later Andrew had called. By her haggard face he divined that something was wrong.

'Ailsa!'

The moist, pain-ridden eyes were focused on him.

'Has — has he gone, lass?'

'Ay, gone — for ever.'

'But — '

'He believed it, Andrew. He believed I — Oh, it was horrible!' she choked.

'But you told him — the truth?'

She shook her head slowly, and Andrew

recoiled with speechless amazement.

'You — you let him go withoot tellin' him?' he gasped at length.

'He didna wait to be told — before he drew his own conclusions. Someone must have met him on the way here. He saw the bairn — he — Oh, God, the way he looked at me!'

Andrew put out his hand and steadied her.

'Lass, lass, keep calm. It's a matter that can be put straight. You'll hae to write — '

'Not a line — not a word. He believed it all without giving me a chance to explain. That's not the love I expected. That's not the trust that love should breed. If it had been the other way round, and some terrible lie had been told about him, do you think I would have believed it? Not if the minister himself had told me. I should have wanted it from his own lips before I accused him as he accused me.'

There was something magnificent in her pride — a vital force which seemed to radiate from her. It overrode her mental agony and blazed from her eyes.

'He's young,' said Andrew. 'You maun mind that.'

'I am remembering, Andrew.'

'And when a lad's young his passions are

70

red-hot. Maybe he cam' here wi' his heart brimming wi' love. You've got to imagine what it would mean to him to hear this lie, and then to find you here wi' the bairn in your arms. By now he'll have had time to reason things oot. He'll hate himsel' for thinkin' what he did.'

'It makes no difference, Andrew. I could never look at him again. To my dying day I shall remember the look he gave me. I — I think it has frozen my heart for ever.'

'Ailsa, you maun pull yersel' th'gither, lass.'

'There are things in one's nature one can't help, Andrew. In mine there is my — my father's stubborn pride. I know you will say cast it aside, but you might as well ask me to cast my skin — or — or do Peter here some injury. It's impossible, I tell you. I'll forgive him, but in forgiving him I shall have to forget him.'

She was speaking quite calmly now, and Andrew, who was a good judge of human nature, saw to what depths she had been wounded. Yet he believed it was not impossible to put things straight, and already his brain was working at a plan. But he reckoned without Ailsa's feminine intuition. She saw the furrows in his brow, and as through a mirror divined his intentions.

'You mustn't interfere, Andrew.'

'Eh?'

'I know you love me, and would do anything to secure my happiness, but to interfere by communicating with Stewart would hurt me more than you can guess.'

Andrew pulled a wry face.

'This isn't going to break me, Andrew. I'm going to live every second of my life. For all the love I've lost I'm going to be compensated. Peter has cost me all this, and Peter is going to repay me. I'm going to make him love me, love me, until the cup runs over.'

'You're a brave lass, Ailsa.'

'Brave! It isn't brave to be happy. I'm going to be happy though the village eats its head off in talking about me. And I'm going to the kirk every Sunday with Peter, and I'll sing the praises loud to let them know I'm there.'

'I wonder?' mused Andrew.

'Wonder what?'

'Whether you winna find public opinion ower strong.'

She looked at him with disappointed eyes.

'Even you, Andrew, and I thought — '

'It's no' your courage I'm underrating, Ailsa. It's this thing they call ostracism — it's a monster difficult — to contend wi'.'

'Not when your conscience is clear. I'm going to look them all in the face bravely.'

But when he had left her she found it much more difficult to be calm and careless of the forces that were arrayed against her. To her Stewart had been a stalwart beam. So long as she retained his love and confidence other things seemed of comparative unimportance.

She had scarcely expected a letter from him, but two days later one arrived. It was some time before she could summon up courage enough to open it, and when she did the words were like tongues of fire.

'Dear Ailsa, — I feel that the whole world has slipped away from under me. Everything I held dear, everything which made life worth living gone — gone. It is not for me to judge you, or to attempt to discover how this terrible thing came about. Though it renders any future impossible between you and me, I shall always try to think well of you, and to put the blame where I feel sure it must chiefly lie. Whoever he is, wherever he is, may he be brought to pay the full price — Yours sorrowfully, Stewart.'

She could almost feel the restraint with which he had penned the words. He was trying to be kind, generous, when all the time he despised her. With a sob she tore the letter into fragments and flung them into the fire. That night she returned the engagement ring without an accompanying word.

The last link having been severed, she set herself to forget the past and to lay the foundation stone of a new life, in which Peter should be the pivot. True to her resolution, she went to the kirk on the following Sunday, taking the baby with her. It was the testing time of her courage, and she felt her position keenly. In the hushed silence a sense of great loneliness swept over her. She could not help noticing that, although the place was rapidly filling, the pew in which she sat was practically empty.

People were avoiding her. They came up the aisle, glanced from side to side, and preferred to squeeze themselves into the already packed pews. She had expected that, but it stung much more than she had anticipated.

At the last moment help came in the figure of Andrew. His feet echoed through the place and his figure seemed almost too large for the small building. He made no pause, but came straight to her and sat down beside her. This could not fail to cause whispered comment, for it was notorious that Andrew never came to the kirk. Ailsa knew that quite well, and her heart went out to him as she divined the motive which had brought him there. She met his eyes, and in her own was the deepest gratitude for this kindly act.

It imbued her with new strength. She gave herself up to the service, and her young, clear voice swelled above the organ and rose to heights of ecstasy. Andrew, not to be outdone, added his basso profundo. Together they led the congregation. Never had the little kirk rung with such music.

When the minister delivered his homily she gasped at the subject of it. Judge not, lest ye be judged! She knew it was all for her, who needed it not, and she found it difficult to keep back the tears. But Andrew's hand slid along the seat and touched hers.

In the hallowed atmosphere it was not difficult to be generous, but once outside, such lessons were quickly forgotten, and the minister knew that quite well. When the service was over he managed to overtake Andrew and Ailsa on their way home.

'Glad to see you, Ailsa,' he said. 'And you too, Andrew.'

'Oh, me,' said Andrew. 'I thought I'd drop along to try my voice. I used to sing in the choir when I was a boy.'

'I wish you'd sing in it now.'

Andrew shook his head.

'And how's Peter getting on, Ailsa?'

'Splendid. He's the quietest and most contented baby that ever was born. Look at him.'

She pulled the shawl away from Peter's face and revealed his dimpled cheeks and wondering blue eyes. The minister grinned at him and touched the chubby fists, but in his eyes was something akin to pity. Ailsa saw it, and put back the shawl quickly, and a few minutes later he bade them good-bye.

'A good man,' mused Andrew, 'but a wee bit prejudiced.'

'He was pitying him, Andrew,' said Ailsa. 'Pitying my Peter, who, please God, is going to be as fine a man as ever stepped.'

'Ay, if he takes after his foster-mother.'

She looked at him with brimming eyes. A few minutes later she left him at the door of the farm and watched his big figure go striding down the lane. She thanked God for Andrew, the bravest, truest heart in the whole of the Glen, her dearest and best friend.

But what of Andrew himself? In the clean breast of him something lived which for years he had kept in check. That Andrew had never married had been a great surprise to the people of the village. They did not know that Andrew's heart was given to a dream — a dream he knew could never come true. And the dream was Ailsa.

It had started on Ailsa's return from school, a maiden on the verge of radiant womanhood. She had come to Andrew, as she always did, to talk of the hundred and one things that filled her mind — to ask his opinion on matters innumerable and to gladden the smiddy with her merry laughter. On that occasion Andrew had not kissed her. Gone for ever were the kisses and the cuddles. Three months absence had made all the difference. Ailsa was a woman.

And then grew the secret knowledge that with the death of his paternal friendship something else was born. It had frightened him at first, for he had not wanted that. With all the power of his mind he endeavoured to stifle the whisper. But he might as well have tried to stop Niagara.

He was not the man to evade facts, and this one he met bravely. The upshot was a sworn resolution — she never should know. For five long years Andrew had kept faith with his own conscience. This he knew — that to Ailsa he was the same old Andrew who had nursed her and romped in the meadows. Rather than she should know his secret he would have died a thousand deaths.

8

Jean arrived home a week later, looking more beautiful than ever, and browned by the open-air honeymoon. An hour after her arrival she came across to the farm to see Ailsa.

'You look splendid,' said Ailsa. 'Have you been happy?'

'Happier than I have ever been in my life. Ailsa, Alan's been so good to me. You can't imagine what it means to be married to a man who adores you.'

She took Ailsa in her arms and kissed her fondly, then looked round the room expectantly.

'Where is he?' she murmured.

'You shall see him,' smiled Ailsa.

She went into the garden and brought Peter in her arms. Jean smothered his face with kisses, laughing almost hysterically as he pushed his tiny fists into her mouth.

'The darling! Oh, Ailsa, you don't know how much I have missed him.'

Ailsa was wondering on that point. Had she really missed him as much as she pretended? The love of her husband perhaps was a more vital thing than the love of Peter. Then there was the future — that magical future which dazzled her and filled her dreams.

'Are you going to settle at Aberdinnie now, Jean?' she asked.

'Yes; the housekeeper has engaged most of the old servants. We're to have a big garden party next month, and a lot of eminent people are coming. The Menzies have introduced us to such a crowd. You know, of course, that Sir Angus Menzies is putting up for Parliament at the by-election. The constituency is a very scattered one, and Alan is going to look after this part of it — nurse it, he calls it. It will be a good thing for Alan, because the Menzies are very influential.'

She rattled on for several minutes in like vein, and Ailsa saw in her fervour the newly-planted seed of ambition. She divined that the time was not far distant when Jean would be ashamed to look back into the past, when she had worked with her hands. Even now, although she invited Ailsa to Aberdinnie, it was with some little hesitation, for she knew that Drummond had some scruples about her association with Ailsa.

'You've no use for me at Aberdinnie,' said

Ailsa, shaking her head. 'To a certain extent our ways lie apart.'

'Ailsa!'

'You know it's true. In this village I'm an outcast — a woman beyond the pale. It is difficult to get some of them to buy my butter. All I have in the world is Peter.'

'And Stewart,' added Jean, with a rather shamed expression.

'Not even Stewart.'

'What! You don't mean — '

'Don't — don't ask me anything about that. Stewart got to hear, and it's all over.'

'But he doesn't think that you — that you — '

Jean's amazement was complete. Ailsa merely inclined her head and kept her eyes averted.

'But that won't do,' cried Jean. 'We must tell Stewart, Ailsa, you've suffered so much for me you must not ruin your happiness in that direction. I'll write to him.'

'No, Jean, dear; I've reconciled the loss now. Please, please don't mention him to me again.'

Jean could do no other than accept that. She began to cry, but dried her tears of remorse as Ailsa broke into a laugh and changed the conversation.

The weeks that followed were crowded

ones for Jean. The garden party took place and was a huge success. She had looked forward to it in fear and trembling, but found it much less overwhelming than she had imagined. It was partly due to the dress she wore and to her beauty. Dressed as well as the best of her guests, she felt fortified against critical eyes. As pretty as the prettiest of them, she could afford to hold her head proudly.

'It went off splendidly,' remarked Drummond afterwards. 'Jean, you were a veritable queen.'

'I felt very nervous at first,' she murmured.

'Why? You had nothing to fear. Your father was wellborn and you are as well educated as any of them. But, tell me, have you seen your sister?'

'Yes.'

'And did you mention that matter to her?'

Jean shook her head, and a frown crossed his face.

'Why not?'

'Alan, I couldn't. How can I ask Ailsa to leave the farm, just to satisfy our social ambitions? What justification have I — her own sister — to suggest such a thing?'

Drummond walked up and down uneasily. Ailsa was the fly in the ointment. So long as

Ailsa stayed in close proximity to Aberdinnie she must prove an obstacle to his schemes for social advancement.

'I don't want you to think me hard, unsympathetic, Jean,' he said. 'I am more than sorry for your sister, but it's inconvenient to have her so near. You must see that.'

'It — it may be inconvenient for us,' she demurred, 'but oughtn't we to consider her? She's the dearest girl in the world — '

'Yes, yes, but I'll give her the means to settle down elsewhere in comfort. There's young Morrison waiting to marry her when he can afford it. This would be an excellent change for her.'

'But Stewart Morrison is not going to marry her,' she almost screamed.

'What a hash she has made of her life. And for what — some unscrupulous knave whose name we do — '

He stopped as Jean uttered a sharp cry.

'I'm sorry,' he whispered. 'But looking at it from a sensible point of view, isn't it better for Ailsa to leave the Glen? There's the boy to be considered. He'll never have a chance so long as the people about him know the truth. I'll see her myself,' he decided.

'No, you mustn't. It would hurt her terribly.'

'Then what's to be done?' he asked a little

impatiently. 'Things cannot remain as they are now.'

'If you must put this proposal to her, why not go to Andrew Esplin? He has been like a father to us ever since our own father died.'

Drummond reflected for a few moments. The suggestion was certainly worth adopting, for he knew Ailsa's affection for the big smith.

'I'll see Andrew to-morrow,' he replied at length.

Then Jean began to have qualms. Andrew knew the truth. Suppose that came out? Her dreams were full of this possibility, but in the light of day she gained courage. Andrew had given his promise and could be relied upon. Nevertheless, into this garden of gladness came the spectre that was destined always to live with her — the knowledge that another was paying the price.

Drummond's interview with Andrew was very brief and most unproductive. Andrew had listened attentively while his visitor put forward the suggestion in great detail, explaining with no little embarrassment that his motive was to give Ailsa a new start in life. When he had finished Andrew stood up and pushed his great head forward.

'And ye ask me to tak' that message to

Ailsa Leslie — to advise her to gie up her hame, leave the place in which she was born so that she winna be an inconvenience to you?'

'I never suggested such a thing.'

'Na, but I'm suggesting it. There's a puir lassie wi' a bairn, fightin' bravely to feed it an' clad it, lovin' it as dearly as your mother did you. Ye're no' satisfied wi' flingin' mud, but you want to turn her oot o'the place as well.'

'What are — '

'Oh, I'm a man who speaks his mind on such matters. I don't begrudge you stepping up the ladder a wee bittie, but you're no' goin' to walk ower the body of a woman wi' my consent. That's a' I've got to say to ye, Mister Drummond. Good day.'

Drummond left the house in high dudgeon. His sudden access to money had already changed him a great deal. He felt his position keenly now. He had tried to persuade himself that he was acting in Ailsa's interest all the time, but Andrew had revealed the lie to him, and it was not pleasant to reflect upon.

The visit had not surprised Andrew greatly. Nevertheless, it enraged him as few things could.

'Turn her oot, wad they?' he growled. 'Turn my Ailsa from her hearth and home.

No' while Andrew Esplin has blood in his veins and means to prevent it. What a world it is, to be sure, wi' men and women walking ower each ither to grasp at a shadow.'

Naturally enough he said nothing to Ailsa, and she was left in ignorance of the proposal, for Drummond, on thinking things over, came to the conclusion that for the present things were best left as they stood.

As the autumn advanced, and the morning frosts heralded the approach of winter, folks no longer discussed the lass at the farm, for other things occupied their attention.

9

Summer faded into autumn and autumn into winter. The election took place, and Sir Angus Menzies was returned by a big majority. To this end Alan had helped as far as lay in his power. Jean, too, had assisted him by canvassing some of the farmers in the district.

'It was good fun,' she confided to Ailsa. 'I knew practically nothing about Sir Angus' views, but most of the voters seemed to know less.'

'I'll warrant you never got Andrew's vote.'

'Nobody did,' laughed Jean. 'Andrew is the most cantankerous man alive.'

'Andrew has brains.'

'He reads too much for a man in his position — thinks too much about things, and has prejudices. I'm sure he is not happy.'

Ailsa had often pondered the same point. Andrew certainly was not the care-free man he had been years ago. She missed his hearty laughter and the light that was wont to sparkle in his eyes. She noticed, too, that he was more prone to cynicism and more silent.

'Perhaps it's because he lives alone,' she said. 'Andrew ought not to live alone. He loves children so much he ought — '

'Ailsa, aren't you going too fast?' remonstrated Jean. 'Even if Andrew were to contemplate marriage, who is there in the Glen for him to marry?'

'Oh, the Glen isn't the whole world.'

'It's Andrew's world. He was born in it, and has only been out of it on three occasions.' She shook her finger. 'It's no use your trying match-making with Andrew.'

'I'd like to see him happy,' reflected Ailsa. 'If I knew of a woman who could bring back Andrew's hearty laugh I'd go after her and tell her what a chance she is missing.'

Jean laughed merrily. She could afford to laugh now, for things were going splendidly for the new Laird of Aberdinnie. As a mark of esteem Sir Angus had offered her husband a directorship in a company in which he was interested. It meant that Drummond would have to attend certain meetings in Edinburgh, but Jean was willing to put up with his enforced absence. She had become imbued with her husband's yearning for further advancement.

'Alan has been awfully lucky of late,' she confided.

'He has always been lucky.'

'Yes, but this, perhaps, wasn't so much luck as good sense. He invested a whole lot of money in some industrial shares which were at their lowest ebb. For a time I was terribly nervous, in case something should go wrong. But it didn't. Suddenly the shares commenced to rise. I watched the newspaper every day — it was the most exciting experience I ever had. Then Alan sold them.'

'What for?' queried Ailsa.

'He sold them right at the top of the curve. They went down immediately after, and are now worth little more than when he bought them. He made over five thousand pounds.'

Ailsa gasped. It seemed dishonest to her for anyone to make money by speculating in that way.

'Five thousand pounds,' she mused. 'But if he made it, who lost it?'

'I don't know. Somebody, of course.'

'It might have been somebody very poor — a lot of people with small means. I don't think I would like to make money that way.'

'What nonsense. Everybody does.'

'Do they?'

'Of course they do. How can people get rich otherwise?'

'That's just what Andrew asks.'

'Oh, Andrew. Ailsa, if you are going to let Andrew fill your brain with his strange ideas I shall refuse to come and see you. No, I shall not. Whatever happens to me, Ailsa, I'll still remember you did something for me which few sisters would do.'

'Don't talk like that.'

'I won't. I've sworn to forget it. In a few weeks it will be New Year. My great resolution shall be to forget I was ever unhappy and poor.'

Ailsa looked at her sharply.

'You talk as if poverty were a crime,' she said.

'I never knew what life really meant until I married Alan. Don't you remember how we used to scrape and nearly starve when the crops were bad? Ailsa, to have dresses in plenty, to wake up and find that things are different, to really live — '

She became aware that her indiscreet talk was hurting her sister, and was immediately contrite. But what was hurting Ailsa was not the fact that she was almost as poor now as she had been in the days gone by, but that Jean was changing — that she was making wealth and social ambition an idol.

Three days before the New Year snow set in. It transformed the Glen into the semblance of an oldtime New Year's card. Jean was putting a proposal to her husband which was destined not to meet with approval. She anticipated reluctance on his part to fall in with it, but not the stubborn refusal she met with. She had been playing some old airs from the Scottish song book to him on the new piano after dinner and had brought from his lips expressions of deep appreciation.

'Do you really mean it?' she asked.

'Of course I do,' he laughed. 'I never pay compliments unless they are deserved.'

'Oh, but you do. You just spoil me.'

'Jean, I want to make you the happiest wife in the world. I — I would do anything for you.'

'I wonder.'

He looked up.

'Suppose I ask you to do a little thing for me now?'

He wagged his finger laughingly.

'So you mean to get me at my weak moment? What is it — another new frock, or — '

'I want you to invite Ailsa up here for New Year's Eve. Peter could sleep here and be driven back in the car when we have seen the New Year in — .'

She stopped as she saw the look on his

face. He shook his head determinedly.

'That, Jean, is impossible.'

'Why?'

'Can't you see how impossible it is?'

'I can't,' she retorted. 'New Year's Eve is a time of goodwill and — '

He put out his hand and caught hers, gazing at her tenderly, but nevertheless relentlessly.

'Listen, Jean. You and I are bound to view Ailsa's conduct differently. I do not blame you for standing by your sister. In a way I admire you for it. But, however much she may have suffered, however big a scoundrel this unknown man may be, it does not alter the fact that Ailsa is partly responsible for what has happened. Jean, I would do anything in reason to please you, but this is out of the question.'

Jean's hands were closing and unclosing nervelessly, and tears were streaming down her distressed face. He drew her closer to him and kissed her hot cheek.

'I'm sorry to upset you, Jean. But oughtn't we to consider our own future. As it is, things are said which are extremely embarrassing to me. If Ailsa had any love for you she would save you from this. As it is she seems to delight to live almost next door to us.'

'How deeply you misunderstand her.'

'Well, you must admit that her conduct since that affair has not been blameless. She goes about with that child, with her head in the air as if — as if she were proud of it.'

'Why shouldn't she be proud of him? He's so bonnie, so healthy. Whatever you may say, he is your nephew — '

It was an unfortunate remark. Drummond stood up and paced the room in a state of great agitation. His nephew! It stung him to the quick, and hurt him all the more to hear it from Jean's lips.

'Alan!'

He swung round to find her facing him with her arms out.

'You — you are angry with me?'

'No, no, not with you.'

'You are, Alan, and I can't bear it. I — I want your love more than anything in the world. Won't you forgive me?'

He clasped her to him. A few moments later they were sitting very close together on the couch, talking of their wonderful future, with Ailsa and Peter but faint figures in the background. But neither of them could quite forget her, for she marred to some extent the far horizon.

It was on the last day of the old year that something quite unexpected happened to Ailsa. The day being fine and sunny, she spent the morning in taking Peter for a walk. It was on the return journey that the thing happened. She was emerging from a side lane when a figure came round the corner and almost collided with the perambulator.

'I beg your par — '

The voice set her heart beating furiously. She looked up and saw Stewart Morrison. For a second they stood looking into each other's eyes, both bereft of speech, then with a strangled sob she pushed past him.

'Ailsa!'

She hesitated, half turned, and then, reflecting that any conversation could only end in misunderstandings and recriminations, plunged forward at a rapid pace. The mere glimpse of his face had revived all the past — brought back with painful clearness the myriad incidents of their courtship, the dreams she had once cherished, and sacred conversations. He had friends in the Glen. She had no doubt he had come to stay with them for the holidays — perhaps with the object of seeing her again, or at least to hear something about her. She imagined the kind of thing he would hear — the congratulations that would be poured upon him. And this was the day on which she had meant to be so happy — on which to frame resolutions for the New Year. She hardened her heart, but not sufficiently to quite drown the yearning sensation which dwelled there.

Things could not be forgotten quite so easily. With the knowledge that he was near her again came pulsing the old love. She feared to go out lest she should meet him again — feared to look through the window lest she should see his straight figure in the distance to remind her how great was her loss.

10

Time passed and nothing happened to disturb the natural peace and quiet of Glen Eck.

Ailsa strove to forget Stewart, and all her love and devotion was showered upon Peter, the innocent cause of the great upheaval in her life. Drummond had been a great deal in Edinburgh and London, and Jean had stayed with him there for lengthy periods, making new friends and acquaintances. But in the summer she and her husband came to Glen Eck and kept open house. The Twelfth of August saw a large shooting party at Aberdinnie, eager to kill the grouse with which the place abounded.

Among the guests was the owner of a large portion of the land about Glen Eck — Robert McKinnes. He was a bad landlord, inasmuch as he never worried himself about his tenants and was only interested in the rents.

'It must be five years since I was in the Glen,' he confided to Drummond. 'Nothing appears to have changed. The place wants developing.'

'It wants new houses,' said Drummond. 'A good many of the people are overcrowding.

There's not a single house been erected for seven years.'

'That will soon be altered,' murmured McKinnes.

'Is someone going to build?'

'Quite probably. Land is not worth holding these days — I am about to put mine in the market.'

This was interesting news to Drummond. His quick brain saw great possibilities in this proposed sale.

'All of it?' he asked.

'Yes. I'm tired of being a landlord — tired of reading the terrible things that are said about us. I propose to sell all the freeholds. I saw Benton about it yesterday. He is busy making up the lots. It is a convenient time to sell, as nearly all the leases are running out.'

'And the tenants?'

'They will have an opportunity to buy their farms. The whole thing will go to auction.'

Drummond said no more, but determined to watch events closely. His guests were still with him when the first announcement of the forthcoming sale was published. It created quite a stir in the Glen, for no one had the slightest idea that McKinnes would ever contemplate selling his properties. Men gathered at the village inn and discussed the important announcement.

'That's guid news,' said a burly farmer. 'Leaseholds were aye unsatisfactory. Look at my place; it's no' fit for a pig to live in, and hasna been for twenty years. When it's a man's own he's got some reason for keeping it trim. Will you be buyin', Leckie?'

'If the price is reasonable,' said Leckie. 'But, mind you, there's a big demand for land, and I dinna doot but that we'll see a lot of speculators at the sale to run up prices.'

Andrew Esplin, who had dropped in to while away an hour, opened his ears at the conversation. He was wondering what Ailsa would do in the circumstances — whether she had heard of McKinnes' intentions.

'Seen a plan yet, Leckie?' he asked.

'Aye.'

'Is Ailsa Leslie's place included?'

'Aye — Lot Number 8. I mind that fine. It includes the meadows on the north side.'

Andrew nodded, and after waiting a few minutes longer went over to see Ailsa. He found her putting Peter to bed, and was so immersed in the operation that he almost forgot the object of his visit. A year had made a huge difference to that infant. He now boasted a wonderful mop of golden curls plus six teeth and a winsome smile. When he saw Andrew he put out both his arms and lisped, 'Nunk-ie, Nunk-ie!' Andrew caught him up and slung him round his neck.

'Oh, be careful!' cried Ailsa.

'He's all right,' laughed Andrew. 'Look at the limbs o' him. He's goin' to be a braw lad that. Peter, what have I got in my pocket?'

'Choc-choc,' said Peter promptly.

'Right first time.'

'Don't you dare give him chocolate this time of night,' stormed Ailsa. 'Andrew, you know nothing about bairns.'

'Maybe no. But what can I do? He knows I've got it.'

'Give it to me. He can have it in the morning.'

Andrew parted with a huge bar of chocolate and Peter's blue eyes followed its movement. Ailsa, with wonderful dexterity, pretended to give it him, but put the business end of the feeding bottle into his mouth instead. Then she whipped him into his cot before he could realise the deception.

'Now, what brings you up here, Andrew?'

'Have you heard the news?'

'What news?'

'About the land sale?'

She shook her head and gazed at him questioningly.

'There's to be a big auction in the Glen

in a fortnight's time. McKinnes is selling all his property under the hammer.'

'Are you sure, Andrew?'

'Aye, the bills were posted to-day. Benton is to sell it at the inn. How does your lease stand, Ailsa?'

'It runs out in six months. Does it mean that I can't get it renewed?'

'You might, but not from McKinnes. He has made up his mind to sell. Your farm is Lot 8. Ailsa, you'll have to buy if you want to bide here.'

Ailsa looked very reflective. Her available cash was extremely little, for the harvest was poor, and she had recently lost a cow from some strange illness.

'What do you think the place will fetch?' she quavered.

'I canna say, lass, but it ought to be worth a thousand pounds.'

'A thousand pounds! It's impossible!'

'Of course, you needna pay it all. You can get a mortgage on, say, three parts o't.'

'But that will mean that I must find two hundred and fifty pounds?'

'Aye, about that sum. Can you do it, Ailsa?'

Ailsa went to a drawer and produced her bank pass-book. She made a few swift calculations and then nodded.

'But it will leave me with scarcely anything in hand. I — I never bargained for this. I thought I could get the lease renewed in December.'

'McKinnes has been hit by the war,' Andrew explained. 'If you can buy it at that price, Ailsa, I advise you to do it. At any rate it must be worth twenty-five per cent. more to you than to anyone else, so you are safe to bid for it.'

It came as a blow to Ailsa, who had been struggling to put a little away week by week that Peter might one day have a good education. She saw that it would mean working harder than ever now — producing two ears of wheat where but one grew before, economising even more in her own personal expenditure, which was low in all conscience.

Strangely enough, as if she anticipated the trouble, Jean approached Ailsa two days later with regard to Peter's maintenance. She put her suggestion very bluntly — so bluntly that it aroused Ailsa's resentment immediately.

'But, Ailsa, you must be reasonable. Peter is my obligation — I insist upon paying what is due.'

'I've kept him all this time,' said Ailsa stubbornly. 'I — I feel that he is really mine. I've suffered for him — I've sacrificed my — my whole life for him, and I mean to provide for him myself. He shall never want for a single thing while I live.'

'But — '

Ailsa waved her hand peremptorily, and Jean, who knew her so well, realised that argument was useless. She went to the sleeping child and kissed him softly, feeling for a moment a terrible knocking at her heart. Yet he looked so beautiful and contented lying there that it helped to still the voice of conscience within her. No mother could have lavished more affection, more care on him than Ailsa had done. The cot was draped in white muslin and everything about him evidenced the love and unremitting attentions of his foster mother.

'I — I wish I had him,' burst out Jean suddenly.

'It's too late now,' replied Ailsa.

'Is it ever too late?'

'What do you mean?'

'I don't know. Sometimes I feel that — that — '

She did not finish the sentence, for the premonition she had was not the kind she could discuss easily — even with her own sister. The dread that haunted her was that she might never have a child by her husband — that she had given away the single beautiful fruit of her life.

Ailsa happily did not understand this fear. She knew that the sight of the boy always aroused a queer look in Jean's eyes, but ascribed it to the everpresent fear that Drummond might one day get to know the truth.

The day of the auction drew near, and to Ailsa's discomfort several people came to look over the farm, as if with a view to bidding for it. She had already been to see the bank manager with reference to a mortgage and had calculated that eleven hundred pounds was the utmost she could afford. She hoped that even this would not be necessary.

When at last the day came she went into the village and, armed with a catalogue, entered the big drawing-room of the inn, where a mixed throng had gathered. Benton was acting both as auctioneer and solicitor for McKinnes. He dwelt in the usual way upon the value of the choice properties he was about to offer and reminded the tenants that now was their chance to become owners of their farms for all time.

Ailsa sat and listened to the bidding for the first lots, and was glad to see that they fetched very low prices. It looked as though she would not be called upon to go to the limit already fixed by her. At last came Lot 8, prefaced by a few remarks from Benton. She waited breathlessly for the bidding.

'Shall we make a start at a thousand pounds?' said Benton. 'Come along, ladies and gentlemen — a most excellent property here, well watered by a brook; the house in good repair. Let us make a start. What's that, sir — five hundred? Very well, I am offered five hundred.'

'Five hundred and fifty,' said Ailsa

'Five hundred and — Did you say six hundred, sir? Six hundred.'

'Seven,' murmured Ailsa.

'Seven hundred pounds. I am offered the ridiculous price of seven hundred pounds for the Glen Farm. That is not the value of the buildings. Thank you, sir — eight hundred.'

'Nine hundred,' said Ailsa, somewhat huskily.

'Nine-fifty,' promptly replied the former bidder — a land agent from Perth.

'One thousand,' said Ailsa.

The crowd now began to get interested. All eyes were turned on the agent, but he shook his head. Ailsa began to feel relieved, when, to her horror, a stranger in the corner nodded.

'That's better — I am offered eleven

hundred pounds. Can I say twelve hundred, Miss Leslie?'

Ailsa, who had never anticipated the last bid, hesitated. On top of the small prices fetched by other farms, equally good, this was amazing.

'Don't let it go, Miss Leslie,' advised Benton. 'Can I say twelve hundred? Come, I will make it eleven-fifty. Dirt cheap at the price. Don't lose it for fifty pounds. Very well, I am here to sell the property. I am offered eleven hundred. Going at eleven hundred — going at eleven hundred — '

'Eleven hundred and fifty!' gasped Ailsa.

'Ah, that's better. Now we are really getting near the value. The bidding is against you, sir. May I say twelve-fifty?'

To Ailsa's absolute horror the man nodded. A gasp went up from the crowd. They stared at Ailsa, wondering what she would do, but Ailsa was finished. She saw the place drifting away in the clouds — her home, her mother's home, gone.

'Twelve hundred and fifty pounds — a fair price, but not too large. Am I to sell this lot at twelve hundred and fifty pounds, gentlemen?'

'Thirteen hundred and fifty.'

The bidding came from a little man standing quite close to the last bidder. Ailsa could scarcely believe her ears — thirteen hundred and fifty pounds from a complete stranger! The man who had recently bidden against her stared hard at his competitor, but that worthy appeared to be quite calm, and went on reading the lots in the catalogue. The auctioneer was evidently astonished at this fierce competition. Had people gone mad? What was there about the Glen Farm to warrant this high bidding?

'Thirteen hundred and fifty pounds!' he cried. 'That is something like a price. The bidding is against you, sir. May I say fifteen hundred?'

The other bidder was busy making notes on his catalogue. Despite his assumed coolness, little beads of perspiration were standing out on his forehead. The auctioneer droned away for a few minutes, seeking to raise the price yet higher. The calm little man with the bald head sighed, and then his competitor found his courage.

'Fifteen hundred!' he said hoarsely.

'Sixteen!'

'Seventeen!'

'Eighteen!'

The minister, who sat next to Ailsa, mopped his brow and shook his head.

'It's a mystery,' he murmured. 'Why are they bidding so furiously? The place is not worth that money. Who is the little man?'

'I don't know,' replied Ailsa. 'Is the other man going to bid again?'

'Doesn't look like it. No, it goes to the little man.'

The hammer came down with a dull thud, and it was announced that Lot No. 9 would now be sold. Ailsa, having no further interest in the sale, nodded to the minister and prepared to leave.

'I'm so sorry, Ailsa,' he said. 'What shall you do now?'

'I — I don't know. I want to go home and think about it.'

She made her way out, followed by a hundred pairs of eyes, many of which were sympathetic. Even though she was no longer their idol, they were patriotic enough not to be pleased at a stranger buying the farm over her head.

When at last she got outside she saw to her astonishment that both the strangers had also left. That fact was very significant — it meant they were interested only in her home. With a choke she turned into the street and made towards the farm.

11

Almost simultaneously with Ailsa's return home to wrestle with the big problem of the future a visitor called on Drummond. He was the stranger who had bidden unsuccessfully for the farm. He was shown into Drummond's study immediately on his arrival, and stood there in a quite forlorn attitude.

'Well?' queried Drummond.

'It's gone.'

'Gone!'

'Aye. It fetched eighteen hundred pounds.'

'Eighteen hundred pounds!' gasped Drummond. 'Why, it isn't worth a penny more than thirteen hundred — and that's an outside price. But why didn't you bid higher?'

'You told me sixteen hundred. I went another hundred.'

'Bother! I wanted that place. You told me I could get it easily for that price.'

'I had no doubt about it, but the fellow was determined.'

Drummond looked up sharply.

'The fellow — what fellow? Didn't Ailsa Leslie get it?'

'No. She fell off very early. Another man cut in — I don't know who he was.'

'That's very strange.'

'Aye, he must be mad.'

Drummond walked up and down, biting his lip. It annoyed him greatly to realise that his plan had failed. More than ever he had wanted to dispossess Ailsa, and in the auction he thought he saw a certain means. His intention was to force Ailsa to accept the offer he had previously made, and he had been prepared to lose several hundred pounds by over-bidding in order to bring this about.

Nevertheless, he felt he had cause for gratification, for Ailsa was dispossessed in any case. The more he thought on this the more satisfied he grew in his mind. It was unlikely that anyone would pay such a price and be willing to grant a new lease. By the evening he was quite jubilant. Jean, who had been at Perth, arrived back in time for dinner.

'Did you go to the sale?' she asked.

'No. I had a lot of business to attend to.'

'Then you don't know how Ailsa got on?'

'I — I heard she was not successful in buying her farm,' he stammered.

Jean uttered a little cry of disappointment.

'It was bought by a stranger at a ridiculous figure.'

'Poor Ailsa! Alan, we ought to have helped her. We ought not to have sat still when her home was in danger.'

'Jean, don't you think things have worked out rather well for all of us? We can help your sister now. She'll have to find a new place somewhere. It will enable her to make a clean start among people who do not know the truth.'

Jean turned her head away, afraid to reveal her blushing face. If Ailsa went away it would mean that Peter too must go with her. Now that the boy was beginning to get personality and the rudiments of speech she wanted to be near him. The maternal instinct, temporarily dampened down by the excitement of marriage, was beginning to assert itself.

At the same moment that these two were discussing Ailsa the latter was talking over things with Andrew Esplin. Andrew, who had been too busy to attend the sale, presumably heard the news relative to Ailsa's farm and dropped along to condole with her.

'What am I to do now, Andrew?' she asked.

'Maybe you know the man who bought the place?'

'No. But if I did, what good would that do?'

'Perhaps he's not wanting it himself and would give you a new lease.'

'He must be wanting it himself, or he would not have paid that big price.'

'A body's never sure,' said Andrew. 'Why not get his name and address and write him?'

'It would be a waste of time.'

'Lass, you mauna tak' things for granted. Look you, I'll get his address from Benton if you'll undertake to write and ask him for a lease. It's a chance, Ailsa — you canna miss a chance. Will you?'

She agreed at length, but felt that the time so employed would be wasted. Andrew was as good as his word, and the next day handed her a slip of paper. It bore the words 'David Duncan, 14 Holridge Road, Stirling.'

'Benson gave it to me,' he explained. 'Dinna waste time, lass. Get a letter posted this very day.'

She did so that evening, and posted it immediately. Three days passed, and then an answer came. The contents amazed her and brought a gasp of great joy from her lips. David Duncan begged to acknowledge receipt of her letter, and would be pleased to give her a twenty-one years' lease on the farm at the same rental as she was now paying. She dashed along to Andrew and stopped him in the middle of work.

'Andrew, the most wonderful news. I haven't to go after all. Mr. Duncan is giving me a new lease.'

The tears were streaming from her eyes at this unexpected salvation.

'What did I tell ye?' he growled. 'It's never ower late to keep a scrap o' hope in your heart.'

'But I cannot understand it,' she said. 'He must be losing money on the transaction. My present rent won't give him a fair interest on his money.'

'Interest!' grunted Andrew. 'Every man disna mak' interest the aim o' his existence.'

Drummond heard the astonishing news through Jean. At first he refused to believe it, but in due course its truth was firmly established, for Ailsa got the lease and Jean saw it with her own eyes. Drummond, with his plans finally frustrated, was like a bear for a few days. Then a very unworthy suspicion entered his mind.

'Jean, have you any notion who this David Duncan really is?' he asked.

'Of course not.'

'Nor Ailsa either?'

'No, Ailsa doesn't know.'

'You are sure?'

'Ailsa does not know anyone of that name,' she murmured.

'That might be so, but it's curious that any disinterested person should make a sacrifice, don't you think?'

She saw at what he was driving, and her face grew red with anger and shame. Her husband was linking this incident with another incident in the past — the one that had brought about so much suffering and misunderstanding already.

'Alan, you don't think that — '

'Why not?'

'No, no — it isn't true. I know it isn't true!'

'Jean, how can you know?'

'Because — '

She could get no further. It was impossible to tell him how she knew. From the embarrassed halt he divined that she knew more than she chose to admit. He believed she knew who Peter's father really was, and that despite her assurances to the contrary, it was this same man — this David Duncan.

'Jean, are you perfectly honest with me?' he asked.

'What — what do you mean?'

'This secret of Ailsa's — haven't I a right to know it?'

'No. Ailsa's life is her own. Neither you nor I have any right to interfere. But your conclusions are wrong — she does not know this David Duncan. She saw him at the auction sale, but told me he was a complete stranger to her.'

'Then who is Peter's father?'

She wrung her hands in her agony of mind. It was the first time he had ever put that question, and it hurt her to the soul not to be able to tell him.

'You know. I see you know.'

'Yes, yes; but it's better no one else should know.'

'Is he in Glen Eck?'

'No, he's dead. Alan, if you love me don't put these questions to me. Are you ceasing to love me?'

She turned her large and beautiful eyes on him, pleading with all her feminine charm. Under her spell his sullenness vanished. Despite his occasional domineering ways, he loved her madly, and had the choice to be made, would have placed her even before his lust for position and power.

'You — you do love me?'

'Jean, it's because I love you so much that I cannot bear to think you might be withholding secrets from me.'

'But, dear, secrets and secrets, and Ailsa is

my own sister. If there is anything I withhold from you it is only that which would make for unhappiness. Your love ought to be big enough to surmount that. For your happiness I would give my life.'

He hugged her and imprinted kisses on her mouth and cheeks. The storm-clouds passed away once more. But Drummond was possessed of an incurable curiosity. The identity of David Duncan puzzled him deeply, and he made up his mind to fathom that mystery before long.

The task, however, proved much more difficult than he had imagined. Having occasion to go to Stirling, he invented some excuse to call on Duncan, and found the address without much trouble, but it turned out to be a solicitor's office. He was politely informed that Mr. Duncan was a client, and any communications would be duly forwarded.

Foiled at every turn, he was obliged to give up the quest for the time being. But for Jean's sworn assurance, he would have felt convinced that Duncan was none other than the man of the past, trying to make amends for his conduct. As it was, he was left guessing — wild guesses that led nowhere.

But what of Stewart Morrison, the dis-illusioned, the heartbroken, the poor victim

114

of misunderstanding and giant circumstance? Since that accidental meeting with Ailsa in Glen Eck he had not been near the place. His work at Barrow having been completed, he was transferred to Glasgow and given a post of responsibility.

Nearly a year had gone by since then — a year of unremitting toil and terrible memories. But all the memories were not terrible, for interspersed with them were little things that seemed so trivial at their happening and so large now. It was not possible to forget the Ailsa of the old days — the brown-eyed child of nature, roving the hills with her hand in his and her merry voice calling him to adventure. No feat of the brain could wash out entirely those soft kisses, the tender handgrips, the dreams of the future, when, having found his footing, he and she should set up house together as man and wife.

Ailsa was an ideal girl, to whom falsehood and unfaithfulness were things unknown, so that appalling discovery had driven him almost to madness. To think of it was agony. There was some mistake — some unfathomable mystery of which he knew nothing — and yet — He felt he was trying to delude himself into believing pleasant things. The fact did not warrant this. Beaten, he forced himself to face facts. But all the time the heart within him was unrelenting in its demand for her. For a whole year the battle had raged, and no end was in sight.

Then came a day which was calculated to hasten the issue. He was called before the general manager to listen to a project of the firm. They were starting a branch in the Far East and his name had been mentioned as manager. Despite his youth, they felt encouraged to offer him the post. It would mean three years' residence there, but the climate was not too bad and the terms they proposed were exceedingly generous. Would he accept?

He asked for a week in which to consider it, and was granted it. The chance of his life was here and he was hesitating. At first he did not know why he had hesitated, but a little reflection made it clear to him. There was Ailsa — to be thousands of miles away from Ailsa would be purgatory. But then what was he to Ailsa? What was Ailsa to him? There was no evading the fact. He knew now that he loved her, in spite of everything that had happened.

The child — well, the child was Ailsa's, and whatever was hers was blessed. Could he bring himself to forget — could he? It needed but the slightest push to send him over the gulf, and one evening he took the plunge. With a pen in his hand he sat down to pen the all-important epistle. Once started, the words came fast:

'Dear Ailsa, You will be surprised to hear from me again. In the face of what has happened you may feel like destroying this letter without finishing it. But I implore you to have patience and hear me. For a whole year I have suffered torture. For a whole year I have known in my inner consciousness that I have behaved like a coward. It has taken me all this time to realise that I can never forget you, and that without you life would not be worth living. I know I hurt you with my brutal impulsiveness. I know that you were, and are, as far above me as are the stars above the earth. I shall never cease to think of you as the dearest and sweetest woman in the world. That terrible day when I let my baser impulse override my love I implore you to forget.

'To-day I have been offered a post abroad — a managerial position. This mark of appreciation I cannot refuse to accept. But to go away for three long years and leave you — Ailsa, darling, is it too late? Can you, with all your generous heart, forgive me? I can come to Glen Eck by return — one word from you will bring me post haste. I want to tell you with my own lips how much I regret my conduct — how deeply I love you still. Will you consent to marry me and come away with me to the East for three years? We should have furnished quarters, and there would be plenty of room for the boy. I'd be a good 'daddy' to him. I'd make him love me as I'm sure he must love you. Even if all this is but a wild dream, let me still come to see you once again. — Yours devotedly, Stewart.'

He read it several times, and knew it was inadequate to express his emotions. Nevertheless it sounded sincere, and he hoped she would appreciate that. Fearing to entrust anyone else with so precious a document, he posted it himself half an hour later, and set himself to curb his gnawing impatience for at least two whole days.

12

More had happened in the Glen in three years than in the preceding twenty. It was chiefly the outcome of the land sale, which, coming at a time when houses were sorely needed, attracted a small builder from over the hills, who, despite the prevailing high costs, managed to erect half a dozen cottages. It had been a bad piece of business on his part, but good for the inhabitants of the Glen, who eventually got possession at a rental which left the builder a sad loser.

Then Drummond saw an opportunity to do a little good in the village. At his own expense he erected a reading-room and furnished it with a fair collection of books. Sir Angus Menzies laid the foundation stone and a few months later opened it officially for the benefit of the people.

But this was merely a beginning. After that the school received consideration. It was redecorated and considerably enlarged. A meadow was bought and added to the rather cramped playground. In the estimation of the people Drummond rose still higher.

The net result of these worthy deeds was a seat on the County Council and the addition of the letters J.P. after Drummond's name. It represented his first real advancement in local society and received the full approval of the people in the Glen.

'He's a fair-minded man is Mister Drummond,' averred the Glen postie. 'Did ye' read that case that came up before him the other day — that man who treated his wife badly? My, he laid down the law hot and strong. Two months he gave that chiel, and serve him right.'

'I'm no' so sure he didna overdo it,' muttered Andrew. 'If I had a wife like yon, maybe I'd feel like treating her badly. She didna do her best for those bairns. It's no use trying to believe that all women are angels, man, for they're no'.'

The postie curled his lips scornfully.

'What do you ken aboot wives, Andrew Esplin? Why, I had twa wives before I was your age.'

'Then maybe you had my share as well,' retorted Andrew, to the amusement of a farmer who was waiting for a job to be finished. Postie, who never could see a joke, looked extremely fierce, but Andrew slapped him on the shoulder playfully and restored his good humour.

'Thinking of taking a third, Robert?' he asked.

'Well, I wouldn't be above that. When a man gets my age he needs a woman to look after him. I'll be seventy next June. If I was forty years younger maybe I'd — I'd — '

'You'd what?'

'Well, I ken one bonnie lass in the Glen that would be happier wi' a man o' her ain.'

'Who?'

'She's comin' doon the street now. Spite of what some folks say, she's the sweetest lass within fifty miles, and me that's had two wives and fourteen bairns ken what I'm speakin' aboot.'

Andrew handed a mended reaping-hook to the farmer and glanced down the street. His eyes brightened as he saw Ailsa approaching with Peter toddling by her side.

'You talk plenty, Robert,' he muttered. 'Better get your letters delivered, or there'll be trouble.'

Robert gave him a queer side glance, put his delivery bag firmly on his shoulder, and trudged off, touching his cap to Ailsa as he passed. The farmer, who also left, walked in the opposite direction. Peter ran in at the door and almost fell into Andrew's open arms.

121

'I'se come to see you, Uncle Andrew. Can I see the sparks?'

Andrew laughed and ran his hand through the boy's curly hair. Then he began to work the bellows furiously, while Peter clapped his hands.

'There they go, Peter. When you get a big lad, will you come and work my bellows?'

'Yes, yes.'

'And I'll show you how to make horseshoes and steel springs, and — '

'And puffer trains?' lisped Peter.

'Aye, and steam rollers and ocean liners — '

'Oh, no, you won't, Andrew,' said Ailsa from the doorway. 'Peter's going to be an artist — a great artist. Here is his latest portrait of Andrew Esplin.'

She laughed as she handed the smith a weird and wonderful collection of circles and strokes.

'That,' she explained, 'is your head. You are holding it upside down.'

'This is fine,' said Andrew, 'but I've only got one eye, little lad. Aren't you ashamed of yourself.'

'No,' said Peter; 'I draw'ed it all myself.'

Andrew gave Ailsa the drawing and looked at her keenly. Three years had not changed her in the slightest. The warm, brown eyes may have been slightly less brilliant, but her cheeks still glowed with virile youth — dimpled and smooth and round.

'And how are things?' he asked. 'I haven't seen you for over a week.'

'I've been busy, Andrew; so busy I haven't known which way to turn. Munro has been ill for over a fortnight.'

'Ought to get rid of him.'

'Andrew, isn't that callous?'

'I don't mean now that he's ill — you ought to have got rid of him years ago. He's too old, and never was a good worker.'

Ailsa sighed plaintively. She knew it was true, but she hadn't the heart to discharge a man who for forty years had served her family.

'I couldn't get a new man without turning Munro out of his cottage, and surely you don't expect me to do that?'

'It would be hard, but I was thinking of you, Ailsa. Munro disna earn his wages — not only that, but he disna even do his best for you.'

'I know — but I can manage. It's this lack of rain which is ruining everything. How long is it since it rained?'

'Nigh on three months.'

'If it would only rain.'

Almost every person in the Glen was wishing for the same thing.

'How you can stand this heat is beyond me,' said Ailsa, moving nearer the door. 'Why do you work so hard?'

'I'm planning for a day when I can lay doon my hammer. 'Mak' hay while the sun shines' is my motto.'

'You ought to have saved enough to be able to stop now, Andrew,' said Ailsa mischievously. 'You're a thrifty man, and must have a long stocking after twenty years of hard work.'

Andrew pursed his lips and shook his head several times. He never talked of his own financial affairs, but it was common knowledge that he kept a tight hold of his purse strings. Peter, who was roaming at large, was suddenly discovered half way up the ladder which led into the loft at the back of the forge.

'Come down,' roared Andrew. 'You'll break your neck, you young rascal.'

He seized Peter by the back of the loose jumper which he wore and hauled him into safety. Ailsa took him and brushed the dust from him.

'It's a sailor the lad'll be,' said Andrew.

'No, an artist. Don't you go up there again, young man.'

'What's up there?' asked Peter, with wide-open eyes.

'Rats,' said Andrew.

'I like rats,' replied Peter. 'We's got lots in our house.'

'Unfortunately we have,' said Ailsa. 'I detest them. One actually jumped on to Peter's bed this morning.'

'That's bad,' said Andrew seriously. 'You should complain to the landlord. It's up to him to get rid of them.'

'I haven't the — the impudence. It was only last spring he had the whole place decorated. Andrew, I'll never say a bad word about landlords again. He painted it inside and out, papered every room, and let me choose my own papers. He even put me in a new stove because the old one was not working well.'

'It improved his property,' replied Andrew. 'I don't see why you should make foresight a virtue. Anyway, you'd better write him about those rats, or they'll eat away all the foundations, and he'll be angry.'

Ailsa had never looked at it in that light, and reluctantly promised to communicate with the landlord, who was as mysterious as the sphinx. She was about to leave when Peter pulled her head down and began to whisper very audibly.

'You hasn't asked Uncle Andrew about Sunday, Mummie.'

Ailsa laughed.

'It's his birthday,' explained Ailsa, 'and I promised to take him for a picnic in the woods.'

'And Unkie's tumming — you said so.'

'I said I'd ask Uncle,' corrected Ailsa.

'Go on, then,' said Peter. 'Go on.'

Ailsa's eyes filled with fun. She kneeled by the side of the anvil, and with arms outstretched said in dramatic tones:

'Oh, Uncle Andrew, will you take Peter and me for a picnic on Sunday?'

'I will,' said Andrew, in a deep bass, upon which the boy leapt to him and kissed him excitedly.

'I knew he would — I knew he would.'

'Did you?' said Andrew. 'Young Peter, you ken ower much.'

Sunday came at last. Peter awoke to discover a toy engine at the foot of his bed and crept over to pull at Ailsa's arm, that he might show her this treasure. But that wasn't all, for when Andrew turned up after breakfast he carried a big parcel under his arm. It was another engine. Peter did not in the least regret this duplication — a dozen of them would not have been too many.

Then came a messenger from Aberdinnie with a parcel containing an assortment of things which brought cries of joy from his lips. They were from Jean, and accompanying them was a note, 'To my darling Peter.' Ailsa took that and disposed of it, lest anyone might wonder at the rather unusual phraseology.

Half an hour later they started out, Andrew driving the trap and Peter holding his presents, which he insisted on bringing. They took the road which led beside a dried-up watercourse and passed beneath the stately pile of Aberdinnie on the hillside. Ailsa turned her eye up to it and wondered what Jean was doing at the moment. Of late she had seen little of her sister. It seemed to her that, despite all Jean's assurances to the contrary, they were drifting apart. The wife of the Laird of Aberdinnie had different interests in life from plain Ailsa Leslie. Periodically she called to see Peter, to fondle him and inquire about him, but conversation other than that directly connected with Peter was rare.

Drummond Ailsa saw scarcely at all. But had it not been so it would have made little difference so far as she was concerned. Drummond had never forgotten the past.

'It's bonnie day for a picnic,' said Andrew.

Ailsa awoke from her reverie and smiled.

'It'll be cooler in the woods.'

'Aye, Aberdinnie looks fine on a day like this — all white among the green.'

'Jean must have a wonderful view from her

window, right over the hills.'

'That's the place to live, Ailsa — somewhere near the clouds. Our forefathers were crazy to start a village in the valley. I'd build all houses as high as they'd go. One day I'll live up high, and look down on the crazy folks in the valleys.'

'And in the winter, Andrew, when the wild winds come down from the north?'

'Oh, I'm hard,' he muttered.

'The hardest man in the Glen,' she laughed. 'I meant that as a jest, Andrew, but it's a poor one, for you're the softest man at heart I've ever met. Why, I believe I could twist you round my little finger if I tried.'

'You might,' he said, 'but others couldn't.'

He was curiously silent after that, until a bend in the valley brought to view the beautiful spreading woods which was their objective. Andrew pointed at them with his whip.

'It's a pity we let that hill shut this view out from the Glen. It's the best bit of scenery in the district.'

'It's wonderful.'

The horse broke into a trot and the vehicle bowled along the dusty road. The impetus created a wind which fanned their cheeks and was pleasant to experience. Birds were singing in the trees and in the blue. It was indeed the ideal day for a picnic and for Peter's fourth birthday.

Andrew struck off the main road and drove the horse up a steep, winding track, overhung on either side with trees. It led them to the heart of the woods — the place where Ailsa had wandered in the old days with Stewart Morrison. Though she had not been there for four years she remembered every tree, every stone, as if it were but yesterday. Andrew wanted to halt in a beautiful dell beside a small rivulet, but she bade him go farther along, for on that very spot she had once sat with her sweetheart and listened to his promises. For ever that would remain hallowed ground for her.

'What about this?' queried Andrew.

'Splendid!'

Andrew pulled up the horse and leapt down. Peter fell into his great arms, and immediately after Ailsa did the same. She thought that the arms which held her trembled as they touched her, and she wondered why.

13

What could be more delightful after a week of work and worry than to sit in the cool shade of the woods with bird-song all around, to eat from Nature's own green table, with the musical murmur of running water serving as orchestra?

Ailsa was finding great joy in this trip to the woods. In Andrew's company time always passed swiftly and pleasant, for Andrew was the kind of man who never obtruded. He could be talkative enough when he chose, but he respected the silence of others, and scarcely ever interrupted it.

'It reminds me so much of the old days when we used to go picnicking up here,' she said. 'What merry, noisy things we were then — so careless and ignorant of life. Here are the same dear trees; they have not changed — nothing ever seems to change except us.'

'You have not changed much, Ailsa. When I look at you I can see the wee lassie of ten years back; when you speak I can hear that same young voice. There's no reason why a human should change at all in his heart. I grant you one can't always be as frisky as Peter, but a body can store up the things he wants to keep, and keep them still when he's seventy and seven.'

'Yes, one can keep them, but somehow they do change — at least, we see them differently. I used to see fairies in these woods, Andrew. Can you show me a fairy now?'

'Aye, look right down in the water, lass.'

She followed his pointing finger, and blushed as she saw her own reflection there. It moved and changed as the surface rippled slightly.

'You're the dearest, silly thing, Andrew,' she murmured. 'But, see, it changes as one looks. Now I'm all ugly and old — like I shall be when I'm seventy and seven.'

'It's the water that changes, not you.'

'You blessed comforter! Oh, look at Peter!'

She leapt up and ran to Peter, who was trying to sail one of his engines in the stream. To bring this about he was lying on his chest, the better half of him over the bank. She grabbed him and carried him back to Andrew.

'I aye said he was meant for a sailor!' laughed Andrew. 'Come on, laddie, I'll help you to sail your boat.'

He took the boy lower down the stream

where the water ran over a sandy bottom, and a few minutes later Ailsa heard Peter's delighted laughter. Andrew had removed Peter's shoes and socks as well as his own, and the pair of them were capering around the wooden engine, which was floating gaily on the water. A few minutes later she joined them.

It was teatime before they had finished their childish games. A fine assortment of home-made tarts gladdened Peter's hungry eyes. The bare-footed trio sat down and made a hearty meal, Peter collecting what remained for the horse, who would eat anything from bread and jam to gingerbread.

'He grows so quickly I cannot keep pace with him,' said Ailsa. 'School will be my next problem. I want him to learn the things that a man really should know.'

'Only the world will teach him that. What are the things a man should know? Honesty, charity, tolerance and forgiveness!'

'Charity?' said Ailsa. 'That's a hard word.'

'Maybe it is, but it would be a harder world without it, Ailsa. I heard from an old friend last week.'

From the expression in his eyes she divined to whom he was referring. She had persuaded herself that she wanted to hear no more of

Stewart Morrison, but nevertheless she felt an overwhelming curiosity rising within her.

'You — you mean Stewart?'

'Aye. Did you know he was in foreign parts?'

'No; I have heard nothing. Where is he?'

'China. He has been there for nearly three years.'

'Is — is he well?'

'He says so. But you knew he had gone abroad?'

She shook her head.

'That's curious!' he muttered.

'What is curious?'

'He said he told you before he left — wrote you a letter.'

'I received no letter. There must be a mistake, Andrew. Why should he write me a letter?'

'I don't know. Perhaps he thought you might be interested to know.'

'I am interested.'

'And that's all?'

'That's all.'

'He says he's coming back soon.'

He looked to see the effect of this upon her, but her face remained calm and impassive. Whatever she felt was hidden in her heart. She wondered that Andrew could revive this subject on so joyous a day, and yet — yet she was glad to hear about him, and was annoyed with herself to realise she was glad.

'We shall have to leave soon,' she said. 'I think there is a storm brewing.'

Andrew scanned the sky and noticed the peculiar haze which had crept into the blue. The air had become heavier than ever and charged with electricity.

'Let's hope it does come,' he said. 'We want a downpour — a regular deluge.'

'We do not,' retorted Ailsa. 'We want a steady rain that will last a week. If you were a farmer you wouldn't want deluges. Where's Peter?'

Peter was rounded up and the hamper and ground-sheet taken to the trap. In a few minutes the horse was put between the shafts and the party were ready for departure.

'I'll drive back for a change,' said Ailsa. 'You sit with Peter and tell him all the stories you know. I've exhausted my supply.'

'Better hurry,' said Andrew. 'There's certainly a big storm coming.'

Ailsa touched the horse with the whip and the pace increased. A mile along the road they saw two figures on horseback cantering in the direction of Aberdinnie.

'Mister Drummond and Jean,' said Andrew. 'So it is.'

The riders were making straight across

their line of progress, evidently with a view to entering the park by the drive on the western side. Riders and trap almost met in the road. Ailsa waved her hand and Jean halted her horse, but Drummond, upon seeing who the occupants of the trap were, went on a short distance and waited for his wife there.

'How are you, Ailsa?' queried Jean, holding out her hand. 'And you, Andrew?'

'I'm fine,' said Andrew, somewhat shortly.

She backed her horse a step and leaned over to kiss Peter fondly, gazing at him with eyes that expressed a deeper emotion than her actions would convey.

'And so you're four years old to-day, Peter?'

'Um!' said Peter. 'How old is you, Auntie?'

'You mustn't ask. It's never done, Peter.'

'Mummie says one day, if I'm a good boy, I'll be able to see your boo'ful big house.'

Jean flinched a little and shot a glance at her impatient husband.

'You shall,' she whispered. 'I'll send a big motor car and bring you up to Aberdinnie — one day!'

'When is one day?' lisped Peter.

'Soon — soon!'

She kissed him again, and, nodding to Ailsa and Andrew, went trotting towards the waiting man; Ailsa pulled on the rein and the trap moved forward.

'Men are queer animals,' growled Andrew. 'There's a man who last week stood up for a woman who wisna worth defending, but when it comes to dropping his ain pride a little — '

'Andrew — Andrew!' pleaded Ailsa. 'Be careful what you are saying. Peter isn't a bairn any longer.'

'What's that, Mummie?' queried Peter.

'Nothing dear, only Uncle Andrew talking nonsense.'

Andrew relapsed into silence. Drummond's behaviour aroused him to deep anger.

'Still fretting, Andrew?' asked Ailsa suddenly.

'Aye.'

'Then you are silly. I'm not going to fret and spoil a beautiful day. Here we are — home again!

A loud clap of thunder drowned the last words. She bundled Peter indoors and called Munro to take the horse and trap into the stable. Andrew stayed for a few minutes, and then bade her good-bye.

'Thank you, Andrew, for a very pleasant day,' she murmured.

'It was you that made it pleasant.'

'Do you never take credit for anything?'

'Only when it's due.'

A blinding flash of lightning, followed

by an earsplitting crash, hastened Andrew's departure. Ailsa watched him swinging down the road for a second or two, and then closed the door.

All the time she was putting Peter to bed the elements were preparing for battle, and Peter clapped his hands. He was not afraid.

'Say your prayers, Peter.'

He said them word by word after her. She got him into bed at last and whispered a short bedtime fairy tale into his ear. Then she pulled down the blind and went downstairs. Munro had put the horse away and was preparing to go into his cottage.

'You'd better get home quick, Munro.'

He nodded and went across the garden to his cottage, which lay near the dried-up stream on the northern side of the farm. No sooner had he gone than the clouds broke. The air became full of a loud swishing, and out of the blackness came rain — rain, not in drops, but in streams. A peal of thunder louder than any before shook the house to its foundations. A cry came from upstairs, and Ailsa ran to find Peter crying.

'There, there!' she murmured.

'I'se fwightened, Mummie!'

'It's only a storm, Peter. It will go soon.'

But it showed no signs of going. Each minute it grew worse. Never had Ailsa seen such rain. It was about a quarter of an hour later that she heard men's voices in the yard.

'Miss Leslie!'

She left Peter and fled downstairs. Old Munro was standing in the kitchen doorway, with his son close beside him, and both their faces were pallid.

'What's the matter?' she gasped.

'Something's wrong. I'm flooded out, and the water is rising. It's halfway over the meadow now.'

Through the gloom splashed a big figure in an oil-skin coat.

'Andrew!' she gasped. 'What does it mean?'

'A cloudburst in the hills. It's coming down like a water chute. The Glen lies in a bowl, and the water may rise to any height. You've got to leave here at once.'

It was only necessary to look at the rapidly-rising water to realise that things were extremely critical. She slipped on a waterproof coat and saw the water swirl through the door and mount ever higher. Andrew came down the stairs with Peter on his shoulder.

'Away!' he cried. 'Don't wait for anything. Keep close to me, lass.'

She sobbed and followed in his wake towards the sloping land which led up to Aberdinnie.

14

Andrew and Ailsa and Peter struggled through the torrent and ultimately arrived at Aberdinnie. Below them they saw vague forms making for the hill — men and women and cattle all mixed up and drenched with the heavy rain.

'Better go in to the house, Ailsa,' said Andrew. 'I'll have to give a hand to some of those folk.'

She nodded and took Peter from him.

'Don't cry, Mummie,' crooned Peter.

She laughed almost hysterically, and hugging him tightly to her, made up the slope towards the main entrance of the house. She reached it to find Jean emerging.

'Ailsa — what is the matter?'

'The village is flooded. Didn't you know?'

'No. We could hear nothing but the terrible rain. But come inside. I must see Alan and get him to form a rescue party.' Are you cold, Peter?

'I'se fwightened,' replied Peter.

The news quickly spread through the household. While Ailsa got Peter into a bed Drummond routed all the men servants and started off to give what aid he could. He arrived at the point of his land to which the water extended and found there a mixed collection of people and cattle. As he stood pondering the next move Andrew came wading through the water with two children on his back.

'It's six feet in the Glen,' he said. 'Some of the folk are trapped in their bedrooms. If it rises any higher — '

A plaintive sob came out of the darkness.

'Courage!' said Drummond. 'It won't rise any higher. It must be running away now as fast as it can get out.'

A lantern was seen waving in the watery distance, and the eerie 'swish' of water met the ears of the crowd. All eyes were turned in the direction of the nodding lantern.

'It's a boat.'

'Aye — a punt.'

The craft came nearer, and into the light of the big electric lamp which Drummond carried. It proved to be an old punt, and in it was the minister and a dozen women and children. A rousing cheer was given by the watchers as the craft drew near, and several men rushed forward to beach it. The minister, with a pole in his hands, smiled grimly as he helped his cargo out.

'There are six more back there,' he said. 'I'll — '

'No, sir, you take a rest,' said Andrew. 'I'll take the punt across.'

'I'll come too,' said Drummond. He turned to the servant beside him. 'Take all these poor people back to the house and make them as comfortable as possible.'

Drummond took his place in the boat and Andrew pushed off. The party on the land made towards the house.

Ailsa, after putting Peter to bed and hushing him to sleep, came down to find Jean making arrangements for the big homeless party.

'Is everybody safe?' Jean asked anxiously.

The minister, who was close by, nodded.

'Andrew went back for the M'Clures,' he said. 'They were the only ones in any danger. The newer houses are fairly strong, and the water did not rise over the ground floor. Here is Andrew!'

Andrew came forward, but his face was very grim and lined. Ailsa, who knew him so well, realised that something was wrong.

'What — what is it, Andrew?' she murmured.

'It's M'Clure's youngest bairn. She — she's — '

The minister gripped Andrew's arm and

stared into his eyes. Andrew inclined his head slowly.

'How terrible!' moaned Jean. 'Poor little mite — poor little mite!'

'It was the first rush of water,' said Andrew. 'The bairn was in its cradle downstairs and Mrs. M'Clure was putting the other two to bed. She couldn't get down in time. Poor soul, she's half demented.'

The tears rose to Ailsa's eyes. That appeared to be the only casualty, but it was sufficient to cast a shadow over the whole company.

'Have you lost much, lass?' Andrew asked Ailsa.

'Two calves and a pig. But I don't mind much. Peter's safe — oh, thank God, Peter is safe!'

Andrew glanced round the beautifully furnished hall and uttered a short low laugh.

'Don't do that, Andrew,' pleaded Ailsa. 'What makes you so hard these days? You seem so different — so changed.'

'I'm not hard, Ailsa. But a man can't help thinking and wondering at the queerness of life. Look at this cloud-burst — it's ruined almost everyone in the Glen. The poorer the man the worse his loss, but the richest man for miles around gets off scot free.

The ways of Providence take a mighty lot of understanding.'

She caught his big hand and held it in hers, smiling into his face the while.

'That's not my Andrew who is speaking. Why, you used to tell me that a person's first duty in life was to shoulder his troubles without complaint and to present a smiling face to the next batch that came along, didn't you?'

'Did I?'

'You know you did.'

It was impossible to resist the infection of her good nature. He smiled cheerfully and strove to put behind him his drab reflections. When she saw the minister later in the evening Ailsa asked him about Mrs. M'Clure.

'Poor body, she feels it dreadfully.'

'Of course,' she murmured. 'Do you think I could do anything for her?' '

'No, no,' he replied hastily. 'She is quite hysterical. You'd better not go near her, Ailsa.'

There was something so emphatic in his speech as to cause her to wrinkle her brows.

'Men don't understand women much,' she mused.

'That is true, but this poor woman is completely beside herself. You know she was always excitable and — and imaginative.'

'Imaginative!'

He twisted his hands nervously.

'At such a time it is better to leave — '

'I'm sure it isn't. At such a time a woman needs comforting. I — I think I would like to see her. We were such good friends — in the old days.'

She blushed a little at the last words, for all she could not fail to remember that the suffering woman had cut her dead recently. But it was no time to think of that. She could well imagine the anguish of the bereaved woman, and the desire to bring her some small grain of comfort was obsessive.

'I think I will go to her,' she said. 'Is she in the house?'

'No, on the veranda with some others.'

The minister put out his arm, but she ignored it. It seemed strange to her that he should wish to prevent her from offering sympathy at such a moment. It merely succeeded in making her all the more determined. She left the hall and wandered out to the veranda. The northern end of it was occupied by men, but the southern end was given over to one or two families who could not find room inside the house. A score of eyes were turned on her as she emerged, and she could not help noticing that they were fiercely antagonistic. Andrew, who had been sitting in a chair near the railing, rose and came towards her.

'Ailsa, what are — '

But Ailsa did not hear him, for at that moment the demented woman in the corner began to speak, and her words fell like flames of fire on Ailsa's heart.

15

Andrew touched her on the sleeve, but she felt nothing, heard nothing but the choking accusations from the corner.

'It's a judgment on us — a judgment. Just as the Lord destroyed the Cities of the Plain so He'll destroy Glen Eck. This is a warning, I tell you. We've harboured a sinner in our midst these four years. My little Maggie — He took my little Maggie to punish me, and He sent the flood to warn us — all of us — '

Ailsa gasped, and stood there rooted.

'Come away, Ailsa,' urged Andrew. 'She doesn't know what she's saying.'

The hysterical woman suddenly became aware that the object of her bitter scorn was present. She uttered a wild cry and pointed with a shaking finger.

'You are the cause, Ailsa Leslie — you. Through you I've lost my bairn. Through you a curse has been laid on the Glen. May the Lord deal wi' — '

Andrew, unable to stand more of this, strode forward to her husband.

'Can't you stop her, M'Clure?'

'Maybe there's something in it,' grumbled M'Clure. 'I'm ruined through no fault o' my ain.'

'Then dinna try to put the blame where it doesn't lie,' snapped Andrew.

To his surprise Ailsa began to approach the party. He fixed his eyes on her in a mute appeal for her to go away, but she came forward until she stood but a few feet from Mrs. M'Clure, her face pale and her lips trembling.

'Mrs. M'Clure, you don't mean what you said?'

'Go away! Dinna touch me! You're cursed!'

Ailsa retreated before the inflamed eyes. She understood now why the minister had tried to prevent her from coming out there. Even now she tried to excuse this poor woman who had suffered so much, but there were the others — those who looked on with sullen countenances and spoke no word in her defence. That was what hurt.

'There's no place in this village for you, Ailsa Leslie,' shrieked Mrs. M'Clure. 'So long as you bide here the Glen will suffer.'

'Come away, lass,' whispered Andrew. 'She'll be sorry she said such cruel things when she comes to her senses.'

M'Clure glared at him and Andrew glared

back. Ailsa permitted Andrew to lead her away. Once inside the hall, she sank on to a couch and buried her head in her hands.

'Oh, if they only knew how much they hurt — if they only knew!' sobbed Ailsa.

'For two pins I'd tell them the truth,' muttered Andrew. 'You've borne this for too long. I'll go and tell them. Aye, I'll tell them now.'

'Andrew!'

He looked down at the two hands which were clutching his coat.

'I hold you to your promise. Let them talk — let them hurt me. I've been hurt so often, it — it doesn't matter much now.'

'They're trying to drive you out of the Glen, Ailsa. That must never happen.'

'It shall not,' she sobbed. 'They can keep me out of their houses, but I'll never leave my home. But I'm afraid for Peter. He's growing up and will soon be able to understand things. Already he has asked me about his — his daddy.'

Andrew shut his mouth tightly.

'I — I thought they had almost forgotten,' mused Ailsa. 'This thing has revived it all again.'

There were some grounds for this assertion. Like most villages, the Glen was not lacking in its superstitious element. Such a thing

148

as Mrs. M'Clure asserted appealed to the imagination of a minority, but that minority was big enough to keep the thing alive.

'Forget it, Ailsa,' he whispered.

'I wish I could.'

From the veranda came the loud voice of Mrs. M'Clure. She was apparently talking to Drummond, who had arrived there from a door on the northern end of the house.

'It's a warning from God. Where there is sin it must be rooted out.'

'Hush, my good woman.'

'It's true. Now she's here wi' her bairn. This house will suffer, too, as I've suffered.'

Ailsa put her hands over her ears and Andrew clenched his huge fists, feeling his impotence deeply. Drummond came inside, looking worried. He started as he beheld Ailsa and Andrew.

'You hear what they're saying?' snapped Andrew.

'Y — es.'

'And do you believe such trash?'

Drummond shrugged his shoulders and laughed nervously.

'Do you?'

'Of course it's ridiculous. But I can understand their — their hysteria. This must be a heavy blow for them — and that poor woman has lost her child.'

Andrew stepped closer to him.

'And now they want you to remove — the cause?'

Drummond grew very agitated. He looked at Ailsa and saw that her face was pallid.

'Did — did you hear?' he quavered.

'Ay, I've got sharp ears,' retorted Andrew.

'It's the merest nonsense,' rejoined Drummond. 'To-night this house is a haven, and everyone is welcome.' He directed his gaze on Ailsa. 'I — I hope you won't listen to that — '

But Ailsa had risen to her feet, unable to stand any more. With a nod at Andrew she crept upstairs, and, reaching her room, flung herself on the bed beside the sleeping Peter. She felt that Drummond's sympathy was not very deep and that inwardly he wished she were not there. A knock sounded on the door and Jean entered. She uttered a little cry of remorse as she saw the figure on the bed, and ran and put her arms around her sister.

'Ailsa — Ailsa!'

'I — I'm all right.'

'Alan told me — about Mrs. M'Clure and the wicked things she has been saying. Of course, you are welcome here — to stay as long as you choose. You know that, don't you?'

Ailsa dried her eyes and shook her head.

'I'm only welcome in one place, Jean, and that is my own home.'

'Ailsa,' pleaded Jean, 'don't talk like that; it — it hurts me more than you can know. It's my burden you are bearing, and every stone that hits you wounds me too. Oh, if I only had the courage to confess everything!'

She gave a great sob, and Ailsa's arms went round her immediately.

'It wouldn't do any good, Jean. The thing has gone too far now. If your husband knew you had misled him all these years he would never forgive you. Where we made the mistake was at the beginning. It would have been easy to have spoken the truth then. But don't worry any more.'

'If I only loved him a little less I could do it even now — but to lose him — no, no, I couldn't bear it.'

'You are not going to bear it,' said Ailsa. 'As for me — well, nothing can make much difference to me. Now go to bed, dear; it's getting late.'

Jean left a little later, after kissing Peter fondly and running her hand through his curls. When she had gone Ailsa made no attempt to get into bed. She looked out of the window and saw that the moon had risen and was silvering the landscape. Through the trees in the park she caught a glimpse of her farm lying like a small island in a lake of water. Why not leave this house and go to her own home? Why not? The desire grew and grew as the minutes passed. Ultimately she gave way to it.

She put on her waterproof and wrapped Peter tightly in a blanket, then, turning out the light, made her way down the stairs and out by the back door. The brilliant moon permitted her to find her way to the old punt. She climbed aboard and, tucking Peter into the driest corner, took the heavy pole and pushed off. There was a swift current running towards the north, but by crossing this she got into placid water and began to push the craft towards the flooded meadow beyond which was the farm, and successfully steered the punt through the open gate in the meadow, the top of which was just above the water line.

The front door was still open and the water was half way up it. Deeming it dangerous to attempt to wade through it with Peter in her arms, she tied the craft to the trelliswork outside the door and attempted to climb on to the porch. Having got so far, the rest was comparatively easy.

Half an hour later Peter was tucked in his own bed and Ailsa was clad in a dry nightgown. She was ravenously hungry, but food was impossible to obtain. In spite of this she experienced a great sense of relief. This was her own home, in which no spiteful tongues wagged. Before going to bed she looked out of the window and saw that the water was still receding. She prayed that the morrow might see it all gone.

She opened her eyes to see the sun shining brightly outside. It seemed only a few minutes since she had gone to bed, so tired had she been. Her first thought was of the flood, and she ran to the window to utter a cry of relief to find most of the land about the farm free of it.

The days that followed were occupied in cleaning up the damage done by the flood. Ailsa and the daily woman had worked like galley slaves, and in the end most of the previous comfort of the house was restored, but the walls and paintwork still bore signs of the catastrophe.

She awoke one morning to find four workmen outside with a truck containing wallpaper, plaster, and paint. They greeted her cheerily, and told her they had come at the landlord's behest. If anyone was welcome it was they. Work commenced forthwith, and Ailsa saw with great joy a rapid transformation. She naturally expected that the landlord himself would pay a visit to see how things were going, but he never put in an appearance.

'It's strange,' she said to Andrew. 'He takes such an interest in his property and yet he never comes to look at it. One would think he was afraid of meeting me.'

'He wouldn't have let you the farm if he hadn't known you were the best tenant in the Glen, Ailsa.'

She shook her head in perplexity, and Andrew shot her a quick glance and sighed. When she arrived home she found the painter arguing with his mate over the colour of the windows.

'I'm sure he said green, Jim.'

'Cream it was.'

'No, cream inside, green outside.'

They argued for quite a long time, and in the end Jim suggested that his mate should run up and find out. Ailsa knitted her brows as she heard this. To talk coolly of running along to Stirling to ascertain such a thing was certainly extraordinary. She watched the man start off on his errand, and gasped to notice that he went without his coat. To her further amazement he was back again in less than twenty minutes with the question settled.

'Where — where did you go just now?' she inquired.

The man started and acted in an embarrassed way.

'I — I — only up the village.'

'But is the landlord in the Glen?'

He fidgeted with his paint-brush and seemed reluctant to reply. To Ailsa came a possible solution to the mystery surrounding the identity of her landlord.

'Did you go to Mrs. Drummond?' she asked.

He shook his head emphatically.

'Then who is it?'

'I — I promised not to tell.'

'You needn't worry,' said Ailsa testingly. 'I know.'

The man stared at her, and then went on painting furiously.

'Well, I didna tell ye,' he said. 'He asked me no' to tell onybody. Andrew was aye a canny man.'

Ailsa, who had had no idea of the truth, gasped for breath, and quickly went into the next room. The news astounded her. Grateful as she was to Andrew, she could not help feeling humiliated, knowing that the house was being let at a loss. For her sake Andrew had invested all his hard-earned savings. That it was Andrew made all the difference in the world. Just because Andrew was her dearest friend she could take nothing

155

from him. There was only one thing to do, and that was to compel him to raise the rent to an economic level. Friendship was one thing and charity another.

She saw Andrew that evening as he was closing the smiddy. From the expression on her face he divined that something was amiss, but evidently did not guess what was coming.

'Andrew,' she said, 'we have been great friends, haven't we?'

'Why, of course.'

'And we are going to be friends always?'

'I — I hope so. But — '

'Then why do you try to break our friendship by forcing me to accept things from you in secret?'

'Forcing you — I — '

'That farm — I have just discovered who it was that bought it at the auction sale. You bought it through another bidder, and you let it to me at a loss. Why — why did you do that?'

Andrew's face grew crimson and he fumbled his words.

'I — you see — it's like this — you had to have a house — '

'Not in that humiliating fashion.'

Andrew gripped the end of the anvil and recovered his composure.

'Listen, Ailsa,' he grunted. 'Do you think I would have hurt your feelings if I could have avoided it? I had no idea of bidding for that house until I heard what dirty work was going on.'

'Dirty work!'

'Aye. I heard that a man was coming over to bid high for another person who was willing to drop money to get possession. Do you think I was going to sit still and see your farm bought under your very nose that Mister Drummond might rid himself of an undesirable neighbour?'

'Mister Drummond! Andrew, you don't mean — '

'Aye, that was the game. He tried other means, and they failed. Never mind what they were. Well, in this he failed as badly, and all because Andrew Esplin had a few pounds put by for a rainy day.'

Ailsa's brain swam at the reception of the news. To think that her sister's husband could act in this fashion. She could appreciate Andrew's interference now, and her former anger was changed to deep gratitude. Nevertheless, she felt there was only one thing to be done.

'I — I understand now, Andrew,' she said. 'But I can't let you go on losing money. You must raise my rent.'

'Ailsa, now don't — '

'Yes, yes, I shall feel unhappy if you don't.'

'Very well,' he muttered. 'But now, you can't raise rents in the middle of a quarter. I give you six months' notice from now. That's doing the thing on hard business principles. On January first up goes your rent twenty per cent.'

She could not help but smile through her tears.

'It must have taken nearly all your savings, Andrew.'

'Not quite.'

'Oh, why — why do you do all this for me?'

The misty eyes and the beautiful appealing face sent the flame roaring madly within him. He caught her hands and held her close to him for a second.

'Why?' he murmured hoarsely. 'Because — because I — I am your friend.'

She recoiled from him in astonishment. For the first time since she had known him — since the days when he had carried her in his strong arms as a child — she realised that Andrew, too, had human passions, that something else existed in that breast other than mere friendship. It had striven for expression but a minute ago, only to be choked down by his strong will. It astounded her — frightened her, for she had never thought of Andrew in that way. And yet —

The ravages of the flood, while they almost broke the hearts of most of the people in the Glen, afforded Drummond an opportunity to increase his popularity. His desire to help the sufferers was genuine enough, however, and was not entirely generated by selfish motives.

With this worthy end in view he started a subscription list with a substantial sum, and was wonderfully successful in piling up a long list of subscribers. Jean threw her heart and soul into the work thus entailed and visited all the country gentry for miles around.

'This is splendid,' said Jean. 'We have enough to put nearly all the worst victims on their feet again.'

'Thanks to you,' replied her husband.

'What nonsense! I haven't worked half as hard as you.'

Drummond shook his head, knowing to how great an extent the result was due to Jean's captivating manner. He let his gaze rest on her and smiled as he reflected upon his good luck. Four years of married life had merely succeeded in enhancing Jean's physical charm. Possessing good taste in most things, she carried this out in her dress and in her home. If there had been any reluctance on the part of the country gentry to accept the new Laird of Aberdinnie and his wife, that was all gone now. Drummond was not ignorant of the extent of his indebtedness to his wife. She had filled her new position as naturally as any woman could fill it.

'You really are wonderful, Jean,' he murmured. 'Do you know there was a time when I came to believe that I should never be in a position to ask you to marry me? Out there in Australia I foresaw years of struggle ahead of me. At times I grew a little depressed and hopeless I began to wonder whether you would wait — '

'Alan!'

He caught her hand and pressed it to his lips.

'Of course, I ought to have known that you were not the kind of girl to go back on your word or to regret a promise.'

She trembled a little as she reflected upon the past — that past of which he was ignorant.

'Why do you shudder?' he asked.

'I — I — Alan, sometimes I'm afraid — afraid that you place me too high in your thoughts. Always you put me upon a pedestal. That is so hard to live up to.'

He laughed, but stopped as he saw that

her face wore a strange expression.

'At times, dear, you are just a little — a little puzzling. Why do you continually beg me to underrate you?'

'I don't wish you to underrate me, Alan. What I want you to do is to realise that I am merely a woman, much the same as a million other women, with all their weaknesses and faults — all their temptations — '

'Temptations!' He seemed vastly amused, and refused to observe the deadly seriousness in her eyes. 'I should love to know about your temptations. What is it — another man? Oh, don't tell me that you are thinking of running away with my unknown rival.'

In the face of his ridicule it was useless to try and plant that small seed of preparedness which she had hoped might pave the way for a future confession. She was almost at the point of wishing that his love might be less for her. To be trusted so implicitly — to be looked upon as the embodiment of all the virtues — when her heart held so terrible a secret was painfully disturbing. Yet his love for her was a precious thing, and she was loth to sacrifice a scrap of it.

'Sometimes I think it is not right I should be so happy,' she murmured.

'Then you are happy?'

'Almost perfectly.'

'Only 'almost'?'

'I cannot be completely happy while I know I do not deserve to be.'

'There you go again,' he sighed. 'Why shouldn't you be perfectly happy, Jean? I won't be satisfied until I know that the last obstacle is removed — if there is an obstacle.'

'There is one,' she replied seriously.

'What is it?'

'The past.'

'Oh, I'm not worrying about the past. It is the present that really matters — and the future.'

'But what is present to-day is past to-morrow. Alan, dear, how much do you love me?'

'So much that without you I should consider myself the poorest man in the Glen. You know I have ambitions, Jean — I want to be something. I want to be respected by everyone. I know that sounds like vanity, but it's a natural desire when one has been nobody for so long. But most of all I want to pull you up the ladder. I want you to have everything that a woman should have. Yet rather than lose your love I would be content to plough the fields and live in the humblest cottage in the Glen.'

He spoke with the deepest sincerity, and

it caused her heart to leap madly in her bosom. But at the same time it frightened her, for it was so evident that to him she was an ideal.

'I absolutely refuse to believe that you can be anything but what you are — the best and dearest and sweetest woman in the world. There's never going to be any misunderstanding between us, Jean. So long as we are truthful to each other — so long as we continue to hide nothing from each other — we need not be afraid of the future, need we?'

That put an end to her efforts. What could she do in the face of this but keep her secret hidden? She was glad she had not in a moment of impulse laid bare her tortured heart, for that step would surely have wrecked everything. Ailsa was the rift in the lute. She could not look at Ailsa without realising that her present life was a sweet mockery. Yet to publish the truth about Peter might only make matters worse. It would clear Ailsa's character in the eyes of her neighbours, but would that balance the wreckage elsewhere?

Leaving Ailsa out of it, the fight was between her love for her husband and her love for her child. She could not fail to see that her husband came first in her affections.

Had Peter been less cared for, less happy and contented with his foster-mother, it might have been different. She hungered for him with all the natural instincts of a mother, but that hunger did not yet go so deep as the passions which Drummond had aroused.

'We have to consider the distribution of the Relief Fund,' said Drummond. 'Menzies wanted to leave it entirely in my hands, but I objected. As an alternative he proposed a committee comprising myself, the minister, Mr. Benton, you and another.'

'Better leave me out.'

'Nonsense. We must have a woman to represent the feminine side. You must not decline.'

'Very well. Who is to be the fifth?'

Drummond pursed his lips, and stroked his chin. That question had been occupying his mind for some time.

'Can you suggest anyone?' he asked.

'Yes — Andrew Esplin. Everyone knows and likes Andrew. He is really one of the people, and knows all the circumstances. He'll do it if we ask him.'

Drummond looked none too pleased.

'I'm not sure that Andrew is the best man,' he demurred.

'He is. Certainly he says things at times,

164

but he doesn't mean them. He is the kindest-hearted man in the Glen.'

'Very well. Will you ask him?'

'But surely you should — '

'It will come better from you.'

Jean did not see why it should, but she consented, and that afternoon called on Andrew. As she expected, he had a lot to say about it, but in the end she won him over and he promised to attend the meeting on the following evening.

The meeting was destined to prove a stormy affair. The committee had agreed on most points, and after three hours reached the last name on the list — Ailsa's.

'I believe Ailsa Leslie lost two calves and a pig,' reported Mr. Benton, 'not to mention extensive damage to crops.'

'Did Ailsa tell you that?' growled Andrew.

'No; her man, Munro.'

'Ah, I guessed that!'

Drummond raised his eyes from the paper.

'Ailsa is no' kind to make noise o' her troubles,' said Andrew. 'Anyhow, you can strike her name off the list.'

'Oh, no,' retorted Benton. 'Ailsa Leslie has as much right as anyone else to her share of this fund.'

'Certainly!' agreed Drummond.

'I'm no' thinking of rights,' said Andrew.

'I'm thinking of hearts. Have you heard the talk that has been bandied about the Glen since that affair — '

Drummond frowned.

'What has that got to do with the matter?'

'This much,' retorted Andrew fiercely, 'that I'll be nae party to offering charity to a lass whose good name has been trampled in the gutter by those same folk.'

Jean wrung her hands in agony, not knowing what to say or how to act in the circumstances, but Drummond, who was a stickler for formalities, was emphatic on the question of Ailsa's name being included.

'She can refuse it if she wishes,' he urged. 'It is plainly our business to allocate a sum. May I suggest fifty pounds?'

'Fifty lashes!' said Andrew, with flashing eyes. 'That night she was driven from your house by godless talk. You offer her fifty pounds to heal her wounds.'

'I second Mr. Drummond's proposal,' said Benton.

Andrew stood up and pushed his chair aside.

'Then I'm through,' he snapped. 'Do what you like — I'm off this committee. Perhaps Mr. Drummond will feel disposed to go and offer the money personally.'

Drummond's eyes flashed angrily.

'Certainly I will.'

'Fine,' said Andrew. 'That's all I've got to say. Good night!'

Jean stood up and caught him by the arm as he was departing.

'One moment, Andrew.' She turned to the others. 'Andrew is right. You must leave Ailsa out of this. It is true she can refuse the money, but is it a kindly act to offer it at all in the circumstances? She has suffered so much already that to do what you propose is like taunting her. I know your intentions are good, but you don't understand Ailsa as I do. You don't know how much she has suffered from the cruel and merciless gossip — '

'But we cannot help that,' argued Drummond impatiently. 'She would have been forgiven long since if she had — '

He stopped abruptly as Andrew smote the table with his massive fist and caused the ink to fly out of the inkstand on to the list of subscriptions.

'Careful!' he roared. 'Things have a way of coming home to roost. I warn you, Alan Drummond — the taller the castle, the greater its fa'. The stones you fling may break your ain windows, and — '

Jean's face had gone as pale as a sheet. She thrust out her hand pleadingly, and Andrew halted in time to save the situation. He bit his lip, grabbed his hat, and with an almost inaudible 'Good evening' left the room. Jean sank into her chair with a great gulp.

'We must proceed without him,' said Drummond. 'Evidently he cannot control his temper!'

'If you don't mind I will go too,' said Jean. 'I — I am not feeling very well.'

'My dear — '

'It is all right — the heat, I think.'

'I will see you home — '

'No, no. I shall be quite all right in the open air. Please continue and do — what is right.'

So, as the matter was rather urgent, the committee continued with the business and settled it in their own fashion. Despite what had taken place, Ailsa was voted fifty pounds, and Drummond himself signed the cheque.

16

In the meanwhile Ailsa was face to face with a certain fact, and how to deal with it she did not know. For several days she had deliberately avoided meeting Andrew. The knowledge which had so swiftly dawned on her had literally set her brain awhirl. Andrew loved her! It was easy now to realise that this love of his was of no recent origin. She could trace it back over three years.

She had at first wept at consciousness of this. It was like losing the old Andrew who had nursed her in his arms. Whatever he might be in the future, he could certainly be adopted parent no more. Yes, the old Andrew was dead and buried, and here was this new figure reaching down to her heart —

It brought her to think about Stewart Morrison, and with that memory certain facts were made clear. Her love lay buried with him — nothing could bring it back again. She had nothing to give Andrew in exchange for the passion which so clearly swept his breast, nothing but an everlasting gratitude for his friendship and unwavering loyalty.

'Perhaps he doesn't think I know his secret?' she confided to Peter. 'But to think it was only a few days ago that I discovered it!'

'What's a secret, Mum-mie?' lisped Peter.

She stared at him in astonishment, for she had overlooked the fact that Peter was gaining intelligence at a remarkable rate. It meant that her one little confidant was passing away like so many other things. Stewart had gone, the old Andrew had gone, and now Peter, into whose ear she had loved to pour her troubles, was going. She felt very much alone in the world.

In the afternoon the minister called with the object of handing her the cheque drawn the day before. She was quite ignorant of this fact, and wondered why he appeared a trifle uneasy.

'I haven't seen you for some time, Ailsa,' he said.

'I've been very busy.'

'Too busy to come to the kirk?' he asked, with a kindly smile.

'Yes, too busy for that.'

'You are sure that is the only reason?'

She looked at him squarely and shook her head.

'There is another reason — and you know it,' she said quietly.

'I know what you mean, but it's no real reason.'

'It's real enough to me. My presence there would not be welcomed by quite a lot of people. I have no wish to create any spirit of discord. After all, I suppose God can be found in other places — if one wishes to find Him?'

The minister apparently found it a little difficult to reply to this. He looked round the tidy and comfortable room.

'There is not much sign of the flood here,' he mused. 'I see you have had it entirely redecorated — and very nicely too.'

'The landlord sent some workmen along.'

'I wish the other landlords were equally interested in their property. And how are you, Peter?'

Peter, who had heard the strange voice, had entered the room and was gazing at the visitor with wide interested eyes.

'Go and shake hands, Peter,' said Ailsa.

Peter toddled forward and put his small hand into the minister's, then he slipped his other hand into his pocket and extricated a piece of chocolate, offering it with a bashful smile.

'I mustn't take your last piece,' said the minister, whereat Peter put it back with a huge sigh of relief. Ailsa laughed merrily.

'He'll be going to school soon?' he queried.

'Next year.'

Peter disappeared then with a toy engine in tow.

'I almost forgot the real object of my call,' began the minister. 'It has to do with the Relief Fund.'

'Oh, yes. I heard something about it. I hope it was a success?'

'Quite, quite. We — we held a meeting last night to apportion the amounts. It is the earnest wish of the committee that you accept this — this small token of public sympathy.'

He took the cheque from his pocket and placed it on the table. Ailsa's indignant eyes rested on it for a moment and then swept up and fixed him unflinchingly.

17

'Did I appeal for assistance?' asked Ailsa hoarsely.

'No, but — ' the minister stammered.

'Then how dare anyone discuss my affairs? All I ask is to be left alone. Do you imagine I can accept charity from people who have treated me as the folk here have done?'

'My dear Ailsa, I beg — '

'You beg me to forget that I have a soul. You ask me to forget that not long ago a woman called down curses on my name. A large portion of this money was given by someone who tried to buy my home over my head that the Glen might be rid of me for ever — '

'Ailsa, what are you saying?'

'Only what is true. Now you come to me to heap further humiliation upon me. When I want help from my neighbours I'll ask for it, but I shall be dead and buried before that happens.'

The minister had scarcely expected such a display of angry resentment. It rendered him dumb for a few minutes, for in a way he sympathised with her and regretted that he had not agreed with Andrew and not listened to Drummond.

'Who voted me this money?' asked Ailsa.

'The committee.'

'And who is the committee?'

'Myself, Mr. Benton, Mr. Drummond, your sister, and Andrew Esplin.'

Ailsa's lip quivered.

'So my own sister knew no better. And Andrew — '

'No, Andrew would have nothing to do with it, and your sister agreed with him. They both left the meeting, and we settled the matter after that. Ailsa, I assure you that we acted with the best motive in the world. It never occurred to me — '

'I suppose not. Please say no more about it, and take that cheque away. I'll have no one fight my battles.'

'But Peter — wouldn't this money be of great help to him — later?'

It was an unfortunate remark, and he regretted it immediately it was uttered.

'Peter! Do you think I would let Peter be a child of charity? The only person in this world whom Peter is going to be indebted to is me — his — his mother.'

She gave a gulp and turned her head away. The minister took the cheque and placed it in his pocket-book. Then he stepped across to her and touched her on the shoulder.

'Forgive me, Ailsa; it was all a wretched mistake. I ought to have listened to Andrew; he is a wise man.'

She smiled at him through her tears and gripped his hand. She was glad when the door closed behind him, for she wanted to be alone. That Andrew had acted as he had was a great relief to her. It was always Andrew who understood. God bless him for his kindly heart. She wished he would call soon, for she missed him greatly. The past week had been strangely dull, and each day she had experienced an almost irresistible desire to call in at the smiddy. The memory of that last parting prevented her, for what could her presence do but add to his heartache? Yet the situation had to be faced. They could not act now as if they were strangers. She decided that the only thing to do was to attempt to revive the old friendship — to pretend she did not know his secret. But she detested subterfuge and masquerade. Instinctively she felt that they could never be the same again towards each other.

She was on the brink of calling on him, when Andrew took the situation into his own hands. He called at the farm the following evening, and by every means in his power sought to act as he had acted in the old days. She noticed, however, that he kept his eyes averted from her, and gave most of his time to Peter, who had welcomed him with open arms.

'Ailsa,' said Andrew suddenly, 'did you hear anything from Drummond about — about the Relief Fund?'

'Yes. Didn't you know?'

'No. I resigned from the committee when I heard that — that — '

'I know. The minister came here with some money, but I — '

'Refused it?'

'Yes. So long as I have strength and health I will fight my way through life.'

'I believe you can, Ailsa, but it's another woman's battle you are fighting.'

'That makes no difference,' she replied quickly.

'No, I suppose not. I'd be the last man to ask you to turn back now. But bad times come without warning, Ailsa, and with all your brave heart you have only one pair of hands. If ever you want help — '

'I shall never cry for help.'

'But if you find the road too rough, don't let your pride stop you from accepting a helping hand from — from an old friend.'

She noticed that he laid a lot of emphasis on the last two words, and all her heart went out to him. At such a time as this he could come humbly and lay his strength and assistance at her feet, asking nothing in return.

'If I were as abandoned as most of them think me, Andrew, I believe you would still call yourself my friend,' she murmured.

'Of course,' he replied simply. 'What right has any man to set himself up as a judge in such matters? Friendship was meant to weather all storms. Let me help to pilot you through if the rocks are many.'

'You have already helped me so much, Andrew.'

'No more than you would have helped me if it was necessary. I only ask to do what you would insist on doing for me.'

'I will remember, Andrew.'

He left her soon after, and with his going she thought he had taken something with him — some indefinable part of her being. No, it was not love — but something mighty near it. Then she trembled to reflect that her heart was beating rapidly.

18

Old Robert, the postman, was facing the greatest problem that had ever happened in his extremely placid existence. Like so many others, he had been a victim of the flood, the house in which he lodged having been inundated to the ceiling. He possessed two official coats, one of which had been so damaged by mud and water that he had sent it to Perth to be cleaned. On this particular day it had been returned looking brighter than ever, but to his amazement a large envelope accompanied it, containing an unopened letter, which, judging from its condition, had been found in one of the pockets.

'My guidness!' ejaculated Robert.

The letter was addressed to Ailsa Leslie, and bore the Glasgow postmark. Robert gasped as he realised it was dated three years back. How it had got into his pocket he could not remember. Indeed, at this moment he was almost incapable of thought at all, for to him his crime seemed tremendous. He propped the letter against the cruet on the table and stared at it blankly. His appetite was quite gone.

'What's to be done?' he muttered.

It occurred to him that he might slip it into Ailsa's letter-box and say nothing, but even his bewildered brain was capable of seeing that such a step might have severe penalties. Ailsa might put a complaint through, and then for all he knew his pension might be stopped, and his pension was due in less than six months.

Another idea came — to go to Ailsa and confess his carelessness. But aged as he was, he had not a little pride, and it rebelled at this. In all the years he had served the G.P.O. nothing like this had happened. It was awful — terrible. He magnified the thing until it took the semblance of a capital offence.

'I canna face it,' he muttered. 'I daurna.'

He picked up the letter with trembling fingers and turned it over in his hand. He found that he could raise the flap sufficiently to extricate the letter itself.

'Maybe it's no' important,' he thought. 'Might be only a bill — or a circular.'

In this event he could destroy it without much compunction and preserve his peace of mind. How great the temptation was. No, his fingers refused to do the work. His brow was wet with perspiration. He could not do it.

During the rest of the day he had no peace. He completed the evening delivery as in a dream and came home to find himself confronted with the same distressing problem. It was nearly midnight when he took his courage in both hands, and, seizing the letter, extracted its contents.

'To-day I have been offered a post abroad — a managerial position. This mark of appreciation I cannot refuse to accept. But to go away for three long years and leave you — Ailsa, darling, is it too late? Can you, with all your generous heart, forgive me? I can come to the Kirkton by return — one word from you will bring me post haste. I want to tell you with my own lips how much I regret my conduct — how deeply I love you still. Will you consent to marry me and come away with me to the East for three years? We should have furnished quarters, and there would be plenty of room for the boy. I'd be a good 'daddy' to him. I'd make him love me as I'm sure he must love you. Even if all this is but a wild dream, let me still come to see you once again. — Yours devotedly, Stewart.'

It was Stewart Morrison's last letter to Ailsa. Robert, who was a poor scholar, had to read it three times before he got the full sense of it. When he did he almost collapsed. He remembered that soon after that date Stewart had gone abroad and knew that Ailsa had not received another line from him. Here was the reason.

Ashamed, he racked his brains to find out what to do in the circumstances, but no idea came. To confess to Ailsa was out of the question. To confess to Stewart was even more impossible. He would destroy it. Yes, that was the only thing to do now. With a great gulp he tore it in two, but he could go no further. The words swam before his almost blinded eyes. It was as if he were committing murder. With a groan he put the two pieces back into the envelope and secreted it in a drawer.

All unaware of this important incident, Ailsa was carrying on as usual, trying to make good her recent loss by additional toil. Andrew, who watched the struggle in silence, wondered what the end would be. He knew that Ailsa, in spite of her promise, would not come to him for assistance. He got to know that Munro's wages had not been paid for a period.

'It's not for me to complain,' said Munro. 'The young mistress has got enough troubles o' her ain. I'll get my arrears all right when better times come roond.'

Both he and his son were staunch enough in their stolid fashion. What they lacked in energy they made up for in fidelity to the niece of their old master.

'Lost three pigs yesterday,' growled Munro. 'It'll be a blow to Miss Ailsa.'

Andrew wrinkled his brow and thought deeply.

'Munro, I've got three pigs on my small holding. I've no time to attend to them. Suppose you put them in your sty and say nothing.'

Munro opened his eyes.

'Better go and drive them over right away,' said Andrew casually. 'And there's a dozen chickens — better take the lot. I'm tired of keeping live stock.'

He walked away before Munro had recovered from his surprise, but the old man was intelligent enough to put two and two together, and chuckled mightily as he mixed this new stock with the old. Ailsa was fighting the lean times with all her wits and energy. In spite of the enormous amount of work about the farm, she still contrived to give Peter some of her time, and that infant, in all the sublime ignorance of childhood, never knew the sacrifices that were being made on his account.

'We'll win, my darling,' she crooned. 'Your

mummie isn't going to be beaten while she has you to spur her on. But I wish we could add another six hours to the day, so that I could spend them with you.'

Jean called one day with the news that Drummond had gone to Edinburgh and would not return until the following evening. She saw Peter playing in the garden and called him to her, cuddling him to her bosom almost ferociously as he climbed into her lap.

'How he grows,' she murmured. 'I — I suppose he'll soon be going to school?'

'Next year.'

'Here?'

'Of course.'

'He ought to go to a better school than we have here. I want him to grow up a gentleman.'

Ailsa turned round from her butter-making and looked at her sister keenly.

'I want him to grow up — a man,' she said.

'Yes, yes; but later on he'll have to go to a better school. How are you going to manage — '

'I've managed so far, and please God I'll meet needs when they arrive. He shall have opportunities, never fear.'

Jean bit her lip and gazed down into the boy's face.

'He looks — like me,' she whispered. 'Every time I see him he looks more like me.'

Ailsa held up her finger as she saw Peter opening his eyes and wrinkling his forehead.

'Run out and play, Peter,' she said. 'There's your poor horse fallen on his back.'

Peter was off like a shot, with Jean's eyes following him. She sighed as he vanished through the open door.

'If only I had your courage, Ailsa.'

'Courage!'

'To confess all. I've tried so many times and failed. The risk is too great. I made up my mind the other day to tell Alan everything, but he wouldn't listen. In his tremendous trust he made it so clear that to breathe a word of the truth would wreck everything. Yet I want my boy — I want a — a child of my very own.'

A little moan left Jean's lips. Ailsa saw in the moist, pained eyes the tragedy of unfruitful wedlock.

'Four years have passed, and now all hope has — gone. It seems like a punishment for what I have done.'

'Jean!'

'Yes, yes, that's it. I am caught in the net which I spread. God gave me a beautiful

184

child and I — I knew no better than to relinquish the substance for the shadow.'

'The shadow!' gasped Ailsa. 'Jean, is it a shadow, then? Aren't you happy?'

'I oughtn't to have said that. No, it isn't true. My love for Alan reaches up to the stars, but — but I miss the prattle of a child in the house. The corridors — the rooms — seem so — so cold and lifeless. At nights when I am sleeping I see Peter's face — '

She stopped and hung her head as if she were a little ashamed to give voice to her intimate secrets. Ailsa left her work and sat beside the distraught woman. She had never seen Jean in that state before.

'You mustn't lose heart,' she murmured. 'I did not know you felt — that way.'

Jean gazed at her with swimming eyes.

'I didn't — at first. The new life dazzled me. It was wonderful to have a beautiful home, plenty of clothes, and money to spare. The flattery and compliments were sweet enough, but I've changed somehow, Ailsa. Those things seem negligible almost. Married life is beautiful when you are loved as I was, and am, but after a year or two all the passion that intoxicated one — that swept to oblivion all other considerations — changes into something less absorbing but more permanent. It causes one to think, and in thinking a lot of truths are made known.'

'And so the care-free Jean has been learning truths?'

Jean nodded slowly.

'It's useless to deny that love without the fruits of love is not enough.'

Jean dabbed her eyes with her handkerchief and tried to smile, for she felt that she was burdening Ailsa with her troubles when Ailsa had quite enough of her own.

'Now tell me about yourself,' she begged.

'There is nothing to tell you. My circumstances are just about the same. Money comes and goes — chiefly goes.' She laughed gaily. 'But why grumble? Things could easily be worse.'

'Ailsa, have you ever heard from Stewart since — since — '

'No, I shall never hear from him again. He went away three years ago to take up a position abroad, people say. There is a rumour that he is about to return, but whether or no it makes no difference to me.'

'Are you sure it makes no difference, Ailsa?'

Ailsa avoided the searching eyes and shook her head.

'You don't love him now? You have forgotten you ever loved him?'

'Y — yes,' huskily.

Jean was silent for a few minutes. The thing she had really come to ask was not easy to put.

'Ailsa, isn't there another person you ought to consider?' she said suddenly.

'Another person!'

'There is someone in the Glen who worships the ground you walk on — someone who would give his life for you if need be. Is it impossible that you — you might — '

Ailsa got up and walked across the room agitatedly. That Jean should have said such a thing literally took her breath away.

'I didn't mean to be rude.'

Ailsa turned her face round. It was crimson with embarrassment and lined with indecision.

'You mean — '

'Andrew.'

'How — how did you know?'

'It wasn't difficult to guess. Andrew has been so different this past year. He tries to hide his heart, but he couldn't hide it from me, because I've lived for four years with a man who loves a woman. Andrew loves you, Ailsa. You know that?'

'Yes, but he doesn't know I know. I have

watched him crushing it down, because he has made up his mind never to speak.'

'But why shouldn't he speak?'

'He is afraid he might hurt me. He knows all about Stewart, and would rather die than obtrude into any — any memories I might cherish. It is terrible to know this, and to be impotent to help him.'

Jean glanced at her swiftly, reading in the words Ailsa's inner feelings.

'So you — you still love him? In spite of all that has happened, you love Stewart?'

'No, no. All that is over and done with, but what Andrew asks I can never give. Jean, I shall never love anyone again.'

'Andrew may know that.'

'What do you mean?'

'Andrew might be prepared to accept something a little less. Ailsa, in married life friendship and understanding occupy a large place. Oh, I know — I know. The hot flame that we call true love isn't the only thing, nor the most lasting. Suppose Andrew, too, was aware of this, and offered you companionship, respect, fidelity, and his good name, wouldn't it be worth considering — wouldn't it?'

'Perhaps — perhaps. But he may never ask.'

'But if he did?'

'I — I might — I might consider it. No
— no, it is all impossible. Please don't
mention that again.'

Jean had no intention of doing so, but she
had made up her mind in another direction,
and that was that Andrew should speak, and
speak soon.

19

Ailsa's talk with Jean had left her more undecided than ever. It had not needed Jean to make her aware of Andrew's virtues. These were as plain to her as the hills. But what Jean had hinted at had never occurred to her — that is to say, the possibility of marrying someone whom she did not really love. She had always believed in facing facts, and this one she faced with her usual courage. Into the scale she placed all the pros and cons, and she found they balanced.

Andrew was ten years older than she. In many ways he was different. His outlook on life did not harmonise with hers in every respect. But at least she knew him as well as it was possible for one being to know another. Andrew, she felt sure, had no secret life. His very nature was against it.

Then there was Peter to be considered, and it was this consideration which counted a great deal. Much as a mother might be to a boy in his younger years, a father became necessary to enforce that discipline without which any boy's character becomes warped. Peter already regarded Andrew as a father.

Why not take the comparatively short step which would make the thing a reality?

In the meantime Jean had been exceedingly busy. She began to find innumerable jobs for Andrew to tackle. That worthy certainly did wonder why so big a lady should delight in visiting his smiddy in person to bring in jobs which the gardener at Aberdinnie could have done quite well, but he never guessed what was at the back of Jean's mind until conversation was subtly led into the desired channels.

'Have you seen Ailsa of late, Andrew?' she asked.

'Not a great deal,' replied Andrew. 'Both Ailsa and I are in the same boat — overworked.'

'You should take things easier, Andrew. You work too hard.'

'Hard work never did a body ony harm.'

'I'm not so sure. You're not the man you used to be.'

Andrew stared at her, and then laughed amusedly.

'I'm as fit as ever I've been in my life,' he averred. 'No man could run a smiddy like this if he wasn't fit in wind and limb.'

'Is that all you think about — wind and limb?'

'Now, see here, Jean,' said Andrew,

wagging his finger, 'you may be a great lady these days, but in the matter of hard thinking you're not qualified to give me lessons.'

'Don't be so sure,' retorted Jean. 'Bigger brains than yours have been at sea where a woman is concerned.'

'Aye, women,' growled Andrew. 'I'll admit I'm a dunce there. No man can tell what a woman will do next. She doesn't act logically as a man does. When by all the force of reason she ought to do one thing she more often than not does the opposite.'

'And she may be right.'

'She may be, but you canna run the world on those lines. A woman's final appeal is to her heart and a man's to his reason.'

'And you think the heart is a poor guide?'

'Aye, emotion will work all kinds of wrong — like Mrs. M'Clure when she called down vengeance on an innocent girl — '

'And afterwards came begging for forgiveness. You didn't know that, Andrew, but it's true. Oh, don't disparage the heart as a guide to happiness, Andrew. What you call logic has made as many mistakes as intuition.'

Andrew shook his head and wondered that she should choose to discuss such a subject.

'Look you, Jean,' he added as a final bolt,

'if I ran my business on emotional lines I'd be in a bonnie mess. When your heart runs agin your reason let the first go and trust the second.'

'You're wrong, Andrew. I could almost prove it.'

He wrinkled his brow as he met her direct gaze. It held something which puzzled him deeply.

'You could prove it — in my ain case?'

She nodded her head, still keeping her eyes on his querulous face.

'Go on, then.'

'You might not like it.'

'I'm not the man to shy at a truth — if it is a truth.'

'It is so true that you cannot deny it. Andrew, why don't you do what your heart has been urging for the past year, and more? Why listen to this deluded voice of reason which succeeds in persuading you that what you hope for can never be attained?'

Andrew's face grew crimson. He turned from her with a great gasp and began to work his bellows, but when he glanced round he saw that she was waiting patiently. He flung aside the wooden handle and faced her.

'So — so that's what you have been trying to say these past few days?' he growled.

'Yes, and why shouldn't I? Ailsa is my

own sister, who has sacrificed a lot of her happiness for me. Like a drowning woman, I will clutch at any straw that may possibly save her from — from bitter disappointment.'

'Disappointment! Do you imagine that Ailsa with all her youth and beauty could care for a man — '

'I don't imagine — I know — and it's because I know that I am impertinent enough to intrude. Andrew, your stubborn logic will lead you astray where Ailsa is concerned. Only your heart can reach her. Don't let it ask in vain for the thing that is so near to hand.'

She vanished with the swiftness of a shadow, leaving him gasping with amazement.

20

Andrew sat down on the wooden block which supported the anvil, and mopped his brow. What surprised him most was that Jean should know his innermost desire.

He shut up the smiddy and went indoors to think. It required a lot of will power to cancel his earlier resolution, but if Jean was right, and Ailsa was really in love — Oh, it seemed impossible — yet was it so unthinkable? She must know at least of his devotion to her. Surely she must know that her happiness meant more to him than his own! If that was so, it were better to speak without further delay.

He made up his mind by the time he went to bed. His one great fear was that he might hurt her feelings; but with Jean's encouraging words still ringing in his ears that probability seemed less certain than before.

'I'll tell her,' he muttered. 'I must tell — I must. Please God, she'll understand why I didn't speak before!'

And Andrew was not the only man in the Glen who had a restless and disturbed mind at that time. To the ordinary dweller in the

Glen, accustomed to look upon the Laird of Aberdinnie with somewhat envious eyes, it would have seemed impossible that a man so fortunately placed as Drummond could have troubles of any kind. They had only to turn their eyes to the hill to see the big house gleaming among the trees, encircled with spreading lawns, and almost perpetual flowers.

'A lucky man yon,' quoth Robert.

'Aye, and I remember him when he was as poor as a church mouse. It's mighty strange how Fortune favours some and passes others by. To think of young Alan Drummond coming into money and owning Aberdinnie!'

'Well, it must feel strange to waken up o' mornings without a single care in the world.'

That was the common view concerning Drummond, and it was in the circumstances a very natural one, for these people of the Glen worked hard for a livelihood. It had never occurred to them that a moneyed man with an adoring wife and a magnificent home could be anything else but sublimely happy and contented, but then they merely saw the imposing exterior and were not afforded a glimpse of the yearning heart in Drummond's breast.

During the past year Drummond had

changed considerably. A lot of his exuberance had vanished and he looked much older than his years. To his wife he was not one whit less considerate. Jean always came first — even before his financial interests, which by this time were considerable. Jean held his love as fast as on the day of their marriage. She alone was aware of certain changes in his spirit, and she felt she knew the cause.

'Aren't you going to town to-day, Alan?' she asked one morning.

'Not to-day, Jean.'

'Then let us go riding. We haven't ridden out for weeks.'

'Would you like to?'

'Immensely.'

'Then that settles the matter. I will tell Donald to bring the horses round. But it looks like rain.'

'Let it; I don't mind.'

They started off half an hour later under a frowning sky, riding side by side over the springing bracken. She tried to induce conversation, but failed miserably, for Drummond was in one of his moods — a kind of depression from which it was always difficult to arouse him. Jean put her heels to her mount and went galloping madly forward to relieve the tension. He came cantering after her, and she waited for him on the brow of the hill with her face flushed and her eyes gleaming.

'Isn't it glorious?' she said.

'Yes, the open air is good.'

But there was little enthusiasm in his words, and she looked disappointed and dejected. They rode on for nearly an hour in silence, and then dismounted near a brook and permitted the horses to graze on the grass nearby. Jean seated herself on a rock and began to throw stones into the running stream. She looked up, to find her husband beside her gazing at her in strange fashion.

'You've been awfully quiet,' she murmured. 'I — I thought you were annoyed with me.'

'How absurd! Why should I be annoyed with you?'

'That's what I am wondering.'

She smiled and put her arm round his shoulder.

'Alan, haven't you been happy of late?'

'What a question to ask! Whatever put it into your head?'

'Your behaviour. Alan, is anything worrying you — some financial trouble, perhaps?'

'Nothing — nothing.'

'Then it's worse than finance?'

'What do you mean?'

'Oh, you can't hide it from me. I've seen a small cloud gathering for a long time.

Whenever I have looked at you you have always tried to hide it — to act as if things were just as they used to be. You used to laugh with me, tease me, romp with me; but not now.'

He pulled her head closer to him and kissed her then let his hand wander over her curls.

'What a girl you are, Jean. So you want me to romp with you, just as if we were eighteen?'

'Need we be much more than eighteen?' she pleaded.

'I am afraid so. Time is merciless in its march. Why, it won't be long before I shall be counting the grey hairs in my head, and these days will be but mere memories — '

She uttered a little cry and a tear gathered in her eye.

'Why conjure up visions of old age and loneliness?'

'That is it,' he muttered. 'Loneliness — being alone in our old age.'

A tremor went through her body as she divined what lay behind the remark. The same thing that was torturing her was torturing him too.

'Jean!'

She choked back a sob.

'Suppose — suppose it turns out that way?' he asked.

'What way?'

'You know — we've never spoken of it before — but we've thought of it, haven't we? Our house is strangely silent. In the slums of the big cities there are children that should never have been born at all — some unloved, uncared for, others deformed and diseased — '

'Alan!' she almost screamed.

'It's true — and yet here are we with the desire, the means, the love to lavish — '

'Yes, yes — it seems cruel,' she moaned.

He clasped her passionately in his arms and kissed away the tears in her eyes.

'Don't think it makes any difference to my love, Jean. If the lonely days come, surely we can face them together. So let us forget it and go on being all in all to each other. I won't think of it again.'

'Yes you will, Alan,' she said slowly. 'The gap is too great to be ignored. But there is another way?'

'Another way?'

'There are children who are a drag upon their parents — children who might in after years be eternally grateful for an opportunity which they might otherwise not have had. To take a boy or girl from a narrow rut and put him into sunshine — isn't that worth doing?'

'You mean — adoption?'

She nodded, and watched the play of his features. The suggestion evidently startled him.

'It wouldn't be the same.'

'Isn't that a little selfish?'

'Yes; but isn't love of any kind selfish up to a point? Your own kith and kin come first — they must; it's human nature.'

'It should be human nature to love without distinction.'

'You're an idealist.'

'Perhaps; but I want to be a realist, too. Couldn't we do something fine for some child, Alan — something of which we should have the right to be proud? This nightmare of loneliness could be banished. We could watch him as he grew up — share all his triumphs — weep with him in his failures. He might be as close to us as if he were our — our very own.'

He gazed before him reflectively, and she knew that the suggestion was taking root.

'Would it be possible to find a woman who would surrender her own child?' he asked.

'Yes, if she thought it was for the child's good. And — and we might not have far to search.'

He shot her a swift glance.

'You mean in the Glen?'

'Yes — even next door to us.'

In her great desire to solve their mutual problem, and at the same time to satisfy her own heart's craving, she had gone a step too far.

'Oh, Jean! You don't mean — Peter?' he gasped.

'Yes; why not?'

'I wouldn't dream of it. Besides, do you imagine your sister would give up her child?'

'Yes, yes. You don't understand — no, you can never understand. Ailsa loves him, but she won't stand in his way — '

Behind all his good intentions Drummond's puritanical spirit was gathering force. It was the one flaw in his character — an inherent trait difficult to contend with.

'That child couldn't be brought up under my roof.'

'Alan, how can you be so cruel, so relentless? Peter is the dearest child I ever saw. Oh, don't talk to me any more; you are breaking my heart.'

She leapt up from the rock and ran swiftly along the river. His anger subsided, leaving him wondering at her strange conduct. In a way he could understand her sticking up for Ailsa's child, but her agitation seemed scarcely warranted.

With a sigh he went along the river, and eventually found her on a fallen tree, dabbing her eyes with her handkerchief.

'Jean!'

'I'm sorry, Alan,' she said quietly; 'but you don't know how much you hurt me.'

'I didn't mean to. Why did we allow ourselves to quarrel?'

'It's foolish, I know, but we seem to look at things differently. Let us go home.'

The ride home was extremely irksome to both of them. Each of them was realising how swiftly discord could be bred when intolerance got in the way. To Drummond his wife's suggestion was monstrous, and to Jean her husband's prejudices were cruel. The idea of getting possession of Peter by such a subterfuge had seemed promising enough. In the circumstances she had imagined he would put no obstacles in her path. Now that great hope was shattered for all time.

'You are still angry with me,' he remarked.

'Not angry — disappointed.'

'If I could do what you ask I would. But I can't bring myself to it — my whole nature is against such a possibility. But I'm willing to consider the adoption of another child.'

'A child with no mystery attached to its birth?' she retorted a little icily.

'I am not blaming the child.'

'No; but you punish it, which is just as cruel.'

'You are saying very hard things, Jean.'

She did not reply, anxious as she was not to let this friction develop into a quarrel. With all his narrow-mindedness she still loved him deeply. What hurt her most was his antipathy to Ailsa. To banish that censure she would have sacrificed much, but to achieve that would mean nothing less than the loss of the thing she held dear — his faith and trust in her.

That night she lay awake for a long time, examining the situation from every point of view; but whatever remedy she sought to apply, always there loomed before her the only true solution — the whole truth concerning the parenthood of Peter.

'I can't do it,' she moaned. 'Alan, if I lost you it would break my heart.'

21

It was Saturday afternoon, and Andrew had closed down the smiddy for the day. Adjourning to his cottage next door, he ate his dinner with a complete lack of his customary appetite, changed his working clothes and wandered aimlessly up and down his small garden. The woman who kept house for him gazed after him pensively and shook her head.

'Worryin' aboot something!' she remarked to herself.

This, up to a point, was true. Andrew was steeling himself to face something which in his opinion was far more frightful than physical ailments. Since Jean's outspoken remarks he had been seeking an opportunity to put into practice his resolution, but whenever the opportunity came he grew nervous and afraid.

'Suppose it's all wrong?' he muttered. 'But Jean must know — she couldn't make a mistake like that.'

He was still striding round and round his cabbage patch, when Jean herself came into view. She was seated in a trap with the reins in her hand and the excited figure of Peter by her side. She pulled up the pony outside Andrew's garden and nodded as he touched his cap.

'Hullo, Uncle Andrew!' chirped Peter. 'Aunty is taking me for a beautiful drive.'

'You're a lucky chap.'

'Yes, and when we come back I am going to the big house for tea.'

Andrew looked at Jean, and Jean endorsed this by inclining her head. She guessed that Andrew was wondering what Drummond was thinking of this, and was quick to explain.

'My husband has had to go to Edinburgh on business, so Peter and I are having a picnic all on our own.'

'And there'll be cakes with chocolate over them,' whispered Peter. 'Don't you wish you was coming, Uncle?'

Andrew laughed and shook his head. Then he noticed that Jean was regarding him strangely.

It was, she said, a beautiful afternoon, and Ailsa might be glad of a respite from toil. He nodded his head silently and waved his hand to Peter. Jean smiled, and nodding to him, set the trap bowling down the dusty street.

Half an hour later Andrew went swinging through the lane which led to the farm. At the door his heart thumped madly in his bosom, but having got so far, he meant to see the thing through. He knocked and saw Ailsa's face at the window. It lighted up as she saw the visitor, and her finger beckoned him inside.

'You're off early to-day, Andrew?'

'Aye, it's been a busy week for me, and I was mighty glad to put the key aside until Monday morning.'

'Peter has gone driving with Jean.'

'I met them; that's hoo I'm here.'

She glanced at him swiftly, but Andrew's face was perfectly calm now.

'I came to drag you away from cream bowls and things. Nobody ought to be indoors on such a bonny day. Let's go for a walk.'

'I'm really awfully busy.'

'That's nae excuse. Are you coming quietly or must I tak' ye by force?'

'You wouldn't dare!'

'Wad I no'? You'll see if you dinna mak' up your mind quickly. Ten minutes to get ready!'

'She laughed amusedly, and then nodded her head. In truth she welcomed his suggestion, but from some inexplicable motive she had demurred at first. 'I'll come,' she cried gaily, 'but not in ten minutes. Give me fifteen at least!'

Andrew sat down and waited impatiently. Despite his outward calm his heart was in a turmoil.

Ailsa came in a few minutes later and signified that she was ready. She wore a rather short plaid skirt and stout walking boots, with a red tam o' shanter on her head. To-day her eyes seemed unusually bright, as if the projected trip filled her with joy.

'Where to?' she asked.

'Anywhere.'

'Oh, let's go to that place along the valley where you and I and Peter had our picnic — you remember?'

Andrew agreed, and they set off at a good pace. The warm sun smote down from a cerulean sky, and all the woods were vibrant with the song of birds. It was such a day as to make sadness, regrets, and gloomy aspects impossible. The cooling breeze played about their cheeks and all Nature seemed in gay mood.

All the way to the woods they talked and laughed as beings act who have no single care in their lives. It was as if they had both determined to be happy in spite of everything. Andrew almost succeeded in forgetting the real object of this excursion. Ailsa seemed so happy, so light-hearted, that he hated to reflect he might soon be the means of bringing fear and doubting to her sparkling eyes.

They found the very spot where they had held their former picnic, and eventually sat down by the bank of the musical stream.

The time sped along on magic wings, and still Andrew had not mentioned the thing he had come to say. But the desire to do so was no less strong than when he started out. To look into Ailsa's face, to almost feel her presence beside him, was like to being transported to some dreamland Paradise. But how difficult it was to speak!

'How are things goin' at the farm?' he asked.

'Quite well — now. I got fearfully behind, but little by little things are straightening themselves out. Munro is working better than he has ever worked before. It's astonishing what one can do if one only has the incentive.'

'What incentive?'

'Peter, of course.'

'Does he mean so much to you?'

'Yes; almost everything in life. I think if it hadn't been for Peter I might have given up the struggle.'

'Ailsa!'

'That sounds terrible, but it's true. When

Jean got married it left me very much alone. I had no one to think about but myself, and it isn't enough to think merely of oneself. There is nothing so depressing as being alone — living for nothing but the uncertain future — watching yourself grow old with no one to care — '

She stopped with a gasp as she realised that Andrew had turned his head away. It came like a stab to realise that this was Andrew's lot, and that unwittingly she had administered a blow at him. Her hand went out and touched his.

'How thoughtless of me, Andrew. How selfish!'

'You couldn't be selfish, Ailsa.'

'Yes, yes, I could. I only know one person who is not selfish,' she said quietly.

Andrew's big hand closed on hers and his head came round. His deep eyes surveyed her intently and his lips moved as if they were trying to say something in vain.

'Andrew, you — '

'Ailsa, you mustn't say things like that. I'm just like all the rest — '

'I shall never believe you are selfish — never, never, never!'

'Perhaps that is the wrong word,' he replied hoarsely. 'For behind all my thoughts, all my actions, is the knowledge that — that — '

He stopped as he saw her eyes open wider and realised that she divined what he was about to say. He wanted to snatch any warning she might be able to give before he spoke words that could never be withdrawn, but she said nothing, only continued to gaze at him with an expression on her face which he failed utterly to interpret.

'Ailsa,' he continued, 'am I going to hurt you? Stop me before I utter a word that is better unspoken.'

'What — what were you going to say, Andrew?' she quavered.

The encouragement sent the words bubbling from his lips.

'I love you, Ailsa. I've loved you for years — ever since I realised that you — you were a woman. Ailsa, I've tried to choke it down, to act just as I used to when you were a child, but it's no use pretending any longer. I love you with a passion that knows no rest. I know I'm not worthy of your love — '

'Andrew!' she choked.

'But all I have to offer you, Ailsa, I offer you. Can you find a little room in your heart for me?'

'A little room in my heart!' she repeated. 'Is that all you ask, Andrew?'

'It's all I have the right to expect in the circumstances. Oh, Ailsa, don't misunderstand me. What I want is the joy of being with you, always, caring for you — working for you. I have all the passions that poets sing of, but I don't ask you to return those, because — '

'Because what?'

'Because I feel that you can never be that way to me. I should be contented with a little less than I might be were I younger, but with that little less I should be the happiest man in the world. Ailsa, am I asking too much?'

The proposal, sudden as it was, came not as a complete surprise, and in a way she was glad to be forearmed, for she wanted to act with clarity of mind. Most of all she wanted him to understand exactly her own feelings.

'You have already smoothed the path, Andrew,' she murmured. 'I want to be frank with you. I think you are the best man I have ever known. If I had not already loved — someone else — there might be no need to think of that 'little less.' Perhaps the day might come when even the past could be forgotten.'

'Ailsa — Ailsa!'

'But not now, Andrew — wounds take time to heal.'

He found it difficult to interpret this, and she saw that he was waiting in silent agony for a clear reply.

'You have tried so much to depreciate your love,' she said. 'For fear you might hurt my feelings you have tried to leave an avenue of retreat for me. But I don't want to retreat, Andrew. I believe you can make me happy, Andrew. Take me and make me happy — and yourself, too!'

He gave a great cry and seized her in his arms passionately, kissing her for the first time for many years.

'Oh, Ailsa, Ailsa, it sounds too good to be true. Then there's Peter — he shall have a father who'll put him on the road fully equipped.'

'You're a dear,' she murmured. 'I'll try hard to make you happy, Andrew.'

'I'm that already. Wouldn't any man be happy with the sweetest, dearest lass in the world to share his home? Ailsa, can I tell my good news?'

'If you want to,' she replied. 'But I'd like to keep it secret for a wee while. I'd like to know that you and I have one great secret between us.'

'Yes, yes; but we ought to tell Jean.'

'Yes, Jean, and nobody else.'

The return journey was made in the dusk of evening. They walked as lovers do — hand in hand down the verdant valley, wrapped in their dreams of the future. The miles seemed ridiculously short, and they arrived at the farm long before they realised they were near it.

'Come and see me to-morrow, Andrew.'

'Early?'

'As early as you like.'

He gripped her two hands tightly in farewell. But she smiled and raised her face that he might kiss her. Then he strode away. Now that it was done she was glad. It had stirred her much deeper than she had expected, for his love was so clear and certain. Yet she could not help reflecting it was all so different from that other occasion when Stewart had whispered passionate words into her ear and sent the hot blood scampering through her veins. Could Andrew ever succeed in arousing that emotion?

But she did not wish to remember that. It lay in the past that she meant to forget. Perhaps the greatest joy of all was the knowledge that Andrew was happy. That was sufficient to balance any doubting she might have had.

She waited for Jean to bring Peter back, but the hours passed and he did not come. A little apprehensive, she was on the point of going up to Aberdinnie when Jean called alone.

'Where's Peter?' gasped Ailsa.

'He's all right. He was so tired I didn't trouble to bring him back. He is sleeping at Aberdinnie.' She did not like to confess that the need for Peter was becoming an obsession — that her husband's love was not enough. 'You — you don't mind, do you?'

Ailsa made no reply, but she could not miss the deep emotion in Jean's words and actions, and wondered how the battle would end. Jean, anxious to change the subject, inquired about Andrew.

'He's gone,' said Ailsa, blushing furiously. 'I — I've got something to tell you, but it mustn't go any further.'

Jean stepped close to her and kissed her fondly.

'I can guess what it is, dear. I prayed this might happen. I am sure that it will turn out happy.'

'Yes, yes; we are going to be the happiest couple in the world,' replied Ailsa emphatically. But all the time there loomed before her eyes the figure of Stewart. Why could she still think of him at such a time — why?

22

For two glorious weeks Ailsa and Andrew's secret was kept. During that period the two saw much of each other. Almost every evening Andrew came across to the farm, and with his sleeves rolled up helped Ailsa to make butter and cheese, after which they would walk down the valley and talk of the magic future.

'I shall give up the smiddy,' said Andrew.

'Give up the smiddy!'

'Aye. There's a man in the village willing to pay a tidy sum for the business. I've been inquiring about those meadows behind the farm, and have got an option on them. With another twenty or so acres we ought to do quite well, Ailsa. There'll be no rent to pay, either.'

'But you don't know much about farming, Andrew,' she teased.

'What I don't know you can teach me. Anyway, what I lack in experience I'll make up for in energy. Why should I be running a smiddy when I've a farm of my own?'

She laughed lightly. Andrew was going to do just the thing she hoped he would do. She had the utmost faith in his business ability and untiring energy. With such a man as Andrew at the helm the farm would certainly develop into a prosperous concern.

'We'll send Peter to a school of agriculture when he's old enough, where he'll learn the scientific side of the business that lots o' farmers know nothing about.

'Including me,' laughed Ailsa.

Andrew caught her hand and raised it to his lips.

'Yes, including you, Ailsa. You must admit there is always something new to learn.'

'Of course, Andrew. I'm not in the least offended. I don't think I could be offended with you, whatever you said.'

'Be careful,' warned Andrew. 'A woman may think nice things about her husband, but it isn't always wise to utter them. He might get swelled-headed and believe they were true.'

'I shall know how to reduce your swelled head, Andrew.'

They laughed together gaily. To Ailsa this new relationship was beautiful enough. To Andrew it was a veritable new life. She saw him at times gazing into space with all the evidence of immeasurable joy suffusing his face. The cynicism which he had been prone to in the past was gone now. Andrew was finding life full of joy.

'Ailsa,' he whispered, 'when can it be?'

'The — the wedding?'

'Yes. There is no need to wait long, is there?'

'No. I'm ready whenever you wish.'

Having fixed the day for just over a fortnight hence, there was no reason to keep the affair hushed up any longer. Jean whispered it to her husband, who evidenced the most complete surprise.

'You are thinking that Andrew is crazy?' said Jean.

'No, no, but — Jean, you mustn't think me hard. Nine men out of ten would view this matter as I view it.'

'Not nine men who knew Ailsa as I know her. Alan, will you never live down your prejudices? However big a mistake a woman might make, surely she is not outside the pale of sympathy and forgiveness?'

'Have I ever said she was?'

'Not in words, but all your actions point that way. It makes me think that if ever I did anything wrong you would close your heart to me for ever.'

He turned his head away as if he were afraid to meet her challenging eyes. Always this drama of Ailsa's came to rear its head between his wife and himself. In his heart he was ashamed of his coldness towards the sister of the girl he had married. Little by little — almost unconsciously — a thawing process was taking place within him. When he reflected upon his repeated attempts to get rid of Ailsa he suffered considerable qualms of conscience.

With all his inherent prejudice, his one great desire was to be a good citizen. True he had ambitions, but they were less vaunting than of yore, and he would have exchanged all of them for a child of his own — a fine romping boy like Peter!

It was this searching into his own soul which impelled him to do something quite notable. One evening he met Andrew on his way to the farm. To Andrew's astonishment Drummond smiled very pleasantly and stopped. Andrew, who really cared very little whether the laird of Aberdinnie loved him or hated him, gazed at him with wrinkled brow.

'I — I wanted to congratulate you, Andrew.'

'Thank you!' growled Andrew, who found it difficult to believe that Drummond could be sincere.

'I only heard last night,' resumed Drummond. 'I sincerely hope you will be happy.'

'Is there any reason why we shouldn't?'

Drummond shook his head and was silent for a few seconds, then he let the more generous part of his nature manifest itself.

'I am afraid some of us have been rather hard on Ailsa. Loving one's neighbour is not such a simple matter as it sounds. Andrew, if there is anything I can do to prove how deeply I regret certain — certain acts of the past, I should be glad to have the chance. I — I think you are a lucky man.'

He made an abrupt departure, leaving Andrew rooted to the spot with astonishment. To hear such things from the mouth of Drummond was surely marvellous. It raised him miles in Andrew's estimation, for the latter knew what a vast amount of resolution it must have required to bring Drummond to such a state of humility.

'Even your brother-in-law is beginning to appreciate you, Ailsa,' he whispered.

'What do you mean?'

'He stopped me and congratulated me.'

'He couldn't have meant it, Andrew.'

'But he did. Something has changed him.'

'Yes, he has been changed of late. In spite of his wealth and position, he is not happy.'

'So you have noticed that?'

'Who could help noticing it? And Jean,

too, is not the girl she was. Andrew, she is hungering for Peter — you can see it in her eyes, in all her actions. She wants to take him from me and dare not.'

'If she dared, would you let him go?'

Ailsa reflected, and then inclined her head. 'I could not do otherwise. She is his mother, and has a right to him. But she dare not claim him, for that would be the end of everything.'

'You think he would never forgive her?'

'I'm sure. It was a great mistake she made in not risking everything and telling him years ago. The blow would be fifty times worse now. If she had had another child it might have made all the difference. She could have lavished on it the love she bears Peter.'

Andrew understood this quite well. The maternal instinct had always been strong in Jean. He could imagine what it must mean to her to watch her only son being brought up by her own sister, and to know that the price to be paid for possession of him was her husband's love.

'I wish we could find a way out,' he murmured.

'There is no way except the way she dare not take. You said once that if one sows a lie it will bring forth a full harvest, and Jean is now reaping that harvest.'

They were glad to drop the subject and talk of pleasanter things — their own approaching marriage, and the days that were to come. Andrew would talk of them with bated breath, arousing in Ailsa an enthusiasm which was perhaps a trifle artificial, for underneath all this natural excitement were queer apprehensions. With all her will she had tried to disperse them, and was successful so long as Andrew was with her to gild the future with his strong personality. But it was when she was alone that her heart began to put disturbing questions. For that reason she avoided solitude and hungered for Andrew's company.

'When you are not near me I feel — lost,' she confessed.

'Soon I shall be always near you, Ailsa.'

'And you will be good to me, Andrew?'

'Good to you? Why, I'll be your slave! You have only to say, 'Andrew, I feel I want to be alone,' and that will be a command.'

She understood the innuendo so carefully wrapped up, and blessed him for the thought. He made it so clear to her that his greatest desire was to leave her all the privacy she desired. By the constant manifestation of this clean and generous spirit he was hoping to banish those painful memories from her mind and to bring her to him with open arms.

The news of the approaching wedding now circulated with lightning speed. The whole community knew of it between sunrise and sunset. The wiseacres shook their heads cunningly and swore they knew all along; but the majority confessed it was the greatest surprise they had ever experienced.

The gossip which had laid so long dormant was now revived, and Ailsa and Andrew represented the leading topic of conversation. Ailsa was perfectly aware of all that was being said, but she let them have their say. She noticed with pleasure that Drummond's attitude towards her had changed considerably. He had of late gone out of his way to be kind to her. One morning the gardener from Aberdinnie came over with a basket of fruit. She had at first imagined that it came from Jean, but to her surprise the gardener informed her that Drummond sent it with his compliments.

On another occasion Peter wandered into the meadow which adjoined the grounds of Aberdinnie. After searching for half an hour she found him on the other side of the dividing hedge talking to his uncle — a being who had hitherto puzzled Peter very much. Ailsa heard part of the conversation before she came into view.

'Are you my other uncle?'

'I'm your only uncle.'

'You're not. I've got an Uncle Andrew. He's bigger than you, and I like him.'

'That means you don't like me, eh?'

'You don't come and see me like Uncle Andrew. My mummy says he's going to be my daddy soon.'

'Indeed! And what do you say to that?'

'I'll be awfully glad. Uncle Andrew says that when he becomes my daddy he will live in our house always; then he can play with me every morning and make engines for me. Is that your big house up there?'

'Yes.'

'I wish we had a house as big as yours. Auntie Jean let me sleep there last week — it was lovely!'

This was news to Drummond, and by the silence that followed Ailsa knew that he was pondering the matter. She came into view a second later and called to the boy. Peter ran across to her and wriggled through a hole in the hedge. She shook her finger at him reprovingly.

'Didn't I tell you not to come here, Peter?'

'My ball went through, Mummie,' he explained.

'It doesn't matter,' said Drummond, with

a smile. 'Peter is welcome to come here whenever he likes. It will be a change to hear a child's voice about the place.'

Ailsa thanked him simply, and he walked away. His last words were significant enough. She felt deeply sorry for him and was grateful for his attempts to bury the hatchet.

Then commenced an exceedingly busy period — the plans for the wedding. The question of a wedding dress troubled her. She would have liked to be married as she stood, but Jean was strongly against it, asserting that a girl's wedding day was the one occasion when she must look her best.

'I'm going to take you to a good dressmaker tomorrow,' she said. 'Andrew is going to have the most beautiful bride in the world.'

'What ridiculous things you say!' retorted Ailsa. 'Nothing will make me beautiful. You monopolised all the good looks in the family. No — I'll make my own wedding dress.'

But she did not, for the simple reason that Jean drove up the next day and hustled her off in her car to Perth. Peter was given in charge of the daily woman, who promised to keep her eye on him all the while. But it would have taken a dozen pairs of eyes to have followed all Peter's movements, as events proved.

At the end of the meadow ran the small

river which watered the land about the glen. Normally it was no more than two feet deep at the deepest part, but any heavy rainfall in the hills had the effect of flooding it. On this day it was quite a considerable stream, and in places had overflowed the bank. It was late in the afternoon when Peter, rummaging among his toys, found a small wooden boat which had been lost for several months. The discovery brought a cry of joy from his lips. His first thought was to sail it on the stream, and immediately he set off to put this into practice.

23

At the precise moment when Peter was wandering towards the stream the afternoon train pulled up at the station outside the Glen and a bronzed figure alighted from it. He carried no more than a suitcase, and gazed about him with the look of a man who has been absent for a considerable period.

With a little sigh he made towards the exit where the ticket-collector-cum-stationmaster stood stroking his chin reflectively. The solitary arrival smiled as he handed the man his ticket.

'Why, it's Mister Morrison!'

'I wondered when you were going to recognise me.'

'My, you're looking that different, it's no wonder you nearly passed me. So you've come home from abroad?'

'Yes, to have a look at the old places again. Why, there are new houses across the way!'

'Aye, there have been changes since you went away. We've even got a reading-room in the Glen. Look, you can see the top of it from here among the trees.'

'And I thought the Glen would never be any different!'

'It was all Mister Drummond's doing. He has been a good friend to the folks hereabouts.'

Stewart nodded his head slowly. The past came swimming in now in vivid fashion. There were a hundred questions he was dying to ask, but he kept them back for the time being.

'Are you to bide long in the Glen?'

'No — just a few days. I suppose there'll be room for me at the inn?'

'Aye; if not, the minister will put you up. He's aye pleased to see an old friend like you.'

Stewart bade him adieu and started on his way. His desire to visit the Glen was due to something more than the homing instinct. Three years of life abroad had certainly succeeded in clothing this small Highland village with an atmosphere of romance, but it was not the Glen itself which called him, but a voice from the past. It had surprised him to find that three years had left him inwardly unchanged. Though all hope had long fled there remained the old longing for the girl he knew he could never forget.

He walked along nervously, fearing that he might suddenly come across her. For a few minutes he actually regretted having succumbed to the temptation of revisiting a spot that could only succeed in causing him painful reflections, but he persuaded himself that he was now master of his emotions. Over three years ago she herself had written finis to his life's romance by maintaining silence in the face of his appeal. He thought she might have written, even though it were but to bid him 'Good-bye.' How he had waited on the post! With what bated breath had he watched the postman going from door to door, only to pass his own!

'I never thought she could be so hard,' he muttered. 'And yet perhaps I drove her to it with my brutal impetuosity. Confound! Why can I not forget it?'

He stopped and gasped, as through the trees he caught a glimpse of the roof of Ailsa's cottage. The road to the Glen led right by it — within fifty yards of the very door. He felt he could not pass that way. What had impelled him to come at all? He passed his hand across his brow and entered a gate with the object of taking a field path from which the cottage would be invisible.

He was some fifty yards down the path when a curious sound met his ears. It was like the scream of a child, and it appeared to come from the river to his right. He turned his eyes in that direction and uttered a little hiss of horror as he observed a small figure struggling in the water and being carried away by the swift current.

Dropping the suit-case, he ran like a deer to the river bank. The struggling figure was no longer in sight, and his heart thumped in anguish as he gazed on the face of the turbulent water. Then some distance below him a saturated blue smock appeared. He leapt forward, reached a spot immediately opposite, and plunged into the stream.

A few yards from the bank edge the water suddenly deepened, and he found himself out of his depth. He struck out with powerful overarm strokes and grasped at the blue smock, but on the verge of getting a grip of it, it sank again. Knowing that no time was to be lost, he dived deep into the muddy water and groped about with his hands. They struck something soft and yielding and gripped it. The next instant he was on the surface with the child's body held in his left arm.

He swam towards the bank and ultimately succeeded in mounting it. Without a moment's delay he laid the child on the grass and commenced to apply 'first aid.' Water bubbled from the mouth, and after ten minutes the blue eyes opened and gazed at him.

'Keep still, sonny!' he whispered. 'There's nothing much wrong with you. There — there, how do you feel?'

'I — I want my mummie!' cried Peter.

'You shall have her presently. Where do you live?'

'Over dere.'

'Over dere,' could only mean one place, and that was Ailsa's cottage at the far end of the meadow. Stewart gasped as he realised the truth — this was Ailsa's child — the dimpled baby of three years ago.

'Is your name Leslie?' he asked hoarsely.

Peter nodded between his sobs. Stewart hesitated for a second, and then took him in his arms and walked briskly towards the cottage. As he approached it a woman came running into the meadow.

'Oh — oh!' she gasped.

'It's all right,' assured Stewart. 'The only danger is that he may catch cold. Run in and get some warm blankets ready.'

The woman, almost scared out of her life, did as she was bid. Stewart took Peter inside and had his clothes off in less than two minutes, by which time the woman appeared with two big blankets. Stewart wrapped them round the boy while the woman went for some embrocation. The somewhat fierce rubbing which followed banished the last scrap of fear. Peter, with that wonderful recuperative spirit of childhood, was himself again.

'He's all right now,' said Stewart. 'Is his — his mother away?'

'Yes. It was all my fault. I forgot him for a few minutes, and he slipped away.'

But Stewart was looking round the room which he remembered so well. There was the couch on which he and Ailsa had once sat side by side, dreaming of things so sweet.

'You're all wet,' said the woman. 'Hadn't you better change your clothes? I can get you some rough things to wear.'

'No, thanks,' replied Stewart hastily. 'I was on my way to the inn. I have another suit in my bag. I must get the bag — I left it in the meadow!' He walked across to Peter and shook him by the hand. 'Good-bye, you little rogue, and don't try to drown yourself again.'

Peter grabbed at his arm and put up his mouth to be kissed. The woman wrinkled her brows as she strove to recall where she had seen the tall, athletic figure before.

'I shall have to tell Miss Leslie,' she said. 'She'll want to know who it was that saved Peter.'

'Tell her it was an old — no, it doesn't matter,' he stammered. 'I must go now. I hope Peter will avoid a chill. Good-bye!'

'But — '

The woman stopped as the noise of a car was heard from outside. Stewart stared through the window and saw Ailsa and Jean coming up the garden path. He hesitated for a few moments, and in the hesitation his chance of escape passed. The front door opened and Ailsa stepped inside, followed by her sister.

'Mummie!'

Ailsa's eyes swept the room. They rested on Peter for a brief second and then slowly turned to the saturated figure of Stewart.

'What — I — '

Jean, less agitated, came across and held out her hand, which Stewart took somewhat limply.

'This is a great surprise,' she said. 'But has anything happened — you are all wet?'

'I nearly got drowned,' chirped Peter. 'And he jumped right in and pulled me out. Isn't he brave?'

Ailsa ran to Peter and clasped him in her arms with a glad little cry. Stewart, seizing the opportunity, made for the door.

'Wait!'

The almost frenzied cry came from Ailsa's

trembling lips. She put Peter down and walked slowly towards his rescuer with her hand extended. Stewart stared at it and gripped it for a second.

'Thank you! Thank you so much!' she stammered.

'It is nothing,' he said. 'I happened to — to be passing. I really must go — I have left a bag in the meadow. Good-bye — Good-bye!'

He walked swiftly to the door and went through it. Ailsa stood staring after him in stony silence until Peter's voice brought her to her senses. She turned and sat down beside him.

'Don't stay, Jean,' she pleaded. 'I — I feel — oh, Peter — Peter — Peter!'

The woman left immediately, and Jean stood gazing at the distraught figure. She ultimately crept across and touched her on the arm.

'Ailsa, what is the matter?'

'Nothing — nothing!' She brushed the tears from her eyes and, removing her coat, caught Peter up in her arms. 'It's all right, dear,' she said to Jean. 'It was the shock of hearing — about Peter. I'll get him to bed now. Thanks so much for a pleasant day!'

Jean kissed them both and left the cottage. All Ailsa's acting could not hide the truth from her. Ailsa, who was engaged to Andrew, who had only that day been measured for her bridal dress, was as much in love with Stewart as she had ever been. She went home with aching brain, wondering how fate could be so ironic as to bring about this meeting at such a time.

Ailsa's thoughts traversed similar channels. It needed only this unexpected meeting to transform what had been but a fleeting doubt into a gigantic certainty. When she had set eyes on Stewart again an emotion like a flame had swept her breast. In spite of his treatment — in spite of his apparent neglect — in spite of everything that had happened since, her heart whispered the incontrovertible fact — she loved him as she had never loved, nor ever could love the man to whom she was betrothed.

'Andrew — Andrew!' she moaned. 'It shall make no difference. This you shall never know — never, never! Please God I'll make you a good wife. Oh, help me to forget — help me to forget!'

24

On leaving the farm Stewart recovered his suit-case and made for the inn. The meeting with Ailsa had set his brain in a whirl. He had imagined that he was now proof against almost anything, and it was extremely discomforting to find how wrong he was. During the past three years he had thought of her at times a little bitterly, not because of what had happened, but because she had closed her heart to his sincere attempt at a reconciliation.

How different were his feelings when he had set eyes on her again! Her first glance had shaken him like a leaf in the wind. All the old fire broke through the thin partitions. When her hand had touched his a great thrill went through his heart. He knew he wanted her just as much as he had wanted her in the old days.

It was painful to reflect that but for a momentary loss of confidence in her she might now be his wife. If any man regretted an action he regretted that one. The intervening years had done much to broaden his views and to leaven his former intolerance.

He had suffered not a little since those days, and not once, but a thousand times, he had realised that it could have been avoided by the display of a nobler spirit.

Then the thought came to him — Was it too late even now to put things right? All the way to the inn his mind repeated the question. Had Ailsa quite forgotten those happy days? If so, why had her hand trembled in his — why had she averted her eyes in that way? His heart gave a bound as he began to draw obvious conclusions from these facts.

He reached the inn and entered it. It was just out of licensed hours, and the bar was deserted. He knocked on the counter, and the landlord appeared from an inner room and uttered a cry of astonishment as he recognised him.

'I'm going to stay in the Glen for a few days,' said Stewart. 'Can you accommodate me?'

'I wish I could, laddie, but I have just let all my rooms to a motoring party. Sakes, you look as if you had swam hame frae abroad!'

'Had an accident,' explained Stewart. 'But I'm sorry you can't fix me up with a room.'

'So am I. But dinna stand in these wet clothes. You're welcome to use my room to change.'

Stewart thanked him, and decided to take advantage of the offer. In half an hour he came down stairs, feeling much refreshed. The landlord was busy in the bar, so Stewart was spared a thousand questions, and after a few words of explanation regarding his movements, left for the Manse.

The minister, like everyone else, manifested extreme astonishment, and was delighted to accommodate him until a room could be obtained at the inn. It was just before dinner-time, and Stewart, who was ravenously hungry, accepted the invitation to dinner.

While the meal was being prepared they sat in the cosy study of the Manse and talked of things mutually interesting. Strangely enough, Ailsa's name was not mentioned. While the minister considered it wise to keep her out of the conversation, Stewart was equally reluctant to discuss her until he had time to sort out his rather confused emotions.

'I suppose you are on holiday now?'

Stewart nodded, as he filled his pipe from the minister's pouch.

'Your trip doesn't appear to have done you any harm?'

'No, I'm feeling well enough. It's good to be back in Scotland again. I've dreamed of this for the past year. I used to keep a calendar and block out the days as they passed. Many times I've wondered what was happening back here.'

'Quite a lot of things have happened. Of course, you know that Drummond bought Aberdinnie from Sir William — that happened before you went away, didn't it?'

'Yes. I heard he had done a great deal for the Glen.'

'He has, indeed. It was he who built the reading-room — you must see that — and it was due to his generosity that we were able to enlarge the school. With all due respect to Sir William, I may say that his successor is even more liked than he was.'

'And Jean — Mrs. Drummond?'

'As bonnie as ever.'

'I know that,' laughed Stewart. 'I met her as I came from the station, but is she happy?'

The minister laughed at so unnecessary a question. He, like a great many other people, was ignorant of the inner life of Jean.

'Wouldn't any woman be happy in her circumstances? Her husband worships her. She has health, wealth and — '

'Children?'

'As a matter of fact, no.'

'That's a pity,' mused Stewart. 'Jean was always keen on bairns. So Drummond now fills an important place in the Glen?'

'Yes, he has a fine social spirit, and will do anything for the common good. Really the Glen is fortunate in having so good a friend near at hand.'

Stewart was not very interested in these eulogies of Drummond. He was anxious to hear about Ailsa, but still experienced a reluctance to talk about her. Their conversation was interrupted by the entrance of the minister's wife, and a girl of about twenty years of age, who bore a slight resemblance to the minister himself.

'My dear, you remember Stewart Morrison. Here he is come home to roost like the hen — '

'Or the bad penny,' put in Stewart.

Mrs. Forrester laughed merrily and shook him warmly by the hand. The minister led the somewhat shy girl forward.

'This is my niece — my brother's one and only daughter. Kitty, you have heard me speak of Mr. Morrison?'

'Oh, yes,' she murmured. 'How do you do?'

Stewart smiled as he took the white, slim hand of the blushing girl. There was something arrestive about her, despite her pallid cheeks and frail figure. Stewart could not help comparing her with Ailsa, who was her exact opposite.

'Are you staying here long?' he asked.

'Only for a week or two. My uncle is so proud of the Glen he insisted I should spend a holiday here.'

'And do you like it?'

'I think I shall, but I only arrived yesterday. I suppose you are glad to be back again?'

He nodded as the gong went and summoned them into dinner. The meal passed pleasantly enough, for the minister was full of amusing anecdotes connected with his work. Occasionally Kitty's laughing eyes met Stewart's, and were turned away swiftly, as if she found his gaze discomfiting.

'We had a bad time here earlier in the summer,' said the minister. 'There was a cloudburst in the hills, and it played havoc with the Glen. Everybody had the water in their houses, and a great number of cattle were lost. It was quite a unique experience, and I pray it will not happen again.'

'It was awful,' added his wife. 'I can see it all now — the fearful rain and the struggling men, women, and children. For quite a time some of the folks averred it was a punishment for — '

'Mary!'

She stopped at the word of warning, realising too late her indiscretion, but neither Stewart nor Kitty understood in the least, and both looked at the minister interrogatively.

'Punishment for what?' queried Kitty.

'Of course, it — it was all nonsense,' stammered the minister. 'The Glen did not merit any Divine punishment.'

'A poor woman lost a little one,' added Mrs. Forrester. 'That started the childish theory.'

'What theory?' asked Stewart. 'What did they imagine the punishment was for?'

The minister hesitated, but was ultimately driven to some explanation by the two pairs of questioning eyes.

'It was a rather painful incident which I would prefer not to dwell upon,' he murmured. 'I think it might have been forgotten long ago but for this deluge. Suffering is apt to harden people's hearts, and to cause them to hunt out the imagined Jonah. But let us forget it.'

Stewart suddenly saw daylight. He uttered a little gasp and half rose from his chair. Kitty looked at him in astonishment, and the minister shot his wife a swift glance. After that a queer silence reigned, and Stewart was mightily relieved when Kitty and her aunt left the room. He took the cigarette which the minister offered, lighted it mechanically, but made no attempt to smoke it.

'Mr. Forrester,' he said suddenly, 'I want

to know about — Ailsa.'

The minister looked at him keenly.

'Has she suffered much? It was she of whom you were speaking, wasn't it?'

'Yes. Things have been hard for her, Stewart. I am sorry her name was brought forward because of — '

'I understand, but I want to know about her. All the time I have been abroad I have been thinking about her. It never occurred to me that the people among whom she has lived for so long would treat her badly. I was so wrapped up in my own interests that I forgot that others could be as merciless as I — '

'My laddie!'

'Please don't try to find excuses for me. You know we were engaged to be married; you know what happened. I went to her; I accused her as if I were some spotless creature fit to judge her. On that day I flung away the jewel which I held in my hand.'

The minister looked embarrassed, but he remained silent in face of the younger man's passionate outburst.

'When I had hurt her as much as I could I had the audacity to write and ask for forgiveness. She never replied. Of course, I blamed her for that, but I see now that I had trampled on her so roughly as not to merit any forgiveness.'

'Yet I think she has forgiven you, Stewart.'

'That I mean to find out.'

The look in the tense face caused the minister to become terribly agitated.

'What did you come here for?' he asked.

'I don't know — I couldn't resist coming. But during the few hours I have been here I have learned a few things.'

'You have learned that she — '

'I believe that she still cares for me. I saw her this afternoon. Chance brought it about. I saved the boy Peter from the river and carried him to the farm. Then — then she came in and — and saw me — '

The minister was holding up his hand, imploring him to desist.

'What is it — '

'There is something I ought to have told you immediately I saw you. I refrained with the best intentions. Stewart, don't you realise it is over three years since all this happened, and that many things may happen in three years?'

'I don't understand you.'

'Haven't you considered the possibility of Ailsa falling in love with someone else?'

Stewart started violently.

'You don't mean that — that has really happened?'

'Yes.'

The blow fell with crushing weight upon the unsuspecting shoulders. The minister's mouth twitched as he realised how painful was the news to his guest.

'Who — who is it?' gasped Stewart.

'Can't you guess?'

'No; tell me!'

'Andrew Esplin.'

'Andrew! Why, he has always been a kind of stepfather to her — '

'Yes, until she blossomed into womanhood — until she was left all alone. Andrew isn't so very old, and he is young enough to love. I wish I had told you this sooner.'

Stewart sat as if petrified. The thing seemed impossible; and yet he could find no argument to bring against it. He had always admired Andrew — had known that Andrew literally worshipped Ailsa, but this possibility had never occurred to him. To think of Andrew succeeding where he had failed.

'Are they engaged?' he asked hoarsely.

'I am to marry them in less than a fortnight.'

'Marry them!'

The minister stood up and came round

245

the table to place his hand on Stewart's bent shoulders.

'Is it so bitter a disappointment?'

'It — it hurts a little. You see, I began to imagine all kinds of things this afternoon when I saw her. Before that I considered the past a closed book, but the sight of her — Oh, what's the use of repining? I've got all I deserved.'

'Don't let it embitter you, especially towards Andrew.'

'That shall not happen. Andrew has the right to be happy. But I wish I had never come back.'

Mrs. Forrester poked her head round the door and asked if they intended to sit and smoke the whole evening away. Stewart could do no other than join the ladies in the drawing-room and chat over the coffee, as if nothing had happened to shake his heart to its foundations.

When eventually the two women retired to bed Stewart uttered a sigh of relief. He felt he wanted to be alone for a while to steel himself to face the future with as stout a heart as possible. He walked to the window and saw that the moon had risen, and was flooding the Glen with its mystic light.

'Do you mind if I take a walk before turning in?' he asked. 'My head aches a little — the fresh air will do me good.'

The minister understood, and inclined his head. He felt deeply for this young man, but could find no solution to his problem.

Stewart emerged from the house and gulped down the cool night air into his lungs. He soon found that his desire to be alone was a mistaken one, for being alone meant thinking, and thinking in the circumstances was a painful process. It astonished him to find how this love of his youth had taken hold of him. He was old enough to know that many men succeed in recovering from a first love, to love no less passionately in the not far distant future and to look upon the first affair as a mere prelude.

But this was no prelude. He knew that no one could ever take Ailsa's place. There was some charm about her that was entirely her own. It had not ceased to exert its influence, despite the incident which had maddened him for the time being.

His next ar   nediate step was fairly   get out of the Glen for   hour spent here was an hour of torture.   here might be forgetfulness in hard work far away from the place where she lived. He laughed grimly as he reflected that he had six months' holiday ahead of him. There could be no holiday now. Better to forgo it and return to harness.

He found himself by the side of the stream where but a few hours before young Peter had nearly met his end. He walked on and on until he realised that it was time to return and seek the oblivion of sleep, if such a thing were possible. So he turned on his heel and cut across the field in the direction of the Manse.

He was entering the road from a field when a big figure emerged from the lane opposite. In the light of the moon the face was quite clear — it was Andrew!

25

The two men recognised each other at the same moment. Stewart saw Andrew's eyes contract and then open wide and light up with his usual smile. He stopped and held out his hand.

'How are you, Stewart? I heard you were back again.'

'I'm all right, Andrew, thanks. I was just taking a stroll before turning in for the night.'

'Staying at the Manse, aren't you?'

'Yes — the inn is full up for a day or two.'

'Staying long?'

'No. I'll be away to-morrow or the next day. I only came to have a look round.'

'I see!'

Both were striving to act normally, but it was a palpable failure, and each knew it. Andrew, with his customary bluntness, was eager to get to the point.

'I heard you got young Peter out o' trouble this afternoon?'

'Yes, I happened to be passing when he had an accident. I hope he is all right?'

'Doesn't look a bit the worse.'

'You've seen him?'

'Aye, I've just left him. Ailsa is a little upset, but that's natural enough.'

'Of course.'

By this time they had reached a point where their paths divided. Andrew stopped and looked at Stewart keenly.

'You — you've heard the news?'

'Yes. I should like to congratulate you, Andrew.'

'You're sure o' that?'

Stewart met the fearless gaze and nodded with a wan smile.

'All's fair in love and war, Andrew. You won her fairly, and you deserve the greatest happiness. Good night!'

He turned to go, but Andrew put out his hand and caught him by the shoulder.

'You're upset, lad. I'm sorry this should greet you on your homecoming. If I thought the past wasna completely dead, I'd — '

'It is,' interrupted Stewart. 'There is no shadow of doubt about that. Only memories are left, and even those will fade — perhaps. Then passionately, 'Andrew, you are not doing this out of kindness — you really love her as she deserves to be loved?'

The light which flamed from Andrew's dark eyes was sufficient answer.

'Well, good luck to you both. Good night.'

He turned round and made up the path which led to the Manse, leaving Andrew standing there reflectively. It was some seconds before the latter strode away, for in his breast were curious forebodings. These were due, not so much to Stewart's evident distress as to Ailsa's attitude that evening. She had welcomed him with a glad cry on her lips; had seemed, in fact, even more pleased to see him than was usual, but somehow she was different, and the change was difficult to analyse. When he had left her at the gate of the farm she had clung to him as with terror.

'Oh, Andrew, don't stay away from me too long. I want your — your help, so much!'

Where now was the old strength of her? Where her calm resignation and self-sufficiency? He was modest enough to search for the cause of this emotion elsewhere than in the affection she bore him. On the top of the castle which he had built so high a little skeleton was dancing.

Ailsa was finding the situation tense enough. She felt as if some mighty stream had lifted her off her feet and was carrying her along to the sea. Always before her eyes was the figure of Stewart, obliterating, to her horror, the bigger figure of Andrew. She moaned to realise that this was happening in spite of her resolution. In a few short days she would be wedded to Andrew in the full consciousness of the fact that the past which she had tried to bury was more alive — more vital — than ever.

She was afraid to go into the village the next day, for fear she might meet Stewart face to face. She prayed he would go soon and leave her at peace to fulfil her vow! Peace! The word mocked her. Could there ever be peace with this secret locked away in her breast?

Then, to her chagrin, she saw the man she dreamed of. She was gazing through the upstairs window when he came into sight — some distance off — with Kitty by his side. Her sight was keen enough to observe that they were laughing together. That small, insignificant thing helped to fortify her. Why should she care?

For nearly three years she had kept her heart open towards him, patiently waiting for some word of regret. Now he could come back and laugh with this girl. No, nothing must happen to rob Andrew of the happiness he so richly deserved. Andrew must come first — always first.

Stewart's departure was delayed by pleadings on the part of the Forresters. The minister had begged him to stay a few days longer, and Kitty had added her voice — at least she had manifested her regret at his proposed departure with such sincerity that he felt he could do no other than agree to tarry a day or two longer.

Kitty proved to be a delightful companion. Her nervousness had passed away now, and she treated him much as she would have treated her brother. He knew there was nothing deeper than this in their friendship, and was glad she looked for nothing but the pleasure of walking and talking with him.

'You are very difficult to understand at times,' she said.

'Am I? I didn't mean to be.'

'But you are. Sometimes I think you must be forty. You aren't forty, are you?'

'Not quite,' he laughed.

'Would you be very annoyed if I said something personal?' she asked.

'I might.'

'Well, I'll risk it. You've had some trouble, haven't you?'

'Perhaps I have. Did your uncle tell you?'

'Oh, no. He never tells me of people's troubles. I usually find them out myself.'

'That is very clever of you.'

She looked at him wistfully, and made him feel ashamed of the unkind retort.

'You think I take a joy in — probing other people's troubles? It isn't that. You can't expect me to walk with you and not notice that you are unhappy, nor to sympathise with you?'

'You are very good.'

'I'm not. But I'm a girl, and I feel very annoyed with the girl who has caused you to be unhappy.'

'You would be more annoyed with me if you knew the truth,' he said. 'I am the culprit, not she. I deliberately threw away the most priceless thing in the world.'

'Then go and pick it up again!'

'Someone else has already done that. Please — please say no more. I want to forget it.'

But he might just as easily have tried to forget his own existence. In the companionship of Kitty he found a temporary solace, for the girl was full of quick life and fun, which were infectious, for periods together, but the moment he turned to serious thinking he found himself caught up again in the toils of regrets, longings and black despair. After a prolonged stay of two days he could stand the strain no longer, and decided to leave by the first train on the following morning.

'Then I shall never see you again?' said Kitty.

'Why do you think that?'

'I am sure of it. You will never come to the Glen again, because — because that is where your trouble lies.'

'You — you know that!'

'Yes, I found out accidentally. I saw the girl, too.'

Her quiet candour astonished him, yet it was impossible to be angry with her.

'You ought to see her before you go,' she said.

'See her! Why?'

'To tell her that you still love her — '

How could he bring himself to place any reliance in her assertions when every fact known to him seemed to prove the contrary? No, to see her, talk to her, would only hurt them both, and serve no purpose whatsoever.

Nevertheless, fate conspired to take a hand in things. He was returning from a lonely walk that evening when he saw Ailsa coming towards him. His first desire was to avoid her, but there appeared to be no means other than retracing his steps. Then came the resolution to speak to her — perhaps for the last time in his life. He stopped within a few paces of her.

'Ailsa!'

She blushed violently, hesitated, and finally halted.

'I just — just wanted to say good-bye,' he stammered.

'You are leaving the Glen?' she asked in a level voice.

'Yes — early to-morrow morning. I only came down for a few days.'

'I hope you have had a good time.'

He drew in his breath with a hiss, and strove to keep back the resentment occasioned by the remark.

'It has been interesting enough,' he muttered. Then impetuously, 'Ailsa, need there be any ill-feeling between us? Of course, I know what is to happen shortly. I wanted to tell you that I shall always remember you. I want, if possible, to feel that you have forgiven me.'

'Isn't it rather late to think of that?'

'Ailsa, how can you be so hard?'

'Hard!' her eyes flashed angrily. 'Can you recall the past and yet accuse me of being hard? Perhaps it all meant nothing to you. You could forget so soon — '

'Forget! Do you think I have forgotten for a single moment? Do you think I have ever ceased to regret the madness that made me act as I did? When I recovered and realised what I had lost, I did all I could to make you see how deeply I — '

'You did nothing!' she murmured.

'Nothing! Was it nothing to have waited and waited for a word which never came? You let me go away — alone, when you might have — But what is the use of recrimination now that the past is closed, and I want you to believe that your future happiness means much to me. You do believe that, don't you?'

His earnest eyes convinced her of his sincerity, but she could not understand his words. In the face of what had happened they seemed strange and uncalled for. He spoke as if she were the one who had set her heart against any reconciliation, as if she had deliberately refused to listen to the regrets which he now voiced.

'You bewilder me,' she murmured. 'Oh, why did you come back and make it so hard for me?'

'Make it hard for you! I came back, hoping — hoping it was not too late to humble myself before you. If I had dreamed that your heart was given to — to another — I would have died rather than embarrass you.'

Her determination to present an icy exterior to him was rapidly ebbing. She found herself hanging on every word he spoke, with her heart leaping madly within her the while.

'Ailsa,' he murmured, 'leaving out that terrible mistake, was there ever a time when

I gave you cause to doubt my love? Did I in any word or deed give you reason to doubt for one moment that you were everything in the world to me? Didn't you know that you were the incentive to success? I thought of you always as the goal. Commercial success was only the means to the end — that end when you and I should be together always. You must know that.'

'Yes, yes,' she almost choked.

'And yet because of a single mistake on my part you could cancel all the past. Because I was stunned by an incident — '

'You mustn't speak of that. Do you want to break my heart?'

He looked ashamed as he realised that he was indulging in the very recriminations which he had resolved should never pass his lips.

'I'm sorry,' he said. 'Please forgive me.'

She was standing like a figure of stone, her face pallid and her hands moving nervelessly.

'Good-bye,' he said hoarsely. 'We part as — as friends, don't we?'

She nodded as if she were afraid to speak, and her hand caught his and quivered in his grasp. The contact set his brain whirling. Almost without being conscious of it he pulled her close to him until her head rested on his shoulder and her trembling bosom was near his own pounding heart. She swayed like some hypnotised, beautiful animal — utterly beyond the power of resisting.

'Ailsa, say it is not too late. Tell me now it's all wrong — wrong. Tell me it isn't true — you are going to marry Andrew!'

The look of horror which suddenly dawned in the moist eyes brought a groan of agony and self-reproach from his lips.

'Go — go!' she wailed, 'before — before I hate you!'

With drooping head he turned on his heel and staggered down the road. He did not even see the stark figure of Andrew standing close by, and perhaps it was just as well, for his burden was heavy enough already.

26

Andrew had come upon Ailsa and Stewart together from round a bend in the road. It had taken him so much by surprise that he found it impossible to retreat and hide the painful sight from his eyes. When Stewart had gone by him like a drunken man he had started to beat a retreat, but Ailsa had seen him, and he could do no other than go to her.

'Andrew, I was coming to meet you when — '

She broke down in her attempt to give some explanation of the incident which she knew he must have witnessed. Andrew took her hands and gazed deep into her eyes.

'It's all right, Ailsa,' he muttered. 'Keep calm, lass.'

'I didn't want to see him — I didn't. You believe me, don't you, Andrew. I wouldn't lie to you.'

'I know that. Let's walk a bit — it will do you good.'

So they walked down the road and made across the fields in the moonlight. No words were spoken for quite a long time, for both their hearts were too full to permit of conversation. At length they found a seat beside the stream and sat down.

'Talk — talk to me, Andrew,' she pleaded.

'What about?'

It was the first time Andrew had found it difficult to make conversation, and it sent a cold shudder through her. Was it possible he could have misinterpreted that last scene?

'Say what is in your mind,' she whispered.

'Ah, if you only knew.'

'I do know. You are wondering — wondering what it all meant.'

'Yes, I am wondering whether it is not all a dreadful mistake.' He caught her firmly by the shoulders and gazed at her fiercely. 'Ailsa, are you regretting — anything?'

'No, no; only that I was unfortunate enough to meet him. But he is going away to-morrow. He'll never come again to — '

'To what?'

'To play upon my weakness — to remind me of the past.'

'Is that past still alive?'

'Not when you are with me.'

'You still want me?'

She clung to him desperately.

'More than ever, Andrew. You are the only being who has served as a firm rock to which to cling with safety. You are the only man who has never heaped abuse and mistrust upon me.'

'Because I know the truth.'

'If you hadn't known the truth it would have made no difference. You wouldn't have spurned me as he did. You wouldn't have gone away without a word. Tell me you wouldn't have done that?'

'It's true I wouldn't,' said Andrew. 'But maybe it's because I'm not so young as Stewart.'

'No, no, it's because you are you. I won't have you depreciate your love.'

'You want it, Ailsa? You're sure you want it?'

For a moment she hesitated. It was as if that rebellious heart were forbidding her to speak what she was trying to believe was a fact.

'I want you still, Andrew,' she whispered. 'Take me and make me forget I ever loved anyone but you.'

He breathed a sigh of relief, but it was not very deep. The incident had shaken him rudely, for it but added weight to an already suspected fact. Yet there was no blame attaching to Ailsa. Had she not told him not to expect anything more than devotion and duty from her? Had she not made it clear that she was not yet capable of the deep love which he himself nurtured?

He went home that night with a weight on his heart, and was pursued by nightmares wherein the idol of his dreams was always lost to him. But the next day brought a better state of mind. He learned that Stewart had gone back to Glasgow. With his departure a more hopeful spirit settled within him. Ailsa, too, seemed more her old self and dropped in at the smiddy to chat to him as he worked. Any doubts which he might have had on the advisability of getting married vanished in this atmosphere of calm now generated.

'Come over early to-night,' pleaded Ailsa. 'I've promised Peter he shall stay up and have supper with us.'

'I'll be over at six. The man who wants to buy my business has been in this morning.'

'Has he settled up?'

'Not yet. He has given me until this afternoon to make up my mind.'

Ailsa opened her eyes in astonishment.

'But I thought you had made up your mind?'

'Well, not quite, you see — '

'Wasn't the price satisfactory?'

'Oh, the offer's fair enough, but — well, the fact is it's like parting wi' part of myself. I never thought it would be so hard to give up my smiddy. But when you've made it yourself and worked at it day in and day out for twenty odd years it gets to be part of you. Still, it's got to be done, lass.'

Ailsa laughed and caught his arm fondly.

'Don't give it up if you don't feel like it, Andrew. I can run the farm and you can still run the smiddy.'

Andrew shook his head.

'It's best the way I've planned, Ailsa.'

'Very well — you know best.'

He turned from her as a man entered the smiddy with a broken bar to be repaired. Andrew examined it and flung it into the corner with a nod.

'I'll do it the morn,' he said.

'That'll dae. Oh, did ye hear o' the accident?'

'What accident?'

'Old Robert got run ower wi' a motor car an hour ago.'

'How terrible!' gasped Ailsa. 'Is he very bad?'

'I dinna ken. The doctor is still wi' him, I heard. He was ower bad to be taken to hospital, and he's lyin' at his lodgings. It was a' his ain fault, they say. He WILL walk in the middle o' the road, though he's as deaf as a stane and short o' sight.'

Ailsa, who had known old Robert all her life, was very much upset by the bad news, and announced her intention of calling at his lodgings with a view to inquiring how he was.

She arrived there to hear that Robert was still unconscious and that his state gave grave cause for anxiety. So far as she could gather there were concussion and body wounds. Taking into consideration Robert's age and feebleness, she could not help feeling that the end was only a matter of time. As she left she met the minister hurrying to the house.

'I have only just heard the news,' he said. 'I hope he is not seriously injured.'

'The doctor is there, and is very anxious. He is still unconscious, they tell me.'

The minister shook his head sorrowfully and turned the conversation to herself.

'Getting ready for the great day?'

'Yes, I wish it were to-morrow.'

'Patience,' he said. 'What are a few extra days in one's whole life?'

Her face did not beam with the pleasure he expected, but he ascribed that to the present catastrophe. He little knew that her anxiety to be wed was due to the ever-growing fear that she might recoil from the ordeal at the last moment. Ordeal! Yes, it had assumed that status now. Her own happiness did not enter her calculations now. It was Andrew that mattered — Andrew, who was suffering from an uncertainty of mind. She had not been blind to that, and she had set herself to disillusion him. Even if she wished to withdraw now there was always Andrew to insinuate his big form between her conscience and her heart's desire.

And the desire itself was not based on reason. Here was a good and worthy man loving her with all the strength of his nature, offering her his name and his protection. Why did she tremble at the thought of the approaching marriage?

'Nothing shall prevent it — nothing,' she had sworn.

She called in at the smiddy on her way home to tell Andrew of Robert's condition and to remind him once more not to be late, although such a reminder was quite unnecessary. When she arrived home there was a parcel awaiting her — the last parcel which Robert had delivered before meeting with his accident. She opened it with bated breath, knowing it to be her wedding dress.

There it lay before her — a beautiful creation in white satin. She fingered it with the tears streaming down her cheeks, but brushed them aside swiftly as she heard a conveyance stop outside, and looked through the window to see Jean approaching the door. She put the dress back into the box, and replaced the lid with nervous fingers.

'Ailsa!'

'Good morning, Jean. This is early for you to call.'

'The dressmaker was writing me. She happened to mention that she had sent your wedding dress home, so I came along to see it.'

'It — It's there,' stammered Ailsa.

'Haven't you opened it?'

'Yes, just now. Jean, did you hear about poor old Robert — he has been run over and seriously hurt.'

'I know,' replied Jean. 'I am awfully sorry.'

She went to the box and lifted the lid to gaze admiringly at the dress. 'Do try it on, Ailsa, please.'

'Not now. Oh, I couldn't.'

Jean turned her head round to observe the confused expression in her sister's face. She let the dress fall into the box and approached Ailsa with inquiring eyes.

'What is wrong, dear? This wedding dress doesn't bring the joy it should. You shrink from it as from a shroud. Can't you confide in me, dear?'

'There's — there's nothing to confide.'

'Oh, but there is. This is not the first time I have seen that look in your face. Ailsa, dear, don't do anything that is going to make you unhappy. Don't take a step that may lead you into a prison from which there is no escape.'

'Why do you say such things almost on the eve of my wedding? Even — even if I wanted to, there is someone else to be considered. But I don't want to back out. Andrew is the best and dearest man in the world. I would die rather than wound him in any way.'

'And yet you are afraid.'

'Isn't every girl a little afraid when she faces such a change in her life?'

This was true enough, but in Ailsa's case the natural nervousness of a prospective wife was overdone. Jean saw more in it than that, and since she had been party to this compact, she felt her responsibility keenly. She had no doubt about Andrew's love — the doubt lay in the depth of Ailsa's feeling for her old sweetheart, and on this point she was in the dark.

It was late in the afternoon before Ailsa could summon sufficient courage to try on the bridal dress. It fitted her to perfection, and her eyes sparkled with pardonable pleasure as she surveyed herself in the mirror. She hoped Andrew would like it — would admire her. Then the feeling that she was a fraud came to sweep away the momentary bliss. She took off the dress hastily and hid it away in a cupboard, determined not to look at it again until the day came on which she must wear it.

Despite the fact that she was busy, time seemed to drag. Of late the fear of being alone with her thoughts had increased. Only Andrew had the power to imbue her with strength and fortitude. She prayed that he may come soon, to banish the hideous doubts from her mind.

'Uncle's coming to-night, isn't he?' queried Peter.

'Yes, dear.'

'Soon?'

'In less than half an hour.'

Peter nodded, and a few minutes later asked if it was time for Uncle to come. Like herself, the boy needed Andrew, and although his desire sprang from a different motive she felt that Andrew held the key to their joint happiness in his hands.

But six o'clock came and went, and Andrew did not turn up. Peter began to get frettish and Ailsa impatient. It was unlike Andrew to be late, and she could think of nothing to account for it. When seven o'clock struck her nerves were on edge.

'Mummie, Uncle will come, won't he?'

'Of course, dear.'

The minutes passed and the hands of the clock moved round to the next hour. Peter began to yawn and to whimper. At half past eight she was obliged to put him to bed, much to his resentment. When at last she had hushed him to sleep a faint doubt began to take shape in her mind. Was it possible that Andrew, the faithful, was going to desert her? She could not bring herself to that conclusion. So with trust and doubt making war in her bosom she sat and waited.

27

Andrew was on the point of leaving home for the farm when something quite unexpected happened. The woman who owned the cottage in which old Robert rented a room called with an urgent message.

'Robert is dying,' she said, wringing her hands.

'Dying!'

'Aye, and the doctor sent me to tell ye to come quick.'

'But how — '

'Robert keeps asking for ye. Ever since he cam roond he has cried out for ye. The doctor says he canna live through the night. Will you come now?'

Andrew inclined his head and followed her reflectively. It seemed to him a little strange that Robert should wish to see him above all others. True, he had known the old man ever since he could remember, but in the circumstances it would have been more natural for Robert to send for the minister.

Ten minutes later they arrived at the cottage. The doctor was in the living-room and nodded to Andrew as he entered.

'He wants to speak to you about something,' he said. 'I gather it is an important matter, but don't let him speak more than is absolutely necessary.'

'I dinna ken what he wants me for,' replied Andrew. 'But I'll try to stop him from talkin' much. Is there ony hope, Doctor?'

'I am afraid not. With a younger man it would be different, but — '

Andrew understood, and made towards the door, behind which old Robert was facing the end. He opened the door slowly and stepped inside. Robert was lying on his back, his head smothered with bandages and his eyes closed. His face was like a waxen mask with the cheeks fallen in, and great blue circles around the eyes. Andrew sat down on the chair at the head of the bed and leaned over the still figure.

'Robert,' he whispered.

The eyelids fluttered and the sunken orbs came to view. They rested for an instant on Andrew's face and consciousness came to the sluggard brain.

'Andrew, you've come.'

The words were almost inaudible. Andrew merely inclined his head.

'I couldna go without seein' ye, Andrew. I've got something on my mind. It's been worrying me — worrying me — '

'You mustn't worry about anything, Robert.'

'Yes, yes, it's aboot you — and Ailsa Leslie.'

'Me and Ailsa!' gasped Andrew.

'You're goin' to marry her?'

'Yes, but — '

Robert tried to rise, but Andrew gently pushed him back again.

'It's important — I tell ye it's important.'

'What is?'

'She used to be in love wi' young Stewart — him that went abroad three years ago — you mind?'

'Aye,' replied Andrew grimly.

'There was a quarrel — he went off, and she thought he didna care no more. Suppose he did care?'

Andrew's mouth twitched as Robert resurrected the spectre.

'If he had cared he would have written or — '

He stopped as Robert's lips moved nervelessly, and from his throat came a groan.

'Robert, are you — '

'He did write — that's hoo I sent for ye, Andrew. I made a terrible mistake. There was a letter for Ailsa. I put it in my pocket — forgot to deliver it. Three years later I found it again. I was afraid — ower there in the drawer. Get it, Andrew.'

Andrew turned and looked in the direction of the trembling finger. Then he looked back at Robert.

'The letter — you must see the letter. Get it — for God's sake, get it.'

'All right. Don't — don't excite yoursel.' He walked over to the drawer and found an envelope inside with Ailsa's name and address inscribed without. Apprehensive, he brought it to Robert.

'Open it.'

'It's a private letter.'

'You must open it — you must read it.'

'It wouldna be right, Robert.'

'But it's opened already. I began tae destroy it when I found out what was in it — God forgive me. You must know what is inside that letter before — before you marry Ailsa.'

Andrew's face went pale and his hands trembled. Yet he could not bring himself to read a letter intended for another person.

'I canna do it,' he muttered.

'Gied to me,' croaked Robert.

He put the letter into the palsied hand and watched in anguish the thin fingers extricating its contents.

'Robert!'

'God knows I'm doing the right thing — now.

274

You must know before it's ower late. After — after that you can decide, for my lips will be closed — ay, closed for ever.'

He placed the two sections of the letter together and brought them close to his nose. Then in a cracked voice he began to read:

'Dear Ailsa, — You will be surprised to hear from me again. In the face of what has happened you may feel like destroying this letter without finishing it. But I implore you to have patience and hear me. For a whole year I have suffered tortures — I have behaved like a coward and a knave. I implore you to forget.

'To-day I have been offered a post abroad. Ailsa, darling, is it too late? Can you with all your generous heart forgive me? I can come to Glen Eck by return. One word from you will bring me.'

A deep groan came from Andrew's lips, but Robert with his fading eyes fixed on the writing, heard nothing, and went on mercilessly:

'Dare I tell you my heart's desire. It is that you will consent to marry me and come with me to the East. We should have furnished quarters, and there would be plenty of room for the boy. I'd be a good daddy to him. I'd make him love me.'

There came a halt, and the trembling fingers lost their grip of the letter. They fell on to the edge of the bed and then blew on to the floor. Andrew recoiled from them.

'Andrew!'

The choking cry brought him to his senses. He turned to find Robert staring at him with an expression that was terrible.

'It's for you to decide, Andrew. Do what is right. I should have given it to Ailsa before — I was a coward — thought I'd get — into trouble. But you'll do what is right, old friend; you'll do — '

The silence which followed could almost be felt. Robert was lying in exactly the same position. His eyes were open still, but they were dead eyes. Andrew ran to the door to call the doctor, but before he reached it he remembered the letter and came back to gather up the torn sheet and the envelope.

Thus did Robert pass, leaving behind him the yet unsolved problem which had worried him for months. Andrew stayed but a few minutes longer. As in a dream he walked back to his cottage, oblivious to everything but the significance of the letter in his pocket. Two dreadful hours passed before he realised that Ailsa was waiting for him at the farm. With a heart as heavy as lead he went out.

Ailsa gave a glad cry when she saw him, but it was not until he entered the room that she realised his face was lacking its usual animation. Though he smiled, it was the wan smile of a tortured soul.

'Aren't you well, Andrew?' she asked.

'Not very, but it's nothing to worry over, lass.'

'You oughtn't to have come at all if you feel bad. How selfish of me to bring you out.'

'It wasn't that,' he replied. 'I was called to Robert's bedside.'

'Is he — '

'Yes, but he passed away peacefully.'

'How sad. Poor Robert, he was such a good soul. I am so glad you were with him. He always thought the world of you.'

Conversation went badly after that, but she ascribed it to the gloom cast by Robert's death. It was when Andrew was about to leave that he put the question which had been simmering in his brain since he entered the house.

'You are still certain about our marriage, Ailsa?'

'Why, of course. How strange you should ask me that now.'

'I ask it because I do not want you to have a regret afterwards.'

'Why — why should I regret it?'

'Ailsa, can I ask you a very personal question — something connected with the past and Stewart Morrison?'

She hesitated, and then inclined her head slowly.

'You loved him very dearly once?'

'Yes — once.'

'Well, after that quarrel — suppose he had come back to you and begged to be forgiven for doubting you. Suppose even that he had written and asked to see you — before he went abroad — would you have seen him? Would you have accepted his love again if he had offered it in all sincerity — in a fashion that could not be doubted?'

'Why do you ask that now?'

'Would you?' he insisted.

'I — I — Andrew. I want to be honest and truthful. Yes, I think I should then. It was his silence — his hardness which — which put an end to everything.' Then she smiled and caught his hand fondly. 'You must never drag that up again. You have to help me to forget everything except that we are betrothed — that we are going to be happy.'

She was scanning Andrew's face to discover the reason why he had asked that question.

'Andrew, is something wrong?' she murmured. 'All the evening you have seemed so — so quiet.'

'Nothing is wrong,' he said. 'Everything is right, or shall be made right. Ailsa, you must trust me to do what is right.'

'Of course, but how strangely you speak.'

'I — I am not myself to-night.'

'I understand,' she murmured. 'I know I am selfish to speak of our interests when an old friend has passed away. I — I wish I had been with him.'

Andrew gasped at the words. If she only knew what had happened in the cottage.

'I — I think I will go now,' he said.

'Must you?'

'Yes. Tell Peter how sorry I was to be late. I'll make it up to him some other time. Good night, Ailsa.'

'Good night, Andrew, dear.'

How strange that he should extend his hand quickly, as if he dreaded a more affectionate farewell. She pondered over this when he had gone, but could discover no reason for his strange behaviour other than the deep emotion he must feel at the death of Robert.

Left to herself, the same old doubting

came flooding in. Somewhere at the back of her mind was Stewart Morrison, with hands outstretched and pleading lips. And in the box not far away was her wedding dress.

Andrew, on leaving the farm, had determined his line of action. Once that was fixed it was as permanent as the hills. With her own lips Ailsa had pointed out the path, though she had been ignorant of so doing. He had not the slightest doubt that had the letter in his pocket reached her there would have been no courting days for Andrew Esplin. Once or twice the temptation to destroy it, and so keep her to himself, came hot and strong. How simple it would be to keep her in this state of misunderstanding, trusting in his great love to win the passion which she had felt for the other man.

But it wasn't so simple as it sounded, for Andrew was not that type of man. Mixed with this new and passionate desire was a nobler feeling. Ailsa's happiness meant more to him than the satisfaction of his own yearnings. How could he cheat her after all these years of alleged friendship? How could he look into her eyes knowing that he had deliberately blinded them to serve his own ends?

'There's only one way,' he muttered, 'and that's the road that leads to the greatest happiness to the greatest number — with peace of mind in the bargain.'

Late as it was, he walked up to the Manse and found the minister on the point of retiring. The latter stared at his visitor with some little astonishment.

'Come to cancel all the arrangements, Andrew?' he laughed.

'Ay, just that,' said Andrew quietly.

There was something in the tone of the voice which caused the minister to start violently. He looked at Andrew to find him very serious.

'I didn't come for that purpose,' said Andrew. 'But it's not impossible that may happen. I came to ask you if you knew Stewart Morrison's address.'

'Yes, he left it in case there should be a letter. I'll find it for you. But, Andrew, what were you hinting at just now?'

'Forget it, Mr. Forrester.'

'Then you didn't mean it?'

'I don't know — yet.'

The minister found the slip of paper which Stewart had given him, and Andrew pencilled the address on an old envelope and slipped it into his pocket.

'Thank ye, sir,' he said. 'I won't keep you up longer. It must be nearly midnight.'

The minister shook the big hand and

looked into Andrew's eyes wistfully. He saw beneath the comparatively calm exterior a terrible storm taking place.

'You're troubled, Andrew.'

'Aye,'

'About Ailsa?'

Andrew nodded and waved his hand to discourage further questions. Then with firm step he went out into the darkness. The next morning as soon as the post office was open a message went speeding over the wire to Stewart Morrison in Glasgow.

28

While Stewart Morrison, in Glasgow, was perusing Andrew's telegram with wrinkled forehead, Ailsa, in the Glen, was staring blankly at an advertisement in an old newspaper which she had taken to light the fire with. It was the name Dunton which first took her eye. It sent her mind back over four years to the time when Jean had made her terrible mistake. Then she read the advertisement in its entirety:

'If the widow of Arthur Miles Dunton, who passed away in Glasgow as the result of a railway accident in 1918, will communicate with Messrs. Stears & Wells, Solicitors, Bank Street, Glasgow, she will hear something to her advantage. Any person furnishing information as to the whereabouts of the said lady will be suitably rewarded.'

She gasped as she realised that it was really Jean to whom this had reference, but why Jean should be wanted passed her imagination. She cut the advertisement

283

out and sent Munro up to Aberdinnie with a note to her sister. In an hour Jean was on the spot, not a little concerned at the peremptory summons.

'What is it?' she asked. 'Your note was so vague.'

Ailsa handed her the newspaper cutting and watched her face go pale as she read it.

'Where — where did you get this?'

'In an old newspaper. It was dated back nearly two months. Jean, what does it mean?'

'I don't know.'

'It must be from his people.'

'Whose?'

'Dunton's parents. You said they had treated you badly; perhaps they want to make amends. It must be that, for it says it is to your advantage.'

Jean's lip curled as she recalled the icy attitude which her first husband's parents had adopted towards her.

'It is late in the day to make amends,' she said. 'When they heard that their son had made what they called 'an unfortunate marriage' they did all they could to force him to get rid of me. They regarded me as something beneath contempt. They refused to meet me — to give me a chance of proving I was not what they believed me to be.'

Even now the memory of that dreadful time hurt her. It seemed ironical that after four years the drama should be revived. She thanked Providence that she was in a position to refuse their assistance — if that was the meaning of the advertisement.

'What shall you do?' asked Ailsa.

'Nothing, of course. If I were starving I would not accept their help. Their conscience must be troubling them.'

'Yes; they even offer a reward for any information which may lead to your discovery. Jean, oughtn't you to write and let them know that you are not in need of assistance? Somehow, it seems harsh to leave them in the dark.'

'If I wanted to do that, I dare not. These people are highly placed socially. Who knows but that one day Alan may meet them? Suppose they know that I — I — '

'I never thought of that,' said Ailsa, with a start. 'What a fortunate thing it is they have never seen you.'

'They don't even know where we were married,' said Jean. 'They were not interested enough to ask. They considered the whole affair as a mad escapade on the part of Dunton, and were only concerned enough to plan to get rid of the unknown woman who was dragging their son down.'

She laughed bitterly and shrugged her shoulders. Ailsa could understand her attitude well enough. As usual, the woman had taken the whole blame and the man had passed away with his name unstained in the eyes of his relatives and friends.

'Forget it, Jean,' she pleaded.

'I could if it were not for the fact that it left a legacy behind. I wish they could know what that marriage meant to me — how even now it haunts me. But for Dunton I should have no secrets from the man I love. Oh, I know I am to blame, too. We are all to blame — Dunton for luring me to a life of misery; Andrew for forcing him to marry me; and I for being a coward. You don't know what it is like to go on living this lie, with my own child denied me — '

Ailsa uttered a little cry and put her arms round her sister's shoulder. In her own tortured heart she held a similar tragedy. While Jean was hungering for the child she dare not claim Ailsa was secretly yearning for her lover. She persuaded herself there was no harm in that. Engaged as she was to Andrew, she was entitled to dwell upon that beautiful interrupted romance.

'Perhaps it will all come right,' she said soothingly.

'It will never come right. Ailsa, my great fear is that one day, after you've married, Andrew may want to move to some other place. Then Peter will go too — '

'Andrew has no intention of shifting from the Glen,' said Ailsa. 'All his interests lie here. This house — '

'This house!' ejaculated Jean. 'You don't mean that it was Andrew who bought it at the sale?'

This information had slipped out accidentally. Ailsa regretted it immediately, and could only nod her head.

'So it was Andrew who ran up the bidding! Why did he do that when you yourself were anxious to buy?'

'It wasn't Andrew who ran up the price,' said Ailsa. 'It was someone else. Andrew stepped in to save me from being homeless.'

Jean's face grew crimson. She recalled a certain conversation with her husband, and its significance was now fairly clear.

'Ailsa,' she gasped, 'was it Alan who was bidding against you — through another man — was it?'

Ailsa was sorely tempted to tell a falsehood, but it would have been of no avail, for her face betrayed her. Jean's humiliation was pathetic. She hung her head and a sob came from her lips.

'To think of my own husband being so — so cruel!'

'You mustn't think too harshly of him,' murmured Ailsa. 'You must remember that he is ignorant of the truth. He believed me to be a — a worthless woman. Wasn't it natural for him — '

'No — no. It was a terrible thing to contemplate. However big a thorn you may have been in his side, he ought to have remembered that you were my sister. I — I feel I can never forgive him.'

'You must. All the fault is not his, Jean. You and I are responsible for so much trouble. We cannot afford to be unforgiving.'

'But why didn't you tell me this before?'

'It was a long time before I knew. Andrew kept it all so quiet, and I discovered it quite unexpectedly. I knew it would make you unhappy to tell you. Isn't there sufficient unhappiness without breeding more?'

It was patent from her expression that she was including herself in the category of the unhappy, and Jean was quick to realise it. She grasped her arm and looked intently into the brown eyes.

'You make me so apprehensive, Ailsa. You look like a frightened deer. Where has your colour gone? Why are your hands trembling? Ailsa; trust me, for God's sake keep nothing from me! You are going to marry Andrew for my sake. Isn't that it?'

'You don't know what you are saying,' retorted Ailsa. 'Andrew is the dearest man in the world — '

'Yes, but you don't love him. You are persuading yourself that you are acting for the best. Because Andrew has done so much for — for us, you seek to repay him by sacrificing yourself. All the time you are in love with another man — '

Ailsa's distraught expression compelled her to stop. If she needed any corroboration it was there in the agonised face.

'Stop — stop!' moaned Ailsa. 'Do you want to drive me mad? It is too late to alter things. But it isn't true.'

Jean said nothing more, for to do so were merely to add to the load of despair in Ailsa's heart. But she appreciated at its full value the battle that was going on, and hoped that there might yet be a chance of disentangling the skein which imprisoned them both.

'Is Peter about?' she asked after a long pause.

'He is playing outside.'

'I'll go and find him. Good-bye, dear.'

But Peter was not to be found easily. He had wandered across the meadow and was at that moment engaged in playing with that astonishing uncle of his who lived in the 'big house.' Drummond had seen him scuttling back through the hedge and had promptly collared him. Peter at first was dreadfully afraid, but on turning his scared eyes on his captor he saw that he was actually laughing.

'Why did you run away?' asked Drummond.

'I don't know,' lisped Peter. 'I think I'm afraid of you.'

'You needn't be afraid, Peter. Why are you afraid?'

'You aren't like my other uncle — he plays with me.'

'Does he? Then so will I.'

With which he put the boy down, picked up the ball, and threw it at him with a laugh. How easy to overleap the barriers of childhood's prejudices! In ten minutes they were the best of friends, and out of this rollicking game Drummond was deriving immense pleasure.

'I think I do like you,' lisped Peter, turning his great blue eyes on the pensive face.

'Then all's well. How would you like to have a ride on a nice little pony with a tail that reaches to the ground?'

'Oh, lovely! When — when?'

'To-morrow. I shall not have him until to-morrow. You come down here after breakfast and I'll have him all ready.'

Peter put his arms round Drummond's neck and kissed him many times. And this was the sight which Jean saw as she appeared on the other side of the hedge. So unexpected was it that it held her spellbound for a few seconds.

'Oh, there's Auntie!' squealed Peter.

Drummond released him with a somewhat embarrassed expression on his face and watched him leap across to Jean, who managed to creep through the hole in the hedge.

'I'm going to have a ride on a pony,' said Peter. 'I'm coming down here to-morrow, and Uncle's going to have the pony all ready. Isn't that just lovely?'

To Jean it was something more than lovely — it was miraculous. She kissed him fondly and sent him through the hedge, as she heard Ailsa's voice calling him in the distance.

Drummond came towards her and took her arm with a smile.

'Been walking?' he asked.

'Only to see Ailsa. She — she is not very well.'

'I am sorry to hear that.'

There was no room to doubt the sincerity of his words. She could not help feeling that he must have changed considerably since he had contemplated rendering Ailsa homeless. That incident rankled deeply, but because of his more recent conduct she was determined to forget it. They walked together through the park and up the steep incline which led to the house, both very reflective.

'Jean!'

She turned her head to notice that his face was flushed.

'Do you remember a suggestion which you made recently concerning — concerning Peter?'

'Y — yes,' she stammered.

'Will you let me take back all I said?'

'Take back all — '

'Will you help me to forget that I uttered the most ungenerous words — about the boy?'

'Alan, I am so glad you said that.'

Her hand wandered down to his and pressed it.

'You said you thought Ailsa would — Jean, I'd like to have a boy like that.'

She gasped with mixed amazement and joy. Since that day when her suggestion had been met with anger she had never mentioned the subject; now to hear it revived with such evident approval!

'You would adopt him?'

'Nothing would give me greater pleasure.'

'Are you doing this for my sake?'

'No, for his — for ours, too, perhaps. But I want to think of the boy first and foremost. He ought to have a good start in life. Do you think Ailsa would agree? To me it seems incredible.'

'You don't know her unselfishness. She will sacrifice anything for Peter's sake. I'll ask her — to-morrow.'

This chance of getting possession of her boy was like a great ray of sunshine from behind some sombre clouds. It was the one means of keeping the two great loves of her life, and she felt sure that Ailsa would raise no great obstacle.

But before she could put into practice her intentions things were destined to happen to complicate matters. That afternoon a familiar figure stepped from the train and made for the village by roundabout paths. It was Stewart Morrison, called to the Glen by Andrew's mysterious message.

He found Andrew in the smiddy working like a trojan under a shower of white-hot sparks. He muttered a hoarse 'Good day,' but Andrew pretended not to hear. Now that the moment had come he felt stunned and bewildered.

'Andrew!'

Andrew dropped the handle of the bellows

and swung round, his eyes gleaming from the dust and grime which covered his face.

'You asked me to come.'

'Aye. Will you go into the cottage? I'll be with you when I have had a wash and locked up this place.'

Stewart nodded and left the smiddy. For half an hour he sat in the small parlour of the adjoining cottage, puzzled and impatient. At last Andrew came in and sat down in the chair opposite.

'You — you got my telegram?' he asked.

'Of course. What — what does it mean?'

'It's about Ailsa,' said Andrew, heavily.

'I guessed that. What is the matter — is she ill? Don't say she has met with some accident!'

Andrew shook his head and stared out of the window. How difficult it was to get to the point.

29

'For God's sake, speak,' cried Stewart. 'Something is wrong, or you would not look like that!'

Andrew lost his vacant expression and, resting his clenched fists on the table, looked almost fiercely at Stewart.

'The only thing that is wrong with Ailsa is something which you can cure.'

'I?'

'You remember the time before you sailed? You wrote a letter to Ailsa asking her to forget the past — to marry you and go abroad with you — '

Stewart inclined his head.

'Well, she never received it.'

'What!'

He was on his feet, his face contorted with incredulity.

'Impossible!' he gasped. 'Why, it was correctly — By heaven, that must be the meaning of her hardness towards me! I see it all now — she believes I went away without caring two straws what happened to her! Andrew, are you sure about this?'

'As sure as a man can be about anything.

There is the letter. It was poor Robert's fault. He forgot to deliver it, and was afraid to confess to either you or Ailsa. He died but a few days ago, and in a last effort to put things right gave me the letter.'

Stewart sat gazing at the envelope on the table. The situation bewildered him. Here was Andrew, whose whole interest in life lay in keeping this letter from Ailsa, actually offering him — But what was Andrew's motive? Why had he brought him here to show him this, when in a few days' time Ailsa would be —

'I — what does it all mean, Andrew? If Ailsa never got that letter, how do you know what it contained? Oh, I see — it's opened!'

'Robert did that. He was scarcely conscious o' his actions. He hoped it would prove to be of no importance, so that he could destroy it. When he knew how important it was it almost worried him out o' his life. He — he read it to me on his death-bed.'

'I see. He wanted you to decide what was best to be done — whether to leave Ailsa in ignorance, or to — to let her know the truth.'

'Aye.'

'And have you told her?'

'No, it is for you to do that.'

'I?'

'If you love her. That's why I sent for you, Stewart. I want to hear from your own lips that you love her as much as she deserves to be loved. I want to know whether, in spite of certain things in her life, you will marry her if she is willing.'

'Marry her!' gasped Stewart. 'But what about you?'

'It's Ailsa we're talkin' aboot,' said Andrew fiercely. 'It's Ailsa's happiness that has got to come first. Can you give her back the past? Can you, armed with this letter, convince her that her future happiness lies wi' you?'

'I can — I could,' said Stewart. 'But I won't.'

'Eh?'

'It's inhuman. I can't take the thing I want most at so great a sacrifice on your part. You love her, too, don't you?'

'No' in the same way, perhaps,' growled Andrew. 'Maybe I was just sorry for her, and had the means to provide for her and Peter. Aye, there was never much more than that in it. How could there be between Ailsa and I? Why, I was always like a father to her.'

He turned his head aside that Stewart should not see the depth of his emotion, but he failed utterly to hide it from the observant eyes.

'You are saying that to help me,' said Stewart. 'Suppose I find I can't go on with this?'

'Then I'll tell Ailsa myself. It'll serve no good purpose, lad. Here's a chance to make at least two people happy. Failing that, all three will be miserable, for there'll be no marriage between Ailsa and me.'

He was master of himself now, and Stewart recognised the deep resolution in his eyes.

'Ought I to do this, Andrew?'

'Ay — if you love her.'

'Love her! You can't know how much I love her.'

Andrew thought he could, but he did not say so. He picked up the letter and thrust it into Stewart's hand. The latter took it as in a dream.

'Go to her now, laddie. Don't waste a second in letting her ken the truth. If there is any hitch, come back to me.'

'Yes, yes. But, Andrew, you are mag — '

Andrew cut him short by flinging open the door, which led directly on to the street.

The interview had been so short and the outcome so astounding that Stewart found it difficult to keep a grip on things. A few hours ago he had been in Glasgow, vainly seeking for some escape from the flood of bitter memories. Now he was on his way to the girl whom he had firmly believed had gone out of his life for ever.

He halted suddenly as he reflected upon the shock which he was about to inflict on Ailsa. In the cottage it had not assumed such terrific proportions, but now he literally quaked in his shoes. In the first place, she would resent his calling on her. He wished it could have been possible to warn her before bursting in upon her and startling her. He mopped his brow and commenced to walk with curious, halting steps in the direction of the farm.

The door was reached all too soon. Would that it had been ten miles away, to give him time to sort things out clearly. Twice he raised his hand to knock, and twice he brought it down again. Then with a gulp he gave a quick rat-tat-tat. Half a minute passed and footsteps were heard inside. To his great relief it was the woman who helped Ailsa. She smiled pleasantly as she recognised him as the recent saviour of Peter.

'Is Miss Leslie in?' he asked in a shaky voice.

'She is aboot the farm. Will ye come inside and wait while I fetch her?'

He nodded, and was shown into the sitting-room. Sitting there waiting for her was a most unpleasant experience. After what happened at their last meeting it was not impossible she might refuse to see him, in which case circumstances would render it imperative that he forced his presence upon her.

This, however, was proved to be unnecessary, for Ailsa came in shortly afterwards and halted by the door with apprehensive eyes.

'What is it you want?' she asked. 'I thought you had gone away for good.'

'I thought so, too, but something has happened to bring me back. Won't you sit down? — I've got a lot to say.'

'What can you have to say to me?'

'Please — please sit down.'

She hesitated for a moment, and then, with a little sigh, occupied the chair nearest him. Though she was striving to be calm he saw that under the surface her agitation was enormous.

'I want to speak about the past — '

'No. I will hear nothing about that. For me the past is dead and buried. How can you come here with no other object than that? I thought you had something — '

'Wait — wait,' he pleaded. 'I must make a start somewhere. Ailsa, in the old days you loved me, didn't you?'

'I won't listen — '

'You must. You refuse to confess that

you loved me then, but I know you did. Why, we were engaged to be married when that terrible quarrel took place. After that life became a very barren thing for me. I realised what I had lost. I realised that, like a fool, I had trampled on your heart and mine. Then came a proposal from my firm — they wanted me to go abroad for a long period. It was a mark of esteem I could not very well refuse to accept, but the thought of being buried thousands of miles away from you was terrible. I knew then that I wanted you as much as, or more than, I had wanted you before. In spite of the fact that I had hurt you deeply, I determined to make an appeal to the old love which I felt might still be smouldering — '

Her eyes were following the movements of his lips, as if she could not trust her ears to intercept his amazing words.

'So I wrote a letter,' he added slowly.

'A letter! I got no letter.'

'No, you never received it. That is really why I came — to give it to you now.'

He slipped his hand into his inner pocket and extracted the letter, which he held out before her.

'Please take it.'

'I — I — '

'Please! I want you to read it now.'

She gulped and caught the edge of the envelope with her nervous fingers. Several seconds passed before she could summon the courage to extract the separate halves. When she did she gazed at them blankly, without attempting to read the writing.

'You must read what is written, Ailsa.'

She began to read, and as she progressed her whole being seemed revitalised. It was evident she had forgotten everything outside the neat, burning words. Her head came up as she reached the last word, and in the soft, brown eyes were tears of joy mingled with the anguish generated by the consciousness of her unhappy position.

'You did write, then — you wrote this. And you waited to hear from me and never heard. What did you think?'

'That you had buried it with the past.'

'I don't — understand,' she moaned. 'Why did I never get this?'

'Old Robert made a mistake. He mislaid it, and found it again after three years.'

'Robert! Robert!' she choked, and hung her head.

'Ailsa, if there had been no mistake — if that letter had reached you — what would you have done?'

She raised her head and looked at him with startled eyes.

'You mustn't ask me that — now. Whatever this mistake may have cost me, nothing can alter it.'

'It can!'

'No, no. I'm glad to know, because it makes you different in my eyes. Stewart; how cruel the fates are!'

Impelled by the agony in her face, he leapt across to her and put his arms round the quivering shoulders.

'Are they so cruel, Ailsa?' he said tensely. 'They have made amends now. At least you know that I have loved you all these years — that nothing has dimmed that love since I was able to think and find myself. When I saw you last I believed that in your heart you still cared. Tell me it was so — is so. Tell me now.'

The dark head came near to his, and the wet cheeks touched his face. Intoxicated by her near presence, he kissed her passionately, and felt her arms cling to him for a second. Then, with a wild cry, she pushed him away and rose to her feet.

'What have you done? You make me forget that I am not free. O God, why did you come here to torture me like this? Go — go now — before you break my heart!'

The horror of being false to Andrew was manifest in every line of her face and figure.

Crushing the letter in her hand, she ran to the door, eager to get away from the garden of temptation.

'Ailsa — wait!'

She halted and looked back at him with swimming eyes.

'There is something you do not know. That letter was given to me by Andrew.'

'Andrew! Does Andrew know — what it contains?'

'Every word. Robert gave it to him before he died. He sent for me to come at once. Don't you — can't you understand?'

'Andrew sent for you!' she muttered. 'Andrew told you to come here — with this?'

'Yes.'

'But — why?'

'Because Andrew is the greatest man I have ever known. When he might have destroyed that letter without a living soul being any the wiser he kept it because — because I think he must love you even more than I.'

She turned and came across to him with wondering eyes. Like him, she felt dumb in the face of this great sacrifice.

'I — I can't let him do it!' she muttered.

'He is doing it for your happiness, Ailsa. Nothing counts above that with him.'

'My happiness?'

'Just that. But it is for you to decide now. If you tell me to go I will leave by the next train and never worry you again.'

'Andrew is always right,' she said in a whisper. 'If he releases me with his own lips, I — I — '

'Ailsa!'

She smiled at him a little wanly, but as he caught her hand and raised it to his lips the wan look gave place to unspeakable joy.

'Stewart, how good God is!'

'Yes, to make men like Andrew. And how base some men are to let a single mistake kill their — '

'I have a great secret to tell you one day, Stewart, but you must be patient.'

'I can wait for ever.'

They parted as a knock came on the door, and the woman entered to announce that a Mr. Strong wished to see Ailsa.

'I don't want to see anyone to-day,' said Ailsa. 'And I have never known anyone of that name.'

The woman was about to leave when a step was heard in the hall, and an instant later a tall, dark man entered.

'I regret — ' he commenced.

'How dare you?' ejaculated Ailsa.

The stranger stared at her as if her face afforded him some little surprise. Then he turned his eyes on Stewart, whose presence appeared to embarrass him considerably.

'I did not know you were engaged,' he mumbled.

Stewart, who considered that some interference on his part was required, stepped up to the man.

'Get outside until you are asked to come in.'

'Very well — but my business is of the utmost importance.'

'Let him stay,' interrupted Ailsa. 'What is it you have to say to me, Mr. Strong?'

The woman went out and Stewart made to follow her, but Ailsa retained him with a movement of her hand. Stewart hesitated, and then sat down, while the visitor extracted a notebook from his pocket.

30

To Stewart the situation was discomfiting, to say the least, but he appreciated Ailsa's action in retaining him. It was evident that she meant to have no secrets from him — that her trust was infinitely great. Strong turned over the pages of his notebook until he found the page he wanted. Then he coughed loudly.

'Go on,' said Ailsa. 'What is the meaning of all this?'

Strong glanced towards Stewart.

'Do you really wish this gentleman to stay?'

'I do.'

'I warn you that I have come on a very private mission.'

'A very urgent one by the manner in which you entered this house,' said Ailsa.

Strong shrugged his shoulders.

'I am sorry I acted in that way, but in my profession one has to wink at conventions. However, despite that, it is possible that I may render you a service. I ought to have explained before that I represent a private detective agency.'

Ailsa started a little, and Stewart uttered a low cry of surprise. He glanced at Ailsa and saw that her face had suddenly lost its colour.

'I am acting on behalf of the trustees in the will of the late Mr. Arthur Dunton. Does the name recall anything, Miss Leslie?'

'Arthur Dunton!' muttered Ailsa. 'But he died years ago!'

'The son — yes. But this has reference to Arthur Dunton, senior, who died less than three months ago.'

Ailsa suddenly saw light. This man mistook her for Jean. He had probably made inquiries and discovered the existence of Peter. That alone would convince him that she was the woman he sought. She remembered Jean had told her that Dunton's parents had never seen their son's wife. In a flash she saw the danger to Jean. If this man discovered that the real widow of Dunton, junior, was within a mile —

'Go on,' she said in a hoarse voice.

'Ah, I am glad there is no mistake. You are the Miss Leslie who married Mr. Dunton's son in Glasgow on — '

An exclamation of astonishment left Stewart's lips, but a pleading glance from Ailsa reduced him to silence immediately. Strong nodded his head in smug conceit.

'You will remember that the marriage came as a shock to your — your husband's people, and, in the circumstances, it was not unnatural that they should feel distressed?'

'They were more than distressed,' retorted Ailsa. 'They did not even give their son's wife a chance to prove that she was in many ways superior to the man who led her into an unhappy marriage.'

'Quite so. Well, to get to the root of the matter, Mr. Dunton always regretted his attitude in that affair. When he died he set aside certain money, which the trustees will be pleased to hand over to you, provided a condition is fulfilled.'

Ailsa's face went crimson as the real object of this hounding down was made clear.

'I see — he wants to buy forgiveness with a cheque?'

'It's a hard way of putting it.'

'It's true, though. And what is this mysterious condition which must be fulfilled before this precious money becomes — mine?'

Strong hesitated for a moment, as if he were a trifle nervous about the outcome of the yet incomplete proposal.

'It naturally occurred to him — er — that there might possibly be a child of the marriage, in which case it will be necessary to surrender it to — '

Ailsa's fierce cry of resentment pulled him up with a jerk.

'There's the whole business in a nutshell,' she retorted. 'His real object was to buy the child from its mother!'

'My good woman — '

'And that is what you call regretting his attitude? I suppose it was because you imagined I was that kind of woman that you forced your way into the house. Well, now you may go back and tell your employers that under no circumstances will the boy be surrendered.'

'So there *is* a child?'

'Surely your methods have been thorough enough to have discovered that?'

'True, I heard there was. But I beg you to reconsider the matter. The legacy represents a considerable sum of money — '

'Money! Is that as far as your imagination goes? If that money was to have been given me unconditionally, I would die rather than touch a penny of it. Go back and tell them that.'

'That is your last word?'

'Yes, and I shall refuse to see anyone else who comes to intrude into my affairs.'

Strong sighed, and picked up his hat. Before he left he stared at Ailsa in strange fashion. Ailsa came back to the bewildered Stewart.

'I have been expecting something like that to happen,' she said. 'There was an advertisement in the newspapers — '

'I can't understand it,' said Stewart.

'Of course not,' she replied, grasping his hand tearfully. 'You are wondering how I could come to marry that — that man. You are wondering how I could trample on your love and keep you in ignorance of all this.'

'If you want to forget all about that terrible affair, here am I to help you. I'll never doubt you, Ailsa, dear.'

Peter's unheralded entry interrupted the endearments. He stood with widely open eyes surveying Stewart, who caught him up in his arms.

'And this is the boy they wanted to buy,' he remarked.

'Who wants to buy me?' retorted Peter.

'Nobody,' put in Ailsa swiftly. 'Uncle Stewart was only joking.'

'Is he another uncle?' asked Peter.

Stewart looked at Ailsa and laughed. Then he noticed that she was greatly agitated, and put Peter to the ground immediately.

'Perhaps you would rather I went and left you for a bit?' he suggested.

'Yes, yes, I am so happy, and yet so worried.'

'Worried?'

'That man — he looked at me so queerly when he left. I can't help wondering — Oh, don't ask me to explain now. Come tomorrow — yes, yes, come to-morrow.'

She laughed almost hysterically as she clung to his hand, and then sped him away, standing at the door until he disappeared in the lane. The whole world seemed topsy-turvy to Ailsa, but mingled with this great overwhelming flow of happiness was the deep and almost painful sympathy which she felt for Andrew. Somehow it was like leaving him at the altar. Then there was that queer look on Strong's face. Was it possible he had been fooling her for some reason?

Had she been able to look into Strong's cunning brain at that moment she might have had ample cause to feel alarmed. When Strong had entered the farm he was convinced that the woman he sought was within. It was the first glimpse of her face which had aroused his suspicions, for in his pocket he carried a photograph which the younger Dunton had sent to his parents soon after his marriage with Jean. He now sat in the inn with this photograph before him.

'Something very fishy about this,' he muttered. 'If she is not Dunton's widow, why did she pretend she was? And to back her up is the fact that she has the boy.'

This was the thing which baffled him, and which had actuated him in putting his proposal to Ailsa after he was convinced that she was not the woman he wanted. Until now he had purposely refrained from making any inquiries about the matter in the Glen itself. What little he had learnt had been gleaned in a neighbouring village.

He was not the type of man to stick at trifles nor to go back and report failure. Everything now depended upon finding the original of the photograph, and to this end he was determined to leave no stone unturned. He called for some refreshment and watched with interest the group of men who had foregathered in the bar. It proved to be no difficult task to get into conversation with them, and before long they were treating him almost as one of themselves.

'I used to fish down here a few years back,' he said. 'There was a good spot for trout near that little farm by the big house. There was rather a pretty girl living there — I used to see her at times. Now what was her name?'

'Leslie?'

'That's it. Is she still there?'

'Ay. And what's more, she's gettin' wed one o' these days.'

Strong raised his eyebrows at this unexpected

news. It, however, led nowhere. The men continued the conversation among themselves.

'Why, I mind Ailsa Leslie when she was nae bigger than my arm. They were a bonnie pair, she and her sister — '

'Her sister?' said Strong in a surprised tone.

'Ay. It's strange how things work oot. Ailsa had all the trouble, and her sister a' the luck. She was engaged to a lad who went to Australia to win a fortune.'

'Who was?'

'The sister — Jean. The boy cam' hame fair burstin' wi' money. He bought the big hoose, Aberdinnie, and — '

Strong gave a violent start at this astonishing news.

'You mean that Jean Leslie is now Mrs. Drummond, and wife of the Laird o' Aberdinnie?'

'That's so, and a kindly couple they are. The Glen has a lot tae thank them for.'

Strong was not lacking in brains. Immediately he began reconstructing the drama as he saw it, and every piece fitted perfectly. If Jean was the woman who had married Dunton, then Peter was undoubtedly her child. Its presence at the farm could only mean one thing — that Drummond was ignorant of her first marriage. What was more natural than that, in the presumably unexpected return of her old sweetheart, Jean should seek the aid of her sister in covering up the result of her broken romance.

'It's very interesting,' he remarked casually. 'And is Mrs. Drummond as fascinating as her sister?'

'She hasna got Ailsa's pluck and spirit, but she's considered much bonnier. There's no' a woman for miles aroond to compare wi' her whaur looks are concerned. Aye, she's a bonnie woman — as fair as a rose, wi' a face like an angel.'

This brief description removed the last shred of doubt from Strong's mind. The photograph which he possessed was that of a superbly beautiful girl, and that that girl was the wife of Drummond he was now positive. But it embarrassed him considerably, for it was certain that Jean could not be bribed with money to surrender the child. Keen to succeed in his quest, he thought of other solutions.

In half an hour he arrived at a decision. He laughed aloud as he reflected how simple the solution was, and it surprised him that he had not hit upon it immediately. The weapon he meant to use was Drummond's ignorance of his wife's past. If she had deemed it essential to keep this from her husband all these years, it must be because she feared the result of revealing it.

Under the threat of that revelation on his part would she not yield to the inevitable? He was convinced she would, for the alternative was the loss of something greater perhaps than this child of an earlier and secret marriage. Much as he disliked having recourse to force of this kind, he persuaded himself it was his duty in the interest of his employers.

'Well, here goes!' he muttered, and set off towards Aberdinnie.

31

When Stewart left Ailsa he went straight to Andrew's cottage. Andrew was busy packing a bag, but when he saw Stewart's figure through the window he pushed the bag under the table, where it remained hidden from view by the overhanging tablecloth. His eyes swept Stewart's face as he entered the room.

'You've seen her?'

'Yes.'

'Well?'

'She — she understands. Andrew — I'm so sorry!'

'Sorry!'

'For you. Even now it seems cruel to — '

Andrew silenced him with a wave of his hand. He managed to conjure up a smile and held out his hand.

'Good luck to you, lad! I ken fine you'll mak' her happy.'

'I will — but, Andrew, she wants to see you — to hear from your own lips that you release her.'

Andrew nodded in silence. Then Stewart remembered the other incident.

'A man called while I was there,' he said rapidly. 'Ailsa wished me to stay, so I stayed. He came from the trustees in the will of a man named Dunton — '

Andrew's eyes opened wide, and a deep growl left his lips.

'Dunton!' he muttered. 'What — what did this fellow want?'

'Peter. Old Dunton is dead, and there was some money to come to Ailsa on condition that she surrendered Peter. They must have guessed there was a child — But what is the matter?'

Andrew was staring before him in bewilderment.

'What — what did Ailsa say?' he gasped.

'Refused, of course. But, Andrew, I didn't know about this. How horrible it must have been for Ailsa to be persecuted when she was legally married! She ought to have protected herself against the scandalmongers by telling the truth.'

Andrew gripped him by the shoulders, and stared into his eyes.

'You are still in the dark, lad!'

'In the dark? I was before that fellow turned up, but not now. I know what Ailsa has suffered.'

'You don't.'

'What do you mean?'

Andrew hesitated as he reflected that he had been sworn to secrecy, but, having gone so far, he could see no good reason to keep his mouth closed.

'You are taking my place,' he muttered, 'and it's but right you should ken the truth.'

'What truth?'

'Ailsa has never been married!'

'But she said — '

'Yes, for a good reason. Stewart, you've seen Peter. Is it possible you have not recognised another person in Peter's features?'

'Another person — what person?'

'Someone who is fairer than Ailsa — someone for whom Ailsa was willing to sacrifice herself. Someone who had not Ailsa's courage nor Ailsa's steadfastness?'

Light came in one great blinding flash. Such a solution to the enigma Stewart had never even dreamed of. He looked like a stunned man as he faced Andrew.

'Andrew! Do you mean that Peter is Jean's child? That it was Jean who married Dunton — '

'Aye, and Ailsa who carried the burden. Did you think Ailsa was the kind o' lass to be led away by dreams of luxury — who would trample on the heart o' the man who loved her?'

Stewart looked sick with humiliation. Andrew caught him by the shoulder gently.

'It is easy for me to reprove you, lad, when I knew the truth all the time. I can guess what it must have meant to you to suddenly find — But we winna talk o' that. Perhaps I shouldna have told you, but I couldna resist removing the ugly blot from your mind.'

'Thanks, Andrew, thanks! But Jean — I can't understand Jean permitting this to go on.'

'She didna mean it to go on. She has tried and tried to tell her husband, but he'll no' listen. You mauna blame her ower much, laddie. Some creatures are made strong and some weak. Drummond is weak in a way — he has prejudices that fight hard; Jean is weak in her great love for him. Between the two is the strong — Ailsa — holding them together by self-sacrifice.'

'I understand. I see now why Ailsa misled that man. Andrew, she is even greater than I thought.'

Andrew nodded and looked at his watch as a hint that he had said all there was to say.

'Are you staying at the inn?' he asked in a casual voice.

'I don't know. I haven't had time to worry about a room. I didn't even guess that I should be called upon to stay the night. Did I leave my bag here?'

Andrew picked it up from the corner and handed it to him.

'Better see about a room, or you may be ower late.'

'Yes, of course. Andrew, I wish I could find words to express what I feel about you. You have gone beyond the limits of friendship.'

But Andrew was busy opening the door, and when he shook hands his head was turned away.

32

When Stewart was hearing the truth about Ailsa and her great sacrifice Jean was sitting with her husband in the drawing-room chatting with him in pleasant fashion. His recent change of front had filled her with a joy impossible to express. The adoption of Peter would mean an end to the tortures which she had suffered of late. The desire for possession of her one and only child had become an obsession. Always had loomed before her the possibility of Ailsa leaving the farm and taking Peter with her. That prospect was now fading swiftly into the distant realms of shadows.

'Why are you so good to me?' she asked.

'I'm not really half so good as I might be,' he laughed. 'But, seriously, Jean, your happiness means more to me than anything in the world.'

'Be careful!' she said. 'That is a sweeping assertion.'

'I know, but I mean it. Jean, when I married you it was the greatest thing that ever happened to me — the greatest that ever could happen. Jean, there is something else which troubles me. It's your sister. Is there anything I can do for her? I've treated her badly in the past — oh, yes, I have. I went so far as to try and buy her farm over her head. God forgive me for that! I think it was Andrew who first caused me to feel ashamed. When in spite of everything a man like Andrew was willing to marry her it caused me to think a little. It's astonishing what a lot of hometruths one learns when one begins seriously to examine one's self. It occurred to me that Andrew was in every way a better man than myself — '

'Alan!'

'It's quite true. Luck made me, Jean — but Andrew made himself by toil and right thinking. The things which I am only just beginning to learn Andrew knew long ago. Oh, it is so, and no honest man can deny it. I confess that Andrew made me ashamed. I tried to look at Ailsa without prejudice. That is a terribly difficult process when one has been accustomed to acting on impulse. Well, to cut matters short, dearie, I have been thinking that this approaching marriage with Andrew might be a splendid excuse for me to do something. You see, one can give a wedding present when one cannot offer — '

'You darling!' she cried. 'But it is going to

be awfully difficult. Ailsa is so sensitive — '

She was interrupted by the entry of a servant, who informed her that 'Miss Ailsa' was waiting in the hall.

'Talk of angels!' ejaculated Jean. 'Will you excuse me, Alan? I expect it has something to do with wedding dresses. I shall not be long.'

'Why not ask her to stay to dinner?'

'She couldn't. Peter would be all alone — the woman leaves about this time.'

'It was about Peter that I was thinking,' he said. 'Don't you think you might put that proposition to her? There is no time like the present.'

'I will if there is a chance,' she promised, and went into the hall to find Ailsa looking more agitated than she had seen her in all her life.

'Ailsa, whatever is the matter?'

'Everything is the matter. I have the most extraordinary news. I did not mean to tell you to-night, but — but I simply can't keep it to myself. Jean, Stewart has come back.'

'Come back? What for?'

'Andrew sent for him. There has been a terrible mistake — I misjudged him. Oh, how can I explain?'

Catching her breath for a second, she rattled off the whole story at a tremendous rate, until Jean's brain literally whirled. When she ultimately finished, she sank on to a couch almost exhausted.

'This is — amazing!' cried Jean. 'But what will he do?'

Ailsa shook her head helplessly.

'I don't know — I wish I did. I mean to see him to-morrow, to learn from him — oh, everything — to know that there is no mistake. Oh, Jean, I'm so happy and yet miserable, because of Andrew — '

'You mustn't be miserable, Ailsa. Remember that Andrew did this for your happiness. If he sees you are not completely happy it will make him feel that his sacrifice is in vain.'

'Yes, I know. And there is something else, Jean — something that troubles me a little. I had a visitor this afternoon — a man from a detective agency. It was about — about Dunton.'

Jean started at the sound of the name.

'Dunton!' she gasped. 'How did he get to know? But Dunton is dead!'

'Yes, and so is the elder Mr. Dunton. You remember that advertisement? This is a sequel to it. Having failed to find you by adve ing they employed this man. It is Pete   ey really want — '

'Peter!'

'Peter!'

'Yes. This man traced you to the Glen, but here he made his mistake. He had probably heard about the scandal, and naturally assumed that I was Peter's mother and young Dunton's widow. The father apparently regretted his treatment of you and left a sum of money to be made over to you conditionally that Peter was surrendered to his trustees.'

'Horrible! But he could not have known about Peter?'

'He evidently meant to take no risks.'

'But what happened, Ailsa — did you let him think — '

Ailsa nodded, and Jean closed her eyes and hung her head.

'It's all right,' said Ailsa. 'I got rid of him — at least I think I convinced him it was no use pursuing the matter. But he looked at me so strangely when he left. That's why I called.'

The hesitating voice and the look in her eyes convinced Jean that something was being withheld.

'What is it that you are afraid to tell me?' she whispered.

'Perhaps it was only fancy — but as I was coming here I passed a man in the lane. It was too dark to see his face, but — '

'You think it might be this man?'

'I don't see why it should, but it's best to be forewarned. If he is a little suspicious he can have no proof that I am not Peter's mother. If he should turn up you must face it out, Jean.'

Jean nodded and tried to smile bravely, but the news was very disturbing, for she was tired of this long-lived masquerade.

'I must go now,' said Ailsa. 'I promised to be back in half an hour. I'm glad I came.'

She was shaking hands with Jean when the front door bell rang. It seemed to her like the knell of doom. Jean's face, like her own, was pale as death. She led Ailsa into a small room on the right of the hall and the pair of them waited anxiously. Ten seconds later a maid entered.

'Gentleman to see you, ma'am — a Mr. Strong.'

'Tell him I am at dinner, and ask him to write and state his business.'

The maid went out, but returned very shortly.

'Your pardon, ma'am, but the gentleman says his business is very urgent and will not wait.'

Jean looked at Ailsa, but Ailsa was as much agitated and doubtful of the next move as she was herself.

'What — what shall I do, Ailsa?' she whispered.

'I don't know. Oh, see him, and let us get it over. We are two to one.'

Jean hesitated, and finally told the maid to show the visitor in.

'Do you think he knows?' asked Jean.

'How can he?'

'But why does he come here?'

That was the thing which was worrying Ailsa. There was no time to say anything more, for the door opened and Strong entered the room. He manifested some surprise at seeing Ailsa, and appeared to be far more nervous than when he had unceremoniously entered the farm.

'I — I regret this late call,' he said.

'You wished to see me on urgent business?' said Jean coolly. 'I shall be obliged if you will be brief.'

'I will. This lady's presence shortens our business considerably, for it is fairly evident that she has warned you I might call.'

It was a random shot, but he saw it go home, and nodded his head in a satisfied manner.

'Naturally I have told my sister of your visit to me,' put in Ailsa swiftly. 'But that does not explain your presence here.'

'Pardon me, but it does, for I am now

perfectly convinced that the lady I seek is Mrs. Drummond, and not you.'

Without more ado he produced his pocket-book and put the photograph on the small table before him. Jean gave one glance at it and realised that further denial was futile. It was the photograph she had given to Dunton years ago, and on the bottom of it was written: 'With love.'

33

Jean took up the photograph with trembling hand. For a moment it looked as if she would break down, but she summoned every ounce of her courage and faced Strong.

'Suppose I do not choose to deny it?' she said. 'Suppose I admit it is true? What right have these people to obtrude into my life?'

'They are naturally interested on the child's behalf.'

'How dare they be interested in my child! Who is more capable of caring for him than his own mother?'

'It is not for me to express any opinion on that matter,' said Strong. 'I am merely entrusted with a mission — '

'To come here and offer me money for the surrender of my boy? Well, you have already heard my answer through my sister. I shall be glad if you will convey it to your — your employers.'

It was evident from Strong's expression that he had quite expected this. Reduced to playing his last card, he attempted to vindicate himself.

'In this matter, Mrs. Drummond, our

interests clash. You are concerned in the retaining of your son, I in fulfilling my mission. My duties do not end with the tracing of you. I was empowered by the trustees to settle the matter if possible, and to take the boy away with me.'

Jean gasped at this, and her coolness gave way to anger. She was about to ring the bell, when Strong held up his hand.

'You compel me to have to resort to a kind of force which I had hoped would not be necessary.'

'What do you mean?'

'I mean that in the event of your refusing to consent to this proposal, I shall try — elsewhere.'

'Elsewhere?'

'Mr Drummond, I feel sure, would not have the same compunctions — '

Both Ailsa and Jean started at these significant words, and the latter's face twitched in agonised fashion.

'You would not dare!' exclaimed Ailsa.

'Why not? In my profession I find it inadvisable to consider individuals. I want that boy, and I mean to have him.'

'Never!' cried Jean.

'Wait!' implored Ailsa. She turned to Strong. 'Is there no other way by which this business can be settled to everyone's

331

satisfaction? Suppose we can satisfy the trustees that the boy is well cared for — that his mother is now fortunately placed — '

Strong shook his head emphatically.

'My instructions were implicit. It is for Mrs. Drummond to decide — '

'I have decided,' said Jean. 'I will never give up Peter.'

Strong gazed at her for a second, and then shrugged his shoulders and made for the door.

Ailsa looked at Jean and saw the dreadful look in her eyes. Strong turned on the threshold.

'I regret you leave me no other alternative but to see Mr. — '

A strangled sob left Jean's lips. She imagined the effect of this terrible story upon Drummond. She saw herself as a cheat through his eyes. She thought of to-morrow with its hideous blankness —

'Wait!' she moaned.

Strong left the door and came nearer the table.

'Why should you have this reluctance?' he said smoothly. 'You will know the boy is well cared for. His guardian will be his father's mother, who will devote the rest of her life to his happiness.'

'What — what do you want me to do?' said Jean hoarsely.

Strong extracted a sheet of paper from his pocket and placed it before her.

'I had this drawn up in case it should be needed,' he explained. 'It is a document which will meet with the legal requirements. Please read it carefully.'

Jean ran her eyes over the wording. It was very brief, but it left the mother absolutely without further claim. 'Complete surrender!' How the words burned into her brain.

'You have merely to sign it,' whispered Strong. 'Miss Leslie can witness it.'

Jean, as if hypnotised, took the fountain pen from his fingers.

'Jean!' cried Ailsa. 'Think what you are doing.'

Jean turned her wet eyes on her sister. In them Ailsa saw fully how much this meant to her. She choked down her own resentment, feeling that it was Jean's affair, and that Jean must make her own choice.

The pen touched the paper, and the signature was slowly inscribed. Strong nodded his head and took the pen from the shaking fingers, handing it to Ailsa to complete the document. Ailsa looked at the bent head of Jean, and with a great gulp wrote in her name.

'Thank you,' said Strong.

He was about to pick up the paper when Jean's head came up. The eyes were fixed in horror, and her lips moved nervelessly. When Strong's hand was on the corner of the document she recovered from her trance. Her hand flew out and fastened on the paper. A second later it was being torn into a hundred pieces.

'I must have been mad — mad!' she cried. 'Now you have my answer — my real answer. Do what you like — I've saved my soul. He's my boy, and I'll keep him if I lose everything else in the world.'

Strong looked dazed and speechless. While he stared at the fragments of the document a soft knock came on the door and the handle turned. Strong swung round and found himself face to face with Drummond.

34

'I beg your pardon,' said Drummond, seeing the stranger. 'I didn't know. Why, what is the matter?'

Strong looked at the distraught figure of Jean. She dashed the tears from her eyes and drew herself up proudly.

'Go on,' she murmured. 'Tell him now.'

Drummond's eyes narrowed as he looked at Strong, but Strong was experiencing strange emotions. He had a very good idea of how much this must mean to the beautiful woman before him, and he accepted failure like a man.

'I made a ridiculous proposal to Mrs. Drummond,' he said. 'I am sorry it distressed her. With your permission I will go.'

Drummond stared at him and nodded coldly. Without another word he went out the door. Jean looked at Ailsa significantly, and Ailsa understood. She smiled wanly at Drummond, bidding him 'Good night,' and made her way out. Immediately she had left Jean went to her husband and took his hands, meeting his perplexed eyes bravely.

'You are wondering what it all means, Alan?'

'Well, of course, I cannot help feeling disturbed. I thought you were alone with Ailsa.'

'That man came unexpectedly. He came to shatter all my happiness.'

'What are you saying?'

'He came to buy my soul, Alan, and I was craven enough almost to sell it.'

'Jean, you talk so wildly — are you ill?'

'No, I'm well, and I'm going to tell you something that will hurt you — something that may make you hate me.'

'Jean,' he said hoarsely. 'Must — must it be told?'

'Yes, it should have been told years ago before I got — got to love you to madness. I was always a coward, but I'm brave now, for though the worst may happen the masquerade is finished.'

'What masquerade?'

'I will show you.'

She picked up the scattered pieces of blue paper, and with great patience arranged them on the table. When they were complete and in order she pointed to them.

'Read!' she whispered. 'It is all there!'

Slowly he approached the mystery as if it were some poisonous snake. While he read

336

she could scarcely contain herself, for she saw his hands tremble and his eyes close and open. When the last word had burned into his brain he sank down on the couch with his hands before his face.

'Peter — your child!' he muttered.

'Yes, mine. And Ailsa took all the blame because she was strong, and I was a coward. I've hungered for him all these years — each day has found my desire more obsessive — '

'And you never told me?'

'No. I was afraid lest I might lose love. How could I tell you that a man came into my life, that he dazzled my foolish brain with words of love? You had been away so long, and I was lonely. He urged me to elope with him, and I went.'

'You went!' he repeated.

'Yes; he had promised to marry me immediately we reached Glasgow, but he never intended to do that.'

'Great heavens!'

'But he did — he did. Andrew followed us, and forced him to keep his promise. After that it was terrible. His people disowned him and I nearly starved. Then there was an accident — he was killed. I came back to the Glen — and there my — my baby was born. Then you came home suddenly. As soon as I saw you I knew that I had never ceased to love you, that for a time I must have been demented. You remember you heard the child; I ought to have told you then, but I was afraid of what I had done. You — you meant so much to me. Ailsa came to my help; Ailsa has faced ruin for me. Thank God the truth is out, for it was burning a — a hole in my breast.'

He hung his head, and, unable to go on, she silently left the room and ran upstairs. It was a full minute before Drummond lifted his head and found himself alone. He rose to his feet and paced the room, his brain aching the while. If Jean had anything to regret, was he not similarly placed? Had he not cast stones at Ailsa, the girl who had suffered that he might reap the happiness of those years. And here on the table was Jean's own absolution.

He opened the door and looked towards the broad staircase. From above came faint sounds — from her room. Slowly he mounted the stairs until he reached the corridor not far from her door. The sounds were plainer now; she was sobbing her heart out in there!

He ran to the door and knocked softly, but no reply came. He knocked again, and the sounds suddenly ceased. Soon after a choked voice murmured: 'Who — is it?'

'I — Alan.'

Without waiting longer he pushed open the door. She was standing facing him, with her right hand clutching the rail of the bed. He moved towards her with a wistful look in his eyes.

'Jean!'

'Why — why do you — '

'What do you expect me to do?'

She shook her head.

'You said you had saved your soul, Jean. Won't you help me save mine from harshness, lack of understanding, unforgiveness? I — I want you so — so much.'

'Alan, you mean — '

'I mean that I can look back on the past without pain — even with joy, for it means that we shall have a child to care for. Perhaps you were right not to tell me years ago. I might not have understood then, but I do now.'

She put out her hands with a wild cry of incomparable joy, and at the same time felt his arms drawing her close to him. Her tears flowed again, but they sprang from vastly different causes.

'Alan!' she murmured. 'I did not know how great you could be!'

'Nor how little,' he said with a smile. 'For I have been the littlest thing in the world. Luck fed me with a silver spoon, and I never knew how much suffering was taking place in my interest.'

'No — in mine.'

'Well, ours,' he replied with a smile. 'How happy Ailsa will be to know.'

'Yes, I must tell Ailsa at once.'

'Not to-night.'

'No, not to-night,' she said. 'To-night is ours — every minute of it.'

'And all the future, with no skeletons in the cupboard.'

So these two who had been married for years spent the evening as lovers do — talking in bated whispers of the child which only that day was theirs, planning for him and unburdening their hearts without reserve.

35

Ailsa's first thought on awakening next morning was for the couple up at Aberdinnie. She had tossed and turned about the best part of the night, with that last scene before her eyes. How it would end she dared not guess, for despite Strong's last good act, she felt that Drummond's suspicions were deeply aroused.

'Your mummie is braver than I imagined, Peter,' she murmured as she dressed the boy.

Peter, who scarcely understood this remark, stared hard at her, but she swiftly kissed away his frown. Then she reflected upon the trials before her — the meeting with Andrew and — the more pleasant but hardly less difficult one — the coming of Stewart.

The first surprise came immediately after breakfast, when Robert's successor delivered a letter. She noticed the local postmark, but did not recognise the writing. She opened it a trifle nervously, and read the contents with fast-beating heart.

It was from Andrew, and it told her all the things she wished to know. In simple but impressive words Andrew made the way clear. He explained that by the time she got it he would have left the Glen for a long holiday. He hoped she would forgive him for not coming to say good-bye in person, but that he looked forward to seeing her a happy and contented wife. He had sold the smiddy, but he did not regret it, for he understood it was not impossible she would go away with Stewart to live near his work, in which case he meant to take over the farm.

The whole tone of the lengthy epistle was one of calm contentment; indeed, he asserted that he was tremendously happy in the knowledge that he had been of some little assistance in bringing her and Stewart together. When she had read it twice she kissed it and thrust it into her bosom.

Andrew again had done the right thing. For them to have met at that juncture would have meant a lot of unnecessary pain. She looked out of the window to see the whole landscape flooded with bright sunshine, and down the road which led from Aberdinnie came two figures arm in arm. She uttered a glad cry as she recognised Jean and her husband.

They arrived at the door a few minutes later, and Jean ran to her with a warm greeting. Every line of her face manifested her great happiness, while Drummond stood in the background smiling contentedly.

'We've never been out so early in our lives,' said Jean. 'But it was so fine and sunny. Alan and I — we've come — we've come to make a terrible request.'

'What is it?'

'We want my boy. Oh, not now — in a week or two.'

'But — '

Drummond came across, and Jean moved aside. He hung his head as he took Ailsa's hand.

'Ailsa, last night Jean told me everything.'

'Everything?'

'Yes. Can you ever forgive me for the way I have treated you? Can you forgive me for the hard things I have thought about you?'

'Of course!' she replied.

'I think you are the greatest woman I have ever met. We want the boy, Ailsa, but in the face of what has happened it seems selfish to ask that. But, Jean, she — '

'Why, of course, Jean shall have him whenever she wishes. I have only been waiting for her to say the word that would make her his true mother. I shall miss him, but perhaps — perhaps — '

She blushed at her thoughts, and Jean ran forward and kissed her several times.

'Darling Ailsa,' she whispered. 'Have you seen Stewart this morning?'

'No, I am expecting him.'

'And Andrew?'

'Andrew has gone away for a holiday.'

Jean nodded and looked round for Peter. She discovered him at last playing hide-and-seek with the cat in the next room.

'Would you like a motor ride, Peter?'

'No, I'm going to ride a real live pony this morning, aren't I, Uncle?'

'Why, I had almost forgotten,' laughed Drummond. 'Well, the pony first and the motor after, eh, Peter?'

Peter was quite agreeable. Jean assisted Ailsa to dress him, and a few minutes later the happy party went up the road, leaving Ailsa alone. Thereafter every minute found her gazing through the window towards the village. At last the person she expected hove into sight, almost running in his great impatience.

She went to the door and opened it as he arrived inside the garden. All doubts, all obstacles had gone now. She was free to tell him everything — to accept whatever he offered.

36

For a moment there was silence.

'Ailsa!'

'Stewart!'

He broke through the door and into the little sitting-room.

'Did you — did you get Andrew's letter?'

'Yes, but how did you know?'

'He told me. I saw him off at the station early this morning.'

'Early this morning!' she ejaculated. 'And you have been all this time getting here?'

The words, the look on her face, the brightness of her eyes, convinced him that the path to happiness was open.

'Ailsa, then it means — it means — '

'Wait,' she murmured. 'There is something I want to tell you. It's about Peter — '

'I know,' he said swiftly. 'Andrew told me that last night. Of course, it couldn't have made any difference in any case, but it was a joy to hear. I couldn't sleep for thinking of this morning. I felt a selfish pig when I thought of Andrew, but he was quite different from what I expected.'

'Quite different!'

'Yes; I could have sworn he was as happy as I. He was looking forward to his holiday — said he had not taken a holiday for ten years, and he meant to enjoy himself. And it wasn't pretence, Ailsa; he really is happy.'

'Oh, if only I could really believe that!'

'You can.'

She was sitting quite close to him, with her fingers almost touching his hand. He moved slightly, and the fingers lay inside his own — warm and trembling.

'Ailsa, this is really the happiest day of all. It is true that one must first suffer before the greatest joy can be appreciated. It is just as if a huge black cloud had been suddenly swept from the sky.'

'That is it,' she murmured, 'a great black cloud!'

'If Jean could only face the issue.'

She looked at him with brimming eyes.

'Jean has faced it and won.'

'What!'

'Yes, last night. She came this morning to claim her boy — she and Alan.'

'Then everybody is happy?'

'Everyone; but I the happiest of all.'

He drew the dark head near him and kissed the hair. Then she raised it, and her expectant lips came within a few inches of his own. He took courage and kissed them passionately again and again; nor did she do anything but cling to him and close her eyes in a swoon.

'Tell me you love me — tell me.'

'I love you.'

'You've always loved me.'

'Yes, yes — every minute.'

'And you'll always tell me that?'

'Till you grow tired of hearing it.'

'I'll never grow tired. How right Andrew was: 'Youth goes to youth,' he said. We are young, Stewart, dear. Let us never grow old except — except in each other's arms.'

The sun crept round the window and a great dazzling ray lighted on their two forms. Ailsa turned her head slightly and blinked.

'What are we doing in here?' she cried. 'Let us go out and play, just as we used!'

THE END

Other titles in the
Ulverscroft Large Print Series:

THE GREENWAY
Jane Adams

When Cassie and her twelve-year-old cousin Suzie had taken a short cut through an ancient Norfolk pathway, Suzie had simply vanished . . . Twenty years on, Cassie is still tormented by nightmares. She returns to Norfolk, determined to solve the mystery.

FORTY YEARS
ON THE WILD FRONTIER
Carl Breihan & W. Montgomery

Noted Western historian Carl Breihan has culled from the handwritten diaries of John Montgomery, grandfather of co-author Wayne Montgomery, new facts about Wyatt Earp, Doc Holliday, Bat Masterson and other famous and infamous men and women who gained notoriety when the Western Frontier was opened up.

TAKE NOW, PAY LATER
Joanna Dessau

This fiction based on fact is the love-turning-to-hate story of Robert Carr, Earl of Somerset, and his wife, Frances.

McLEAN AT THE GOLDEN OWL
George Goodchild

Inspector McLean has resigned from Scotland Yard's CID and has opened an office in Wimpole Street. With the help of his able assistant, Tiny, he solves many crimes, including those of kidnapping, murder and poisoning.

KATE WEATHERBY
Anne Goring

Derbyshire, 1849: The Hunter family are the arrogant, powerful masters of Clough Grange. Their feuds are sparked by a generation of guilt, despair and ill-fortune. But their passions are awakened by the arrival of nineteen-year-old Kate Weatherby.

A VENETIAN RECKONING
Donna Leon

When the body of a prominent international lawyer is found in the carriage of an intercity train, Commissario Guido Brunetti begins to dig deeper into the secret lives of the once great and good.

A TASTE FOR DEATH
Peter O'Donnell

Modesty Blaise and Willie Garvin take on impossible odds in the shape of Simon Delicata, the man with a taste for death, and Swordmaster, Wenczel, in a terrifying duel. Finally, in the Sahara desert, the intrepid pair must summon every killing skill to survive.

SEVEN DAYS FROM MIDNIGHT
Rona Randall

In the Comet Theatre, London, seven people have good reason for wanting beautiful Maxine Culver out of the way. Each one has reason to fear her blackmail. But whose shadow is it that lurks in the wings, waiting to silence her once and for all?

QUEEN OF THE ELEPHANTS
Mark Shand

Mark Shand knows about the ways of elephants, but he is no match for the tiny Parbati Barua, the daughter of India's greatest expert on the Asian elephant, the late Prince of Gauripur, who taught her everything. Shand sought out Parbati to take part in a film about the plight of the wild herds today in north-east India.

THE DARKENING LEAF
Caroline Stickland

On storm-tossed Chesil Bank in 1847, the young lovers, Philobeth and Frederick, prevent wreckers mutilating the apparent corpse of a young woman. Discovering she is still alive, Frederick takes her to his grandmother's home. But the rescue is to have violent and far-reaching effects . . .

A WOMAN'S TOUCH
Emma Stirling

When Fenn went to stay on her uncle's farm in Africa, the lovely Helena Starr seemed to resent her — especially when Dr Jason Kemp agreed to Fenn helping in his bush hospital. Though it seemed Jason saw Fenn as little more than a child, her feelings for him were those of a woman.

A DEAD GIVEAWAY
Various Authors

This book offers the perfect opportunity to sample the skills of five of the finest writers of crime fiction — Clare Curzon, Gillian Linscott, Peter Lovesey, Dorothy Simpson and Margaret Yorke.

DOUBLE INDEMNITY
— MURDER FOR INSURANCE
Jad Adams

This is a collection of true cases of murderers who insured their victims then killed them — or attempted to. Each tense, compelling account tells a story of cold-blooded plotting and elaborate deception.

THE PEARLS OF COROMANDEL
By Keron Bhattacharya

John Sugden, an ambitious young Oxford graduate, joins the Indian Civil Service in the early 1920s and goes to uphold the British Raj. But he falls in love with a young Hindu girl and finds his loyalties tragically divided.

WHITE HARVEST
Louis Charbonneau

Kathy McNeely, a marine biologist, sets out for Alaska to carry out important research. But when she stumbles upon an illegal ivory poaching operation that is threatening the world's walrus population, she soon realises that she will have to survive more than the harsh elements . . .

TO THE GARDEN ALONE
Eve Ebbett

Widow Frances Morley's short, happy marriage was childless, and in a succession of borders she attempts to build a substitute relationship for the husband and family she does not have. Over all hovers the shadow of the man who terrorized her childhood.

CONTRASTS
Rowan Edwards

Julia had her life beautifully planned — she was building a thriving pottery business as well as sharing her home with her friend Pippa, and having fun owning a goat. But the goat's problems brought the new local vet, Sebastian Trent, into their lives.

MY OLD MAN AND THE SEA
David and Daniel Hays

Some fathers and sons go fishing together. David and Daniel Hays decided to sail a tiny boat seventeen thousand miles to the bottom of the world and back. Together, they weave a story of travel, adventure, and difficult, sometimes terrifying, sailing.

SQUEAKY CLEAN
James Pattinson

An important attribute of a prospective candidate for the United States presidency is not to have any dirt in your background which an eager muckraker can dig up. Senator William S. Gallicauder appeared to fit the bill perfectly. But then a skeleton came rattling out of an English cupboard.

NIGHT MOVES
Alan Scholefield

It was the first case that Macrae and Silver had worked on together. Malcolm Underdown had brutally stabbed to death Edward Craig and had attempted to murder Craig's fiancée, Jane Harrison. He swore he would be back for her. Now, four years later, he has simply walked from the mental hospital. Macrae and Silver must get to him — before he gets to Jane.

GREATEST CAT STORIES
Various Authors

Each story in this collection is chosen to show the cat at its best. James Herriot relates a tale about two of his cats. Stella Whitelaw has written a very funny story about a lion. Other stories provide examples of courageous, clever and lucky cats.

THE HAND OF DEATH
Margaret Yorke

The woman had been raped and murdered. As the police pursue their relentless inquiries, decent, gentle George Fortescue, the typical man-next-door, finds himself accused. While the real killer serenely selects his third victim — and then his fourth . . .

VOW OF FIDELITY
Veronica Black

Sister Joan of the Daughters of Compassion is shocked to discover that three of her former fellow art college students have recently died violently. When another death occurs, Sister Joan realizes that she must pit her wits against a cunning and ruthless killer.

MARY'S CHILD
Irene Carr

Penniless and desperate, Chrissie struggles to support herself as the Victorian years give way to the First World War. Her childhood friends, Ted and Frank, fall hopelessly in love with her. But there is only one man Chrissie loves, and fate and one man bent on revenge are determined to prevent the match . . .

THE SWIFTEST EAGLE
Alice Dwyer-Joyce

This book moves from Scotland to Malaya — before British Raj and now — and then to war-torn Vietnam and Cambodia . . . Virginia meets Gareth casually in the Western Isles, with no inkling of the sacrifice he must make for her.

VICTORIA & ALBERT
Richard Hough

Victoria and Albert had nine children and the family became the archetype of the nineteenth century. But the relationship between the Queen and her Prince Consort was passionate and turbulent; thunderous rows threatened to tear them apart, but always reconciliation and love broke through.

BREEZE: WAIF OF THE WILD
Marie Kelly

Bernard and Marie Kelly swapped their lives in London for a remote farmhouse in Cumbria. But they were to undergo an even more drastic upheaval when a two-day-old fragile roe deer fawn arrived on their doorstep. The knowledge of how to care for her was learned through sleepless nights and anxiety-filled days.

DEAR LAURA
Jean Stubbs

In Victorian London, Mr Theodore Crozier, of Crozier's Toys, succumbed to three grains of morphine. Wimbledon hoped it was suicide — but murder was whispered. Out of the neat cupboards of the Croziers' respectable home tumbled skeleton after skeleton.

MOTHER LOVE
Judith Henry Wall

Karen Billingsly begins to suspect that her son, Chad, has done something unthinkable — something beyond her wildest fears or imaginings. Gradually the terrible truth unfolds, and Karen must decide just how far she should go to protect her son from justice.

JOURNEY TO GUYANA
Margaret Bacon

In celebration of the anniversary of the emancipation of the African slaves in Guyana, the author published an account of her two-year stay there in the 1960s, revealing some fascinating insights into the multi-racial society.

WEDDING NIGHT
Gary Devon

Young actress Callie McKenna believes that Malcolm Rhodes is the man of her dreams. But a dark secret long buried in Malcolm's past is about to turn Callie's passion into terror.

RALPH EDWARDS
OF LONESOME LAKE
Ed Gould

Best known for his almost single-handed rescue of the trumpeter swans from extinction in North America, Ralph Edwards relates other aspects of his long, varied life, including experiences with his missionary parents in India, as a telegraph operator in World War I, and his eventual return to Lonesome Lake.

NEVER FAR FROM NOWHERE
Andrea Levy

Olive and Vivien were born in London to Jamaican parents. Vivien's life becomes a chaotic mix of friendships, youth clubs, skinhead violence, discos and college. But Olive, three years older and her skin a shade darker, has a very different tale to tell . . .

THE UNICORN SUMMER
Rhona Martin

When Joanna Pengerran was a child, she escaped from her murderous stepfather and took refuge among the tinkers. Across her path blunders Angel, a fugitive from prejudice and superstition. It is a meeting destined to disrupt both their lives.

FAMILY REUNIONS
Connie Monk

Claudia and Teddy's three children are now married, and it is a time to draw closer together again, man and wife rather than mother and father. But then their daughter introduces Adrian into the family circle. Young and attractive, Adrian arouses excitement and passion in Claudia that she had never expected to feel again.

SHADOW OF THE MARY CELESTE
Richard Rees

In 1872, the sailing ship *Mary Celeste* left New York. Exactly one month later, she was found abandoned — but completely seaworthy — six hundred miles off the coast of Spain, with no sign of captain or crew. After years of exhaustive research Richard Rees has unravelled the mystery.

PINKMOUNT DRIVE
Jan Webster
Twelve years ago, moving into the splendid new houses of Pinkmount Drive, they had thought the good times would go on forever. Then came the recession that would take its toll on all their lives.

EMMA WATSON
Joan Aiken
It has always been a source of great frustration to Janeites that Jane Austen abandoned THE WATSONS after only seventeen and a half thousand words. Here, Joan Aitken has used Austen's characters, but has made them her own.

THE MAKING OF MOLLY MARCH
Juliet Dymoke
Life is never easy for a workhouse girl, and Molly's is no exception. Yet fate has wider horizons in store for her. Molly finds herself following the drum in the Crimea, where her indomitable courage wins the reluctant admiration of Captain Matthew Hamilton.

WITH MY SOUL AMONGST LIONS
Gareth Patterson

When George Adamson was murdered, Gareth Patterson vowed to continue his work. He successfully cared for and restored George's lion cubs, who were once again orphaned, into the wild. Batian, Furaha and Rafiki became his life's work and he became one of their pride.

FIELDS OF LIGHT
Jim Rickards

In 1931, Brian Grover sought fortune and adventure in Stalin's murderously dangerous Soviet Union. In Moscow, he met beautiful Ileana Petrovna, and they began an extraordinary love affair that was to enchant the world. This is the true story of Brian Grover's courage, bravery and unswerving determination to be with the woman he loved.

THE LAST TIME I SAW MOTHER
Arlene J. Chai

Caridad is a wife and mother, a native of the Philippines living in Australia. Out of the blue, Caridad's mother summons her home to reveal a secret that has been weighing heavily upon her for years. So begins Caridad's journey of discovery as she is given the gift of her past.

RETURN TO MOONDANCE
Anne Goring

Miranda enjoys a carefree childhood at Moondance, an old house on the edge of Dartmoor. When she is orphaned at the age of ten, Moondance's new owner arranges for her to work at a Derbyshire cotton mill, where conditions are harsh and pitiless. Miranda dreams of taking revenge on the man who ruined her childhood — but will she choose revenge over true love?

CALEB'S KINGDOM
Essie Summers

After her fiancé's death, Greta feels she must have a complete change. She hears that a sheep farm in New Zealand's Lake District needs help while its owner, Caleb Armstrong is away in Europe. The spectacular surroundings work their magic on Greta, but the return of Caleb Armstrong ends her new-found peace of mind. For her attraction to him is far too disturbing for comfort . . .